DMR-5

The Next Generation

God bless, *L J Pugsley*

By

Dr. Linda J. Pugsley

DMR-5
The Next Generation
by Dr. Linda J. Pugsley

Printed in the United States of America

ISBN 9781626971462

www.xulonpress.com

This book is dedicated

To our American heroes

From the Colonial Patriots

To our present day military

We owe you big!

Freedom has a flavor the protected will never know

Acknowledgments

❧

*I*n writing any book, an author takes quite a journey. That lengthy journey not only includes the tasks to craft the words and flow of the writings, but also finding those willing to go along on the uphill climb to publish the little monster. Sometimes you find the fellow travelers, and sometimes they find you. I am blessed with both.

My abundant gratitude must flow toward the leadership team at my church. The prominent cheerleader to have me finally take the plunge to pen this book was our senior pastor's wife, Dr. Shirley Parsons. She somehow saw the passion and listened to my incessant comments about the seemingly unmitigated swirl of damaging changes in our country and in our world. She hit the nail on the head when she said something like, "Linda, you have to stop talking about this and you need to start writing. Just do it."

I am deeply indebted to the rest of the team, which includes our awesome senior pastor, Mark Parsons, computer guru Carolyn Marshall, and faithful fellow Vietnam Vet, security chief, and passionate Sunday School teacher, Ted Marshall. They agreed to my extended leave of absence, an absence that would increase their ministry workload to cover my regular teaching, counseling, and coordination duties.

A huge thank you must also go to Major Bob Maxey, a fellow volunteer with the U.S. Air Force Auxiliary (Civil Air Patrol), who filled in for me in teaching the Character Development classes to the cadets at MacDill Air Force Base during my hiatus. Bob, also a lawyer, generously continued assisting in this endeavor by helping me wade through the terminology of the varied court cases cited. I can sleep so much more soundly, Bob, now that I understand Petition for Certiorari!

This is not a script for the Academy Awards, so I shall not thank everyone I've known since third grade. But I do have to thank all of our members and attendees at Great Hope Christian Fellowship Church in Tampa, Florida, who sent me off on my writing hiatus, not only with much treasured prayer but also with a boatload of Bath and Body Works "stress relief" lotions, scented candles, and bath needs. I used so much of it during the writing process that the readers will probably catch a faint whiff of Vanilla Verbena!

For a portion of my work on this book, I tucked away up in Atlanta at my sister Barbara's house, and owe a huge debt to her and her husband, Joe Beldycki, as they were ever so kind in opening their home to me. They never even winced when I quickly took over the guestroom and rearranged its decor with a huge worktable full of books and files, my computer, printer and all the hooah gear of a writer. It didn't stop there, either, as I then proceeded to leave a trail of my personal stuff throughout their kitchen and supply area; progressing with boldness to fill the living room with more books and notes. Payback was attempted by doing some laundry and cleaning while they were away at work, and of course, preparing a dinner or two, lest you think I am just a scrounging mooch of a writer!

Now, a sweet, sweet thank you to Mary Beth Blehl, one of my younger sisters. Wa-a-a-y younger, as she always says. With much patience and, might I add, bravery, she told me what was lacking throughout the transcript and helped me find my "voice" out here in this writing wilderness. And another thank you goes out to her daughter, my precious niece, (the newlywed) Mrs. Maggie Kuhn, for helping me keep updated in the jargon of youth.

To the thank you list is added Dr. Steven Augustine (my chiropractor and friend), who kept my old bones in line after so many hours hunched over the computer (which is his job), and was ever so creative in helping me invent fictitious names for the book (which is not his job!).

And, for some unique "guy ideas," a big thanks to Jamie Heggedal, the very best sports massage therapist, probably in the whole world. Well, at least close to that.

The Xulon Press editing team is certainly to be applauded not only for their expertise but for their excellent work and suggestions to smooth out the story presentation. You rock!

A shout out must also go to Donny Brown, Barbara and Joe's neighbor. If not for him, my uncooperative computer would not have been brought under submission, and I would still be handwriting this little sucker. Thank you, Donny; you are a lifesaver.

My final thank you is to Bill Barnhouse and his sons for teaching me how to bale hay. Read the book. . .you'll find out why.

Warning

~

*R*eading this book may alter your worldview. As you read the pages and meet the book's characters and the wisdom, knowledge, and insight they glean from each other, may you also do the same.

I hope you take this opportunity to ponder a moment, reflect on the history of mankind and see if it seems to scream out, "Hey, the nature of man is desperately broken," a lot more than the "I'm okay, you're okay" song!

Many people are shaking their fists at God for all this mayhem, but wasn't it that same God who said these things would happen if we didn't align our lives with His directives? I'm not talking religion here; rather, relationship, but more on that later. And even if you don't believe in God, this book has some juicy meat for you too.

So if you're not too chicken, I double dog dare you to continue reading.

Introduction

❧

*E*ven though dedicated to the military, this is not a book about war (at least not the physical kind). It is a semi-fictitious story; blending actual situations from experiences with my crazy and wonderful family and friends, tours in Vietnam, current and past military assignments, and teaching experiences, with a fictional story about a former military chaplain and a neighboring family. The often-provocative conversations with that family's sons and their friends are a stark reminder of the conversations that many people have forgotten to have with themselves and with each other. Indulge me a moment now, as I give a little background to this book's beginnings.

For eleven years, I served as an Air Force Flight Nurse, resigning with the rank of Major. That resignation was extremely difficult for me, as I loved the military and loved my nursing career. But I had a call from a Higher Commander, and had to go off on the vastly different but equally difficult path of being a Christian, and eventually working in full-time ministry.

In the course of my time in the military, I had the honored privilege of evacuating our wounded soldiers and Marines during the Vietnam War. Some called it a "conflict," but when bullets were flying, I called it a war! I flew with the 34th Aeromedical Evacuation Squadron (AES) out of Kelly AFB, TX, with the 56th AES out of Yokota AB, Japan, and with the 57th AES out of Clark AB, Philippines. I pulled flight duty as well as ground tours in DaNang (mostly), Cam Ranh Bay, and Tan Son Nhut. Those tours, June 1968 to July 1969, and another in 1972, helped shape my life and allowed me to serve those awesome, brave young men, whom I call the finest threads of America's cloth. The events and people of those tours remain a deep part of who I am today.

Because of those experiences, a unique opportunity opened up for me and other veterans of the war as guest speakers in our local high schools in the newly developed History of Vietnam course. About fifteen years ago, a Vietnam Vet teacher teamed up with the county schools and developed the course, with the distinctive part being the actual veterans going to the schools and speaking about what they did and saw while in Vietnam. This certainly brought the pages of those history books to life for them!

For fourteen of those years, I have been going to the classes, speaking to nearly 3,800 kids by now. I call my presentation, "The Other End of the Gun." (Hm-m, is that another book in the making?) I am the only female and nurse among the vets who come to speak in these classes, and I bring a little different perspective about the war and the suffering and sacrifices made. For the first portion of the class, I make a comparison of the stark differences between the culture of the Vietnam Era (and a bit before) and the culture in which these kids live today.

And that is the point made here; these kids are shocked when I tell them that our country has not always been the way they know it today. In their world, they have movies with morbidly violent and sexually explicit scenes, music that denounces civility, fidelity, sobriety, and encourages the debasement of women. Their world has teen-themed magazines with pictures as overtly sensual as an old 1950s *Playboy* magazine; they live in families where there has never been a father or a stay-at-home mom, or they travail in a family that is on its second or third set of parental combinations, grandparents, and siblings. They don't know that divorce was almost impossible in my day, because they only know "no-fault" divorce. They don't know that we used to have everything from laws against abortion, to laws against cursing or even spitting on the sidewalk. Those laws today may seem archaically burdensome to "individual freedom," but I compare a list of "transgressions" of seniors in high school in the 1940s (who lived under those and similar boundaries), and the list found in today's schools. They are glued to the screen, not only shocked, but also appalled at this drastic moral change and the resultant behavior it has promoted. Many even felt cheated that they severely lacked rooted foundations and are living with the hurtful and damaging results.

You'd think that most of them would scoff at this old woman's perspective and the generation I grew up in, but what I found surprised me beyond measure. I spoke of growing up in a country where:

- mostly everyone had a dad who worked and a mom who was at home
- there were censors in Hollywood that ensured the actors who played the roles of larger than life heroes like John Wayne and Jimmy Stewart never uttered a curse word stronger than "hell" or "damn"
- large companies and corporations were more philanthropic, often building and subsidizing hospitals, orphanages, museums, symphony orchestras, community buildings, and memorials, etc. (and not doing so for some underlying, nefarious political cronyism, or eventual profit)
- drugs were unheard of among our youth, and drinking a beer was the worst thing you could do
- sex before marriage was really out of line, not because sex was dirty or bad, but because most of us were on a mission to finish high school and college or tech school and didn't want an unwanted pregnancy to hinder our successful forward progress
- abortion was illegal because people thought it better, that if you did get pregnant, you would go ahead and have the baby, giving it up for adoption rather than just killing it (softly renamed today to "terminate the pregnancy")

It's as if I was talking about another planet, one on which they wish they lived!

Sometimes, as I would start my presentation, there would be a few sleepy heads (especially the classes scheduled right after lunch!), but once I embarked on the comparative analysis of the cultural changes that have occurred, there were few of those sleepers left.

They really perked up when I told them it was foolishness when they heard that the "rich are bad" and the only right thing to do was to get more of their money and re-distribute it to the poor. Rather, I told them that I hoped they all got to be billionaires. And when they were that rich, that they would build a day care center at their factory, and that they would pay their workers $45/hour plus health and dental benefits from the profits of the company. I told them they should be doing that instead of having a union or the government doing it for them (because those entities are often too prone to corruption themselves); that they would establish college trust funds for their workers' children and subsidize the further education of their employees; that they would provide adequate assistance with financial planning and retirement plans, etc.

With fewer employers greedily sucking the company dry, as well as fewer employees doing the same (through false sick days, stealing supplies, lying on forms, etc.), profits on both sides of the picture would soar. Heck, never mind the morality for a moment, with that many great benefits, shared from the honest profits made, there would be fewer workers who would cheat if it meant they would lose that sweetheart of a deal job! Production would soar if each employer could reap the full benefit of the profits (instead of the "post cheating" results) as well as if each worker would receive more and more of the profits. Simple system. . .more work accomplished, more money made, more money earned for all parties involved.

Not "equally" shared, but shared accordingly, because not all people are equally gifted or skilled (more on that later). The man who works eighty hours a week (at a similar job) will always make more than the one who works only ten! The students started to see that it was not the rich, the employer, or the worker that was the problem; it was the eroded moral core.

To my amazement, many of the students absolutely understood what I was saying. Their comments and questions showed that they understood that the teen pregnancies, the lives, jobs and families lost to drugs and alcohol addictions, their perverse and damaging world of "entertainment," and the bribery, lies, and corruption in so many areas of our culture, were the culprits. These things negatively affect the economy, their whole world, even affecting how they themselves think and act. And most importantly, that it was not always like that, at least in the United States. . .and that it didn't have to stay that way. They really saw they do have a choice. If they came from a messed up situation or background, they didn't have to stay that way. They could choose the higher, albeit harder, road based on moral excellence, honesty, and hard work, rather than one of laziness or the finger-pointing, "Woe is me" mediocrity. The result would be a more prosperous people in a steadily prosperous nation.

At the end of the classes, as the students are leaving, I am met with the eager effusion of youth who are ready to go out and conquer the world. . .I am in hopes it is by digging for gold with the shovel of kindness and moral excellence, rather than as miserly, greedy, hedonistic jerks.

My hopes were really raised, when, at the conclusion of one class, a long-haired student clad in a black, Dylan Klebold-type raincoat (of Columbine High School shooting infamy) came up to me, leaned in close to my ear and whispered, "I believe everything you just said," and walked away with a smile instead of his initial sullen expression.

Many of our kids are hurting in families that are falling apart; our government and many businesses are full of corruption and confusion, and at an impasse in so many areas; drugs, sex, and alcohol have even entered our middle schools; people are losing their jobs and homes. . .the list goes on and on. And people are blaming the economy! Hello out there, could it possibly have anything to do with this rapidly declining moral climate?

Whether my comments were in speaking engagements in the more secular setting of a high school history class, or in the more spiritually open gatherings of a church youth group, the reaction has been the same. The young people, for the most part, are sick and tired of the screwed up families in which they find themselves, of the screwed up ideas and expectations of early sexual activities and drug and alcohol consumption, and the incessant yet often uncomfortable and confusing sensual titillation in the current youth media. They are sick of rampant cheating and bullying in the schools as well as the perceived double standards from adults saying, "Do as I say, not as I do." The moral cacophony that surrounds them has been deafening and they are open for some relief.

Their cries for help, and even some of the tears they have shed as I talked about the pain of broken family life and the drastically changed moral landscape of this country, have stirred me to somehow get all this into print. A stirring to organize the thoughts and observations of the effects these changes have had on every aspect of life in our country, which, as of late, has not been change for the better.

It is with great hope, though, that understanding the depth of these changes will result in a life-stirring event for all of you; a moment in time that will offer you the alternative of living by morally strong principles, which will produce a foundation upon which to build your lives for the betterment of our community, state, and nation.

In the present day, pervasive moral weaknesses are profoundly affecting us all, from the pocketbook to politics and beyond. We cannot sweep it under the rug, whistle through the graveyard, or ignore the 800-pound gorilla in the room any longer. We must come to the realization that. . . **It's the Morality, Stupid!**

So, get a cup of coffee, come sit on the porch with me, and listen in on the ponderings of a pistol-packing pastor. (Uh, that was just to get your attention. . .although I really do have and carry a weapon!)

Part I

The Next Generation

1

As I sat on the old wooden planked porch, looking out over the distant mountains that were clinging to their smoky haze, as my friend's three-year-old clings to her lamb shaped "pack-pack," I was struck by the contrast of such serenity existing in our fast-paced world.

For years, I have frequently retreated here for lengthy sabbaticals. As an author, the solitude is almost a job requirement; and for a pastor, this setting brings such relief from the oft-felt "ministerial burn out." It has been almost twenty years now, since I inherited this property from a former military friend. I say former because we had to go our separate ways; he left to live on the West Coast and rightly so after what had happened between us. He was very generous in giving me the property. I think it was his way of apology; I don't know. Shortly after moving out there, he died in a car accident. Strange though, even with all the disastrous details surrounding that awful season of my life, it just oddly still seemed providential that I am able to live at this place with my unique situation.

"Enough of *that* unpleasant thought," I mused.

I reveled in the silence, as it suited me like a cool cloth on a fevered brow. But I must confess it was not just the silence and rest that constantly drew me here. I have a secret that I've never shared, and bear a burden that crowds my heart each day. This is the only place where that burden finds relief and where joy fills this empty void. I race here every chance I possibly can. But I can tell no one why.

My blissful silence was quickly broken with shouting from the roadside. The young visitor is my neighbor's son, Major, a recent high school graduate who is handsome, tanned, and muscular. The girls must swoon when they catch a passing glimpse of him. His features bear a faint resemblance to someone from the distant past, and seeing him brings back those conflicting memories in my inner being. But those memories, of which he has no clue, are assuaged by his cheerful presence. If he only knew what he meant to me!

Major is the youngest of Don Garrett's four sons, and lives on the farm adjacent to my abode. He was adopted by the Garretts when only three days old and is the spoiled treasure of the family. Well, they say I have done the spoiling, and probably so. I smiled as I thought on our blessed and close relationship. He has often called me his "second mom," and I cherish that designation. During my numerous visits to this place, I've had the distinct pleasure of watching this little "seedling" grow into the impressive "oak" that is careening toward me now. Riding tractors, tilling the soil, hauling and slinging everything from manure to seventy-pound bales of hay have a unique way of forming a boy into a man.

"Hey, Chaplain, got a minute? Saw you on your porch and thought I'd stop by", said Major cheerfully.

"Hay is for horses," I jokingly shouted.

"And lots of cows, too, I can vouch for that!" he answered without any hesitation as he came bounding up the porch stairs; his broad, white smile etched in between two long, rugged dimples.

"Well, Major, are you ready to jump off the cliff?" I asked, referring to his upcoming enlistment in the Marines.

"As ready as you were, Colonel when you went in the military," he replied, with a sly smile that grew larger and brighter by the minute.

Over the years, I have shared many a story with my young visitor. He knows I was a Flight Nurse in the Air Force and we regularly kid each other about rank because I was a Lieutenant Colonel and his name is Major.

And with a first name like that, he has been the brunt of much chiding; and even more so may lie ahead as he enters Marine Corps

Basic Training at the end of this summer. At least the military doesn't go by first names, so maybe he'll slide by for a while!

I had always cherished the company of my young neighbor and didn't even mind that he broke the invisible meditation barrier I had just wrapped around myself. He surprised me when he said, "If you don't mind, I thought I'd stop by each morning for a few moments and we could talk. You know, about 'stuff'."

Little did he know that was exactly what I had been praying for; I too really wanted to cover some "stuff" with him before he hurtled headlong into life out there.

Major grew up in a stable, loving family and has so much going for him. In addition to being drop dead handsome, he is one of the brightest lights in the bunch, graduating with honors. This upcoming "stuff" should prove to be very interesting, to say the least.

"Hey, Colonel, what are you thinking, or are you just avoiding my question?" he asked.

"Item one, none of your business what I'm thinking! Item two, I heard your question and yes, I would love you to stop by. I'll have the coffee ready for us both. How about coming by at ten hundred in the morning?" Translation: ten o'clock.

In one leap, Mr. Wonderful jumped from the top step down onto the grass, swirled around and stood at attention, snapping an English-style military, open palm salute and said, "Aye-aye, Ma'am. Ten hundred it is. Permission to leave, Ma'am."

Without hesitation I barked back, "Permission granted, you turkey! As you were." We both laughed. He ran off to finish his chores; I went back inside to prepare for a most interesting summer, one I was sure I would treasure even more than most.

2

As another gorgeous mountain morning burst through the dark of night, I walked over to the bedroom window and gazed at the majesty of the surrounding vista. The peaks must have thought I was bored because I greeted them with a prolonged, full body stretch and a wide yawn.

Young Major Garrett would be coming by each morning for our little chat. . .what could he possibly want to discuss? I wondered if everything was all right at home. Was it girl trouble? Was he re-thinking his upcoming Marine training? I didn't care what it was; I cherished spending time with him. He never knew why I favored him so and I would never tell him.

"Whoa, slow down, Tiger," I told myself and then thought, *try to take every thought captive. . .the runaway imagination is always worse than the actual situation. We do that so often though, don't we! We just pre-figure what we'll say if things go a certain way and, most often, are usually way off target. Don't want to put the cart before the horse. . .let's just see what time brings.*

Speaking of time, I'd better get that coffee going.

While making the coffee, I reflected on how I loved the early mornings up here in the mountains. Cool, crisp, fresh, almost makes you crave taking in a deep breath! Reminded me of the flights I took through Anchorage, Alaska. We picked up the wounded in Vietnam and desperately helped them stay alive through their journey to the hospital closest to their home of record. After flying them out of Vietnam, we took various routes to accomplish that very task, and one of those routes was a crew rest stop at Elmendorf Air Force Base (AFB) in Anchorage. The air there seemed so clean that you wanted to suck in the deepest breath you could, as if to store it up for later use. I'll never forget that; what a gorgeous place, but a bit too cold for me for any long term habitation.

Our crew rests were often short, only eight to ten hours before we were off on the next leg of caring for our wounded heroes. But it was on the longer stays of forty-eight to seventy-two hours that I was able to see a bit of the territory. The Portage Glacier, the salmon-filled streams, and I mean filled; and ah yes, the old Bird House Bar. . .I wonder if that little shack out in the middle of nowhere is still there. I don't partake of the "nectar of the gods" anymore, but in that 65 degrees below zero weather, a good hot Rum Toddy surely warmed the body and soul!

My memories of Vietnam are just as fresh in my mind as if they were yesterday. Maybe time will permit me to share a few of them with my young visitor. I will earnestly pray for him as he launches out on what will often be a dangerous adventure. And this reminds me, there must have been many of my family and friends praying for me while I was on my military sojourn, because I have lived to tell the tale. I did not always live a life that mirrored a morally excellent code, and God's mercy held me until that revelation came my way. We must be careful though not to sit in His mercy thinking that judgment will not come. He has to have mercy, because His justice is perfect, and because that justice is perfect, there has to be accountability for our actions. We shall all stand before His throne one day. . .sobering thought.

Well, well. . .here comes Major, and right on time; that's a Marine for you.

"Good morning, Chaplain," he cheerily said.

"Ditto, handsome, and how are you this fine morning?"

"I feel just great. I worked a bit longer on my chores yesterday afternoon to make sure to have time to be here this morning. That's probably going to be the plan from now on."

This kid was serious about getting here each day for our little talks. I wish more of our young ones were like him. He certainly is a breath of fresh air. . .and, ah, yes, I must tell him about Alaska, he'll probably croak when I mention the Bird House Bar. Ha!

"Well, are you sure you're old enough to have some coffee?"

He growled, "Seriously, Chaplain! I work like a man; I can drink coffee like one."

"Just kidding, Superman, just kidding."

He smiled his precious smile and I knew I hadn't soured our get together. He has a great sense of humor and I am glad of that because I tend to have the same.

"So, what's on your mind?" I cautiously asked.

"It's not so much what's on my mind, as what's on my heart. I read your book, *The Climb*, and realized I have only been going through the motions of being a Christian and not really living it."

"That's a pretty big leap there, big guy. A lot of people way older than you have not reached the wisdom of that conclusion."

His face was somber yet bright, inquisitive. "Chaplain, in that book you said something that really got me to thinking."

"I said a lot of things in that book. What caught your eye?"

"Well, a bunch of things did that really gave me a better understanding of 'what' God said to do, but one thing especially made me think on 'why' God said to do them."

As my gaze went from staring into my coffee mug to looking directly at him, he spoke as seriously as I had ever heard him.

"You were speaking to the youth of our country and you wrote, '*You can do it! You can find what other generations have lost!*'"

"So that kind of touched that wonderful heart of yours?"

"Yeah, it did."

I was glad we could freely speak to each other. His family "adopted" me those many years ago and we had been so very close; I held him in my arms as an infant, watched from a distance as he had grown, and could now talk to him as a young man.

He continued, "You also said that the moral principles in America are prisoners of war and the Christian heritage of this country is missing in action and that only a passionate return to repentance and righteousness will heal the ills of this nation. That hit me, sort of like when my dad slaps me up the side of the head when I sometimes act stupid. He's only playing with me, but it gets the point across, just like what you said."

As he spoke to her, Major painfully thought to himself, *she has no idea what I've done. I hate the pain and shame I feel all the time. We're talking about the declining morality around us and I've done such a wrong thing that nobody knows about. I always feel like such a fake cuz people think I'm this great kid. Oh, help me, God.*

He was silent a long time.

I said, "Hello, anyone in there?"

"Oh, sorry Chaplain. I was kind of lost in some thoughts there" and he continued as somberly as could be.

"Well, Chaplain, I got to thinking how true that statement is. Do you know they don't ever mention anything about moral principles in school? My teacher said that we could all decide for ourselves what's right or wrong. And they never talk about our country having a Christian heritage . . .not at all. Even President Obama said that we weren't a Christian nation. What's up with that?"

"Big questions asked, big answers needed" I replied. "Let's start at the beginning, shall we?"

His face lit up like a flare and he said, "Like at the beginning of the earth while it was still cooling and you were born!"

He laughed so hard at his own joke that he made me howl, too. We both laughed heartily.

"You little jerk; I'll get you for that. You had better watch your back, kid. I'm only a bit older than your mother and she'd probably whip your butt for saying that."

We laughed again at both comments.

I continued, "No, I meant more like the beginning of our country. There are many people who have forgotten what really happened then, or more unfortunately, have only read the twisted accounts being given today. Tell you what; I'll gather some information for you to read over and have it ready when you come by tomorrow morning. Deal?"

"Deal" he said, frowning a bit when I said we weren't going to continue.

"Hey, what's the problem? You look like you want more." Jokingly I continued. "I just can't believe you want to listen to someone so old-fashioned!"

"I don't mind, really," he muttered. "Thanks for the coffee, it's very good."

I moved my hand teasingly to muss up his crew cut hairstyle and he ducked quickly.

"Hey, don't touch the hair, it'll wreck my gel!"

We simultaneously said, "See you tomorrow. Be there or be square!" Both heads shook in disbelief that we uttered that goofy statement. Hm-m, we are more alike than he'll ever know.

Returning inside, I thought, *what a unique circumstance I have. . .young Major is ready to listen to some truth that has been so infrequently shared lately and is quite ready to hear what I have to say. That's encouraging.*

In the scheme of things, life is short, but what we do while we are here is immensely powerful and influential. . .for the good or for the bad. Something and/or someone has influenced our attitudes, behaviors, body language, words used in communication, style of dress, thought patterns, sexual practices, family structure, decision-making, every single aspect of our lives. . . . Even in the womb, before we entered this world, we are affected for the good or for the bad.

Hmm — morality, does anyone even know what that is today? What are an individuals' basic set of values upon which are based their decisions? Well, according to what Major said, he, and so many others are taught that everyone gets to determine what is right or wrong for them. I must remember to relate the comparison of what that type of thinking would do to a football game!

A person's core values frame their thoughts, words and deeds. They are the fabric of their being, the clothes in which they wrap themselves. The Latin saying, "Vestis virum reddit", meaning, "Clothes make the man", figuratively could not be any truer today. I just wish that everyone would take an honest look at the "moral cloth" in which they are wrapped. I believe the tumult in which our society finds itself is the direct result of dis-honoring God, thus sending out our children into a cold world, for at least the last two generations, only dressed in moral rags.

I must make a list for Major to look over. Even though the current philosophy of life is often touted as "progressive", it has really caused "regression" in our culture and our way of life. Instead of moral excellence, we have moral decadence. I hope my young future defender of the nation will stop and think on this list and what the "progressive ideology" has given us:

- an educational quagmire producing fewer and fewer articulate, literate, thinking citizens
- drugs, sex, and alcohol at all levels of our society
- the drain of continuing poverty and ignorance (in spite of governmental safety nets and available public education)
- an entertainment community with an ever inundating emphasis on using sex, drugs, and alcohol as part of a lifestyle
- lying, bribery, and corruption that permeates our society
- poor, selfish, or altogether corrupt leadership, resulting in skyrocketing debts, both in the government and by the individual
- continuing out-of-wedlock pregnancies, leaving hapless children in harm's way with little or no successful future in sight
- marriages dissolving left and right
- continuing school dropouts resulting in a decrease of "independent producers" and an increase in "dependent takers" (a cost that cannot be maintained much longer)
- financial devastation at all levels
- rebellion and violence at younger and younger ages
- widening prison populations
- an overall attitude of disrespect, dishonesty, and hedonism
- and an unhealthy disdain for all that is structured or in any way requiring sacrifice, self-discipline, thoughtful consideration, comparative analysis, or critical thinking

The list would be too long if I wrote it all down! This progressive liberal ideology (whether purposeful or unintended) has sent out each successive generation clothed in thinner and thinner layers of core values. To embrace the belief that our society should exist on moral relativism by which each individual is the decider of what is right and wrong, is a recipe for moral anarchy and, God forbid, eventual civil war.

Is that too much for my young neighbor? I think it best if I saunter over to the old homestead and have a little talk with Don before I continue meeting with his son.

3

I met Don almost twenty years ago when I first started coming up to this area. He had no idea of my true motive for living next door to him and his family. He and his wife had been living on this property since they got married. In fact, Don grew up here with his parents and siblings, and was the only son who wanted to continue farming. His brothers gladly let him inherit the land and all the hard work that went with it. He doesn't begrudge them that, as he loves to work outside and to work with his hands. It's as if some people have certain gifts, you know, like working with the earth and the animals. Don Garrett is one of those lucky few.

As I entered the barn, the familiar, wafting smell of cow dung filled the air. You may think I'm a bit crazy, but I love that smell. In my youth, I spent some summers at the farm of one of my uncles in up-state New York, and loved to be around the barn and the cows. I even loved to shovel the stuff, feed the calves and spread the hay. Just an old farm girl inside, I guess. My mom, who grew up on a farm (and couldn't wait to leave it), often said I should have been her sister's kid, because her sister remained on the farm for all of her days. I couldn't concur more; just think, I might have been a farmer instead of a nurse, eventual flight nurse, combat veteran, college instructor, pastor, chaplain, Christian schoolteacher, speaker and author. Both lives involve a lot of work, but in one, you get to shovel the stuff, and in the other, you get to wade through it! Ah, the vagaries of life!

I shouted out, "Hello, anyone home?"

Don bellowed from deep inside the building, "Yeah, I'm out in the barn. Come on over."

Don is a happy fellow, content with his life and his work and is a refreshing reminder of the seemingly less stressful lifestyle of days gone by. His happiness comes, in part, because he has chosen to do the work he cherishes and is very comfortable in it. He graduated some years ago with a degree in civil engineering, but after a tumultuous stint with a local firm, in which he was traveling 80 percent of the time, and under the tremendous pressure of time-constrained projects, he decided to do what he really loves. . .to manage and work the farm. He endured a lot of opposition for that from family and friends because of the severe financial challenges it posed for him and his newly started family. But Don is a man of convictions and did what he knew best to do. And these same convictions thread throughout the lives of his children.

I wish we had more men like him raising families with love, authority, and discipline, extolling the virtues of hard work, determination, independent thinking, and team spirit. His kids have been a delight to watch as they grow up and come into the fullness of God's plan.

The oldest is his daughter, Rebecca, a pediatrician. Four years ago, she gave up a lucrative practice in New York to be the lone physician in a group of small towns near the Indian reservations in Arizona. She is certainly well prepared for anything, having been the only girl in a family of brothers. And it certainly looks like she is modeling after the generous spirit of her father. She remains single, much to the chagrin of her family. That may be changing soon though, as a young suitor has caught her eye. The young fellow is the supervisor of border patrol agents in the area and is an up and coming local political figure. They are a loving couple, and as far as I've heard, are supportive of each other. It is looking like a favorable situation all around, as they both have fine families in their gene pool. I don't know her young acquaintance, but I know Rebecca and she is the catch of a lifetime. Hope the young man knows that and makes all the right decisions. I must remember to add them to "ye olde" prayer list, which is getting longer day-by-day.

Don's four boys are his pride and joy, too. Major is the youngest and preparing to leave the nest after this summer. The other three boys are hard workers in the local community. Even though reared under the same roof and with the same set of parents, they each display their own set of talents and propensities. Don Jr., the oldest son, is a pilot and flies for a commercial airline. Despite his many travels, he decided a long time ago to make his home base up here in the mountains. His wife, JoAnne, has a degree in Early Childhood Education and homeschools their three girls.

Number two son, John, works the farm with his dad. He has his degree in Agricultural Management and loves his work as much as his dad does. Don is thrilled that he has someone to pass the farm on to when he retires or "goes to the big farm in the sky," as he says. John's wife, Melody, works in real estate, blessed with a very successful sales and investments company. They do not have any children and love to travel, as much as the farm work allows.

His third son, Joshua, is tall, strong, and just as handsome as Major. They are closest in age and spend a lot of time together in the surrounding woods, streams, and ponds; doing all the "guy things" they could think of. Don's wife, Aimee, a former Army nurse, must have had many a mother's adventure with hogs, dogs, and frogs, so to speak, with those characters for sons. Being a nurse should probably be a required qualification to raise those kids!

Joshua has been a great brother and friend to Major, and you can see their admiration for each other as they work around the homestead. Joshua is currently on school break from the university where he is studying law. He playfully says he has to become a lawyer because his brothers are destined for trouble. At which point, they pig pile on him as he tries to escape their feigned wrath. What a great family to know and love. And I am so grateful Major is being raised in such a loving environment.

"Hey, Don, how's it going?" I asked.

"Up to my neck in you know what," he said.

"I know what you mean," I said. "I just wanted to run something by you in regards to Major."

"Sure, what's up? He's not in any trouble, is he?"

"No way. . .your kids are pretty incredible, buddy. It's just that he came by the other day and asked if he could stop by each morning at my place before he leaves for Parris Island. He said he wanted to talk about "stuff." Our conversation got pretty deep about morality and all that, and I wanted to check with you and make sure that was okay that he stops by and continues our chats. And to, uh, make sure he is not just trying to get out of some chores or something."

"Thanks for asking, Chaplain. No, he's not trying to get out of any chores, although he has tried sometimes, but his brothers keep him in line, if you know what I mean."

"Yeah, I've seen those characters in action. You must be very proud of them all."

"They are a treasure beyond measure," he said as tears glistened in his eyes. "I love each and every one of my kids and pray every day for their success in life. They each have given their hearts to Christ at an early age and have been faithful to try to do what is right. We don't get to church as often as I'd like, but we have always had some Bible reading and prayer time as a family. I think God honors that, too."

"You are right on all accounts, Don. I just wish we had more solid families like yours. I don't mean to imply you're perfect; it's just that you have held to a moral standard based on the wisdom of our great God. That used to be the norm in our country, and it seems to be eroding day after day."

Don then said, "I have noted that, too. My kids sometimes roll their eyes when I bring it up, but I know they see some of the changes around them. But it's hard to talk to them sometimes 'cuz they haven't lived long enough to see just how much change has really happened."

"And that's what my question is today, Don. So it's okay with you that Major stops by for coffee out on my porch each morning? He has many questions about this very subject, and from what he said, his other friends do, too. He's old enough to handle the answers and comments, but some of it may be about some deep and personal areas of his life. . .even the birds and the bees stuff!" I chuckled loudly as I said that.

"Chaplain, I have known you for near twenty years, and I would be honored if you would like to take on some of his questions. If anyone can appropriately tackle the birds and the bees stuff, it is you. Your sense of humor helps soften the blow of some of the stark truths of life. It would be good for him to hear some of this from another person and another perspective. I trust you and thank you again for respecting me enough to ask if you can talk to my son."

"Doesn't work any other way, my friend," I said. "Hey, how about you and whoever in your clan is around come on over to my place this Saturday night? I make a mean pot of spaghetti."

"So I've heard," he said as he laughed. "Yeah, you cook like you were still cooking for your huge family when growing up. One of your sisters said you don't make a pot of spaghetti. . .you make a vat of spaghetti!"

"Ha, ha, be careful. . .some of your cow patties may end up in your portion there, bud!"

I didn't hear him laugh, but I saw his shoulders jerking up and down as he said, "Thanks for the invite, Chaplain. I'll check with everyone to get a head count and give you a call tomorrow."

"Good, see you Saturday for dinner."

It was a nice walk back to my cabin. I am so blessed with good health, an awesome family, and so many wonderful friends; I sometimes just burst with joy. Even though there have been many troubles and trials in my life, it has been worth them all and times like these, surrounded with God's pure nature, vividly reminds me of that.

4

$\mathcal{I}$t took me a while, but right after I got up this morning, I ran off some copies of information for Major. I will give him just a bit at a time. Don't want to inundate the guy. It all depends on what he wants to talk about, anyways.

My inner chef shouted, "Let's get to that coffee, girl. I can't be late for that soon-to-be Marine!"

The birds must think they're the Mormon Tabernacle Choir this morning. Their chirping is gentle and hangs in the air like an old hymn. The weather is just perfect, cool, but not too cool to sit outside. Refreshing, just like my young neighbor I now hear whistling as he comes up the walk.

Major stopped at the bottom of the steps and said, "Here I am. . .just as planned. And that coffee smells just as good as it tasted yesterday."

"Flattery will get you everywhere," I said. "It might even get you some fresh baked cinnamon buns, too. Here kiddo, help yourself."

He dove into the plate of rolls like he hadn't eaten in days.

"Whoa, slow down, didn't they feed you breakfast today?"

"Sure did," he replied. "But heck, that was four hours ago and, might I add, was just before milking sixteen cows, feeding a hen house full of chickens, and digging three more post holes."

He said that with a clean sense of pride. Geesh, I love this kid, we sure need more like him.

"Well, I hope you washed your hands after all that!"

"Ha-ha," he said, laughing as he gobbled up his fourth cinnamon bun.

"Well, where shall we begin?" I said eager to get started on our summer adventure.

Major looked up at me with that gorgeous grin of his. He purposefully plastered frosting all over his mouth. The little turkey playfully let it stay there as he said, "Ah, how about a napkin?"

"How about a shower?" I answered.

"Chaplain, you're funny. You know that old TV show M*A*S*H? Well, I watch the re-runs a lot with my dad. And you're sort of like a combination of Major Houlihan and Father Mulcahy!

"That's a good one. I didn't know you watched the old TV shows. Who's the dinosaur now?" I quipped.

"Ha, you still beat me on that score, Chaplain!"

"I'm gonna slap your head, you punk," I joked back. "Let's get going with your 'stuff,' shall we?

First of all, Major, before we get started, here is a list for you to look over. It shows you a few of the effects on our country caused by some of the progressive ideology of late. It's just some food for thought for such a smart dude as you."

"Man, I didn't know I was going to get some homework!" he said, with a tone of worry.

"Don't fret, guy, no tests are involved," I quickly stated. "It's just for your reading pleasure."

"Whew," Major said, as he pretended to wipe his brow.

"Just look it over when you can. I'll give you more information as we go. You're an intelligent fellow. I encourage you not to make too many decisions just based on your feelings. Have to get the facts in there now and then. Too many 'pie in the sky' people just keep on shoving crazy ideas out onto our culture, never basing them on facts, just feelings. Make sure you always let the facts get in the way. Truth has a way of leading us in the right direction. As my friend Ted, a Vietnam Vet says, 'If you refuse to hear the truth, you will soon lose the ability to recognize a lie'."

I saw that my young charge was listening intently, so I continued.

"It really is truth that we all need to seek. Not just what we believe, but what is true. If you believed a lie, wouldn't you want to know it?"

"You bet I would," he said.

"An example is that of long ago. There were scientists, engineers, and very smart thinkers who believed with all their heart that the world was flat. And guess what? They were wrong! So just because you believe something strongly doesn't make it true."

Mustering my best Oriental accent I said, "You must find the truth, grasshoppa."

He just smiled.

I continued, "There are many people who believe with all their heart that there is no God. Many people believe with all their heart that there is a God. One of those beliefs has to be wrong because both cannot be true, so always seek for the truth. Do you understand that?

"I never thought about it that way before, but yes, I understand."

I didn't quote the actual Scripture verse, but I told him, "God gives us a hint when He says in the Bible that Jesus is the way, the <u>truth</u>, and the life. It really is as simple as asking Him to make Himself real to you. . .He has a unique way with every one of us."

"I remember that verse," he chimed in. "Dad just read it the other day."

"Many people, including many Christians, have only proclaimed what they believe and not what is true. They speak from the broken nature they were born with. Deception comes from that brokenness, and the truth can only be known when that brokenness is out of the way."

Major looked a little surprised and asked, "We were born broken? We were taught in one of our sociology courses that man's nature is basically good."

I responded quickly, "Well, if man's nature is basically good, then why does mankind have such an enormously long history of war and mayhem?"

Then I threw in a corker, "And if God is so good, why did He let it all happen anyway?"

He mused, "Never mixed those two thoughts before, either."

"Well, you have to, to understand what's going on, so how about we discuss a beginning time even further back than the one involving our country? We'll get to that later, too, but I want you to think about some things.

Some people will discount what I am about to say, but I know you will understand. God is not only wise and powerful He is also just. His justice is perfect, and because His justice is perfect, there has to be a balance of mercy and judgment. It is hard to believe that God is so powerful that He existed all unto Himself, no beginning, no end, in an existence where there was not even light. Power and wisdom, knowledge, etc., don't need light. But God is more than all that, He is love. Because He is love, He has to be shared. Right from the beginning, if we can call it that, He had a plan of creation. From the depths of His superior imagination, He came up with solid, liquid, air, color, plants, animals, and the crown of His heart. . .humankind. He made Adam and then gave him Eve. Everything was provided for them in a glorious place."

Major interrupted and said, "Sounds like a Hollywood movie when you put it like that."

"And that's the sad part," I remarked. "So many people have their understanding of who God is from what other people have concocted for them, and not from what God Himself has stated."

"Go ahead, Chaplain, didn't mean to stop you."

"No problem. As I was saying, because God's justice is perfect, He also had to give humankind a free will. If He didn't, then Adam and everyone else would have just been some robots forced into doing things. That is far from perfect."

Major's gaze wandered off toward the trees, looking like he was in deep thought. He broke the silence and said, "Well, did God know Adam would disobey Him? Why did God put the stupid tree there in the first place? Did He tempt him on purpose?"

I laughed. "You didn't fall asleep after all, during my 'listen up lecture.' That's what my former students used to call my discourses."

"No, I didn't. . .for sure! Well, did God know. . .did He tempt Adam? C'mon, don't keep me hanging. I'm on the edge of my seat here!"

"Good," I replied. "You're listening, grasshoppa!"

Major smiled again.

I went on, "Yes, God knew that Adam would disobey Him. And, just for the record, He did not 'tempt' Adam. The plan was perfect, not flawed in any way. God made Adam and Eve lower than the angels but higher than the animals. He knew that by giving Adam a free will, there was always the opportunity for Adam, or anyone else for that matter, to choose against God. But remember, God's justice is perfect, so it has to be that way."

"Okay," Major said, "But what about the tree thing?"

"That's another example of perfection, dearheart. It was not only the type of tree, the tree of the knowledge of good and evil that was important, but that Adam had a choice to make. How could Adam even know if he loved God if he did not have to choose Him over something else? The only way we can show God that we love Him is to obey Him. What else are we going to do? Heaven is His home and earth is His footstool; what are we going to get Him, a Rolex watch or a car or something? Dude, He is and has everything, how can you top that? God even tells us that if we say we love Him and don't obey Him, we are just lying. It really was so perfect."

Major looked puzzled. "How can you say that was perfect? Adam and Eve screwed up royally, then God got ticked off and threw them both out of the best place they would ever have! They lost everything and you call that perfect?"

"Boy, you're one tough customer," I responded with a smile. "First, God was not ticked off as we know ticked off. And to us it surely looks messy, but to God it all made sense. I had that same question so I just asked God why He made Adam, knowing that Adam would disobey and lose it all."

Major blurted out, "You talked directly to God? Did He answer you? How did you hear Him?"

I leaned in toward him, eager to take advantage of his heightened interest, and quietly began to speak.

"The main key to hearing God is to be one of His children first, being in His family, so to speak, and then hearing from God is simple. As someone else once said, it's as simple as sitting quietly in His presence, fixing your eyes on Jesus, listening for sponta neous thoughts from Him and then you write out the flow of those thoughts. But that's a whole other subject, sweet pea. We'll get to that another time.

I stopped for a moment. "You sure you want me to continue?" I asked.

"Yup," he said.

"Where was I? Oh yes, I asked God why would He make Adam if He knew Adam would fail? The Lord's answer just floored me. God spoke to my heart and said that He wanted to show Adam — and all of us — that He would love us even when we didn't love Him! Whoa! What a God we have, huh?"

Major just kept staring at me, his chin cupped in his hands, not saying a word.

"God didn't leave Adam out in the cold. Right from the beginning, He had a plan of rescue for us all, or at least for those who would take it."

Major sat straight up and loudly asked, "Why didn't God just come the next day and fix all this mess?"

"Funny thing. I asked that same question, too."

"Yeah, when you talked to God again," he said, with a little skepticism.

"Yes, and do you know what? God gave me another answer, smart one."

"I'm sorry, Chaplain. I'm not scoffing at you, really. I just never heard this before."

"No apology needed, honey. I am just glad you want to listen. So few people even ask the questions, never mind listening to the answers."

"Go ahead, what did He tell you?" he impatiently said.

"God really floored me again. He said He purposely let humanity go through all sorts of stages of self-rule, like having the patriarchs, the kings, the judges, even Moses to whom He gave the law, meaning the Ten Commandments. None of these different attempts to control the broken nature of man worked. And God didn't let just a week pass by to prove this. He let thousands of years go by to prove the point. Boy. . .is He the greatest researcher and statistician, or what! Anyways, we all can see that just making laws doesn't work. People can get around them every time. God knew that, so He set up a plan that was as simple as it was perfect. It's called a 'new and living way,' where God's nature comes inside you just for the asking, and then you have the tools to have a fighting chance to do it His way."

I interrupted myself at this point. "Wait a minute; this is starting to sound like a sermon at church. Sorry 'bout that."

I was surprised at his response. "No, not really. This just feels like a regular conversation. I didn't know anyone could just have a conversation about God. I guess you don't need to be in church to think about Him, heh?"

"You are one smart cookie, kid. Well, let's just let all this sink in. You go ahead and read over the list that I just gave you regarding some of the gnarly things that have been happening lately to our country. Come back with any questions, or maybe even some answers, and we'll see where it goes from there."

He grabbed the papers, dropping the whole pile. They scattered all over the porch, some even cascading down the steps.

What a goofball. I can't help smiling as I watch him grab the now wrinkled and dirty papers stuffing the wadded mess up under his arm.

"Oops, my bad," he muttered, as he went running back to his house, singing, "Off we go, into the wild blue yonder. . ."

I yelled back, "Wrong song, buddy. . .that's my Air Force song!"

"I know," he sang back to me in his baritone voice.

What a character.

After our conversation, I decided to go into town for some supplies. The ride would do me good and give me time to think, hmm, better still, to "pray up," as they say.

I started humming, "Off we go into the wild blue yonder." Oh brother, now that song was stuck in my head!

"Riding high into the sky. . ."

Our conversation had me musing as I drove into town.

I don't know if anyone else feels this way, but I have the strong sense that many of the problems in our country, like the 9-11 attacks, the financial woes, the pain at the pump, the combat zone our schools have become, etc., are a direct result of our nation, and especially its leaders, having left God in the rearview mirror. As I reviewed old newsreels on the History Channel, it seemed that a lot of our previous leaders acknowledged God and asked for His blessings much more frequently, and in every form possible, than is seen today.

And all you hear anymore is how we can fix our problems through another change in the law. . .more taxes, less taxes, more programs, and fewer programs. The bickering between those in leadership is non-stop. Heck, it's at a standstill. Not one voice out there is asking what God would do. That question has just been thrown away into some large religious dustbin.

As I just mentioned to Major, I know that humankind is broken because of what Adam did, and it's restored by what Jesus did, not by what some liberal or conservative think tank came up with.

I recall saying in a sermon one time that we are like Adam's "crack babies." He did the crime and we ended up being born handicapped because of it. . .spiritually, at least. But, that's where Jesus comes in. Because we are born these little spiritually twisted and spiritually deformed babies, God has extra mercy on us. He established a "cure" from that brokenness. That cure is a moment in time, when you stand before God, anywhere on the planet, not just in a "holy place" somewhere, and humbly say, "You know, God, You're right and I am not." A short moment in time to ask God to forgive you for anything you have done that does not meet His measure, His wisdom, His purity. Just ask Jesus to come inside your heart and save you from the results of your brokenness. There are many names in the religious world for that moment, "salvation," "being born again," "redemption," a lot of "Christian-ese" out there to explain it. But it is true.

But what do so many do? They just stumble on through this life. Some get lucky and some are thrown to the wayside. They think it is just chance, karma, or the spread of cosmic beams. The problem is that we forget that our "thinker," which comes up with this stuff, is part of what is broken. Without another and higher "nature" coming inside, everyone is doomed to repeat the same errors, the same misguided decisions, civilization after civilization, nation after nation, person after person. Break that downward death spiral by asking the real God, not the religious god or the one made up from the broken thinkers. . .ask the real God to not only save you from destruction, but be your new Lord and Guide in all you do in the here and now.

Hmm—what a difference that would make! But it just won't work when we keep trying to fix something broken *with* something broken. . .when will this ever end?

I guess I am more convinced that our pressing problems and challenges today are not just because of the economy. We have our major problems today because it's the morality, stupid! Hmm, sounds like a great book title!

It's a long way into town, so I continue delivering the "listen up lecture" to the windshield in front of me.

Not to change the subject, God, but sometimes I want to scream out some common sense things to people. Like. . .capitalism is not the problem, capitalism is just a system of production. The problem is the bribery, lies, and corruption. Being rich is not the problem, being greedy is the problem. We are attacking the wrong thing! The outcry against capitalism and the rich is misdirected. We should be fighting the bribery, lies, corruption, and greed.

Ah, but there lies the challenge. Who decides the moral code? Left to humankind, that code hasn't been all too successful so far, ya' think. Religion hasn't helped much, either. Just because we have a right to choose, shouldn't we be choosing what is right? But then everyone asks, "What is right?" Ah-r-g-g-h. . .such a circle plain reasoning brings us. But what you choose is just as powerful as the right you have to choose it.

It seems that the "business as usual" mentality, from our country's leadership down to each citizen, must come to an abrupt halt. No one seems to have noticed—what we are doing is NOT working. Our families are crumbling; our schools are not producing effective, intelligent, skilled people; poverty is not decreasing but rather increasing, even after bazillions of dollars have been poured out to the poor and almost as many programs have been established to change their plight. . .it hasn't! It costs thousands per poor person in administrative costs to give them just hundreds. If that isn't failure crouching at the door, what is?

For our survival as a nation, it is looking more and more imperative that the tattered American cloth needs to be repaired and the country put back on the more morally excellent road. Isn't it just common sense? But what's the old saying? "Common sense isn't so common anymore!"

As I think about it, someone who does not believe in God can have integrity, sexual purity, and sobriety, serve others before themselves, and pursue excellence in all they do. Those Ten Commandments are annoying things though, eh, God? But even if someone didn't like the first four regarding God, then they could at least do the last six. The whole world would change overnight, at least a little, if they did. Of course, that would be quite a dilemma for the many, who upon their demise, have to face that real God they didn't believe in and explain to Him why they didn't follow the first four! Hmm — free will carries a lot of weight with it.

But again, it is not just about rules and laws. As I just told Major, no laws ever helped humanity to stop stealing, killing, cheating, etc. It still kept happening. Even if someone never murdered or robbed a bank they still were plagued with jealousy or lust, or greed or hatred, dissensions, factions, cruelty. . .oh, the list goes on!

It seems, then, if our basic human nature is broken, and with it, we can never meet the measure God has outlined, then we are doomed to eternal failure. Oh, but what a comfort I have in my heart, knowing that even though that cruddy Adam nature in me will not change, I can still meet His measure because I have asked that God nature to come inside of me trying with all my might to allow it to rule. Wait, then any good I do is not really me doing it, but You inside me, Lord.

As I drove along, a Bible verse came to mind that says if you walk by the Spirit, meaning the nature of God, you cannot walk by the flesh, which is the nature of man. That is the answer; it's the change needed. The broken need the perfect God to be the motor that runs their lives.

On our own, we have come up with the dumbest, most ineffective ways to run a family, community, state and nation. We are not using the most powerful nature, but rather the broken one. Duh!

As I pondered these esoteric waves floating through my head, I hoped I could convey them to others in plain and strong terms. It just seems a given that my young Marine, to understand what life is all about, will need to know that he can only do so much and can only meet God on God's terms. But then again, he may not ask me any of this stuff. He may just want to know how girls think so he can catch a hot date!

As I pulled into town, I forced myself to turn off the faucet of thoughts. "Chaplain, just shut up and get the groceries," I scolded myself, and hoped no one saw me talking to the windshield!

"Oh well, let's just dive into the task at hand," I muttered and went off into the well-stocked supermarket.

5

I was up at the early morn, which is not my usual approach to greeting the world. It's just that up here, I don't want to miss a minute of the sounds, smells, and gentle breezes that come with my little hideaway paradise. It was a magnificent start to the day and I was pumped…but what I was really starting to feel were the effects of the jogging I had been doing in these hills. The old "flatlander" here just ain't what she used to be! So I have relegated myself to the luxury of running only two miles every other day or so, instead of my usual four. I gleefully justified that the shorter mileage on the hills was the same as the longer stints on the flats.

Off I went to run those hills. Returning sweaty and smelly, but refreshed, I did my post-run stretches, had a quick shower and felt ready for anything!

"Good morning there, Chief. Having a good day?" I asked as my daily visitor approached.

"Not as good as it could be. I left one of the stalls open, a calf got out, and got her foot stuck in between two pieces of wood on the framework of the storage shed my dad is building. He is not a happy camper today."

"Uh oh, pal. Not a good day when the boss ain't happy!"

"You can say that again."

I hesitated a bit and then said, "Would it be better if we didn't meet today?"

"No, my dad said to come over still. He needed to cool off a bit before he talked to me again."

"That's pretty wise. It's so true that a kind word turns back wrath. You had better pray hard that your dad keeps his natural nature in check and lets his God nature rule. You're sure to be on the mercy end of things if he does."

Major nodded his head in agreement. "My dad is so good at that. He has always told us to cool off before we try to settle anything. My brothers and I don't have a lot of success in that area yet. But we do eventually get back with each other and make things right. I guess that's a good beginning, anyways."

"Speaking of beginnings," I piped up. "Let's see where we left off yesterday."

He quickly reminded me, "You were talking about the beginning and Adam and Eve and all that stuff."

"Thanks," I said. "Yes, we have to know where we came from to know where we are going. That is not only true on our spiritual journey, but also on our physical one." I quietly thought *you will someday find out where you really came from, dear one.*

"Like I was mentioning the other day," I continued, "an important point that is often missed in our country today is that, as a nation, we have drastically strayed from the strong moral beginnings with which our country was started. To know just how far we have wandered, you have to look at how things were back then as compared to now."

I asked him, "Remember when you told me that they were teaching you in school that each person could make up their own ideas of what is right and wrong? Well, the fancy name for that is 'moral relativism.' And when you think of it, it's not going to work either. Imagine a football game where each player decides where the foul line is, decides whether it was a touchdown or not, etc. That game would be in utter chaos in just a few minutes. No play book, no rules, no fouls. . .and yet, that is exactly what we ask our youth to do. If a mere football game needs standards, guidelines, rules, and foul lines to prevent utter chaos. . .then how much more do we need some guidelines to play and be successful in the most important game. . .the game of life?"

With a furrowed brow and a very serious look on his face, Major just slowly kept on nodding his head.

He was listening attentively, so I continued, "Our Founding Fathers didn't just leave the establishment of this nation up to chance, or whim. They knew where they came from and where they were going. They weren't puzzled about life, rather they held on tightly to their fundamental principles, not weighing them against some trendy philosophy of the day. They espoused a God-honoring Declaration of Independence, then fought to achieve it and eventually drafted a Constitution using a specific philosophy directed to avoid specific problems. That philosophy was intrinsically Christian. There, I said it; the founding of this nation was based on Christian principles. They never said you had to be a Christian to live in this country; they were just operating from a basic Christian perspective. For a long, long time, those principles and mores were the platform upon which the vast majority of our culture made its decisions, including our government. I know beyond any doubt, it was that platform of prayer and honoring God that catapulted our country to the vastness of our abilities, production, and wealth, which we have enjoyed for the past few centuries.

I often wondered if there's anyone else out there, who thinks that our country's drifting away from these principles and moral codes just might be the reason we have the current problems assailing us today. Some people have forgotten that we used to have prayer and a short Bible reading in every classroom across this country. I have charts that show the drastic increase in out-of-wedlock pregnancies, drug abuse, violence, and such; it was a massive change that started in the 1960s, when Christian principles were removed from the schools. Coincidence? I don't think so. Amazing how facts shape the picture for you!"

I lamented, "Uh oh, kid. . .it's starting to sound like one of my history classes!"

"If this is one of your history classes, I'm just sorry I wasn't there," he said with a mischievous smile.

"There you go again. . .all that flattery will get you everywhere!"

We both laughed.

"Please, go on. I'm interested. . .really. I don't have any chores until this afternoon. Remember, I told you I made those arrangements with my dad."

"Oh, yes, the dad who is at your house tying duct tape around his head and mouth right now so he won't explode over the calf mishap this morning."

"Yeah, that one," he said sheepishly.

I went on, not missing a beat.

"In looking back over this history, I find that the original intent of our nation's founders has been quite twisted as of late. This 'original intent' has often been misconstrued, if not outright ignored, by today's contemporary historians. Many current history books depict our nation's founders in the light of today's political correctness. Instead of quoting what the Founding Folks actually said in their own words, the authors interpret for us what they think the founders meant. Even worse, the accounts of the beginnings of our country are sometimes skipped altogether, supposedly as irrelevant or too old-fashioned and too long ago."

With his index finger tapping on his cheek, like some college professor pondering the next philosophical explosion, Major said, "Now that you put it that way, you're right. In our history class, they didn't even cover the founding of our country. They covered everything else, but we never really studied the very beginning. One kid asked the teacher about the Pilgrims and Thanksgiving and the teacher just said it wasn't the school's place to cover things involving religious bigotry. I had no idea what she meant. We just started with labor unions or something and went into World War II and on from there."

I sighed. "Great, now we have a nation full of people who not only have a degraded and deficient moral code, but also have no idea of the true history and philosophy of this great nation. So many educators have fallen for and now have spread this skewed, revisionist version of our history, so much so that the true origin of our nation and its Christian moral code is hidden, confused, or mistaken."

I continued with this deep and serious conversation because young Major was able, more specifically, he was willing to grasp it, unlike so many in his age group.

"This trend has resulted in many national and local policies, wrongly founded, but seemingly justified by this emerging 'moral enlightenment' they think they have 'discovered.' The problem is these new revelations on the meaning of our Constitution and its ideals are sometimes producing the very abuses the Founding Fathers intended to avoid!"

Major interrupted again. "Whoa, can we change this? Is there even any hope?"

"It's looking mighty dim," I sadly replied. "Is there any hope to repair a moral code that sees nothing wrong with 'crony capitalism', 'white lies,' and corrupt business practices used as routine business tactics? Can we change a moral code that condones a fourteen-year-old getting an abortion without even informing her parents? Or a code that has now listed pornography as a First Amendment right to free speech? Or tolerates the sale of crotch-less undies for seven-year-olds, or a doll that comes with dance poles and money, like in a strip club? What moral code allows girls to dress like a skank or have eleven-year-olds getting bikini waxing? [1] Our Founding Fathers are turning over so fast in their graves that they shall surely corkscrew themselves to China!"

Major looked like he didn't know whether to laugh or leave at this point.

I went on. "Hopefully, people will rethink what's going on, and what each one can do to initiate the changes needed. And changes are needed to ensure a vital and healthy future, especially for our youth. Who, may I remind you, oh young one, are the next set of moms and dads. Our youth are the next set of leaders in medicine, education, the military, engineering, construction, research, and every vital facet of this country. You guys are the next generation of thinkers, innovators, and doers. The big question is upon what moral foundation will you build our world? What will the business, political, educational, and medical world look like. What if these areas remain chock full of liars, cheats, and thieves? Will your generation keep hacking away at the threads of America's cloth with the machete of moral relativism and secular humanism?"

Major just sat there, wide-eyed and said, while physically pulling his head back, "Do I have to answer those questions?"

"No, honey. The old chaplain just has some deep concerns about the future. Well, mainly *your* future, because as painful as it may be for me to realize, I have most likely put in more time on the planet than I have left. It's just that with the average American spending well over four hours a day watching TV[2] or sleeping in front of it. . .geesh. . .any 'eye-opening,' 'stirring' changes may not be starting any time soon!

"How can a discussion on the importance of the true history of who we are as a country and what comprises our nation's mission, vision, and the morality covering it all, compete with *Dancing with the Stars* or the antics of Deena, Vinny and Sammi on TV's *Jersey Shore?* It may be a glum future if our youth can usually name the last ten *American Idol* winners, but not know any of the Supreme Court Justices, or worse still, think that success is being in a hot tub with six naked women drinking a rum and Coke!"

My little friend kind of screwed up the corner of his mouth and said, "Whoa, you're kind of hard hitting with all this. I don't mean that's bad, I just mean you don't sugar coat anything."

"Do you want me to sugar coat things?"

"I'm no pansy," he replied. "I want it straight up." He chuckled and continued. "I heard my uncle say that one time when he was at a bar at a wedding. He didn't want ice or anything that would water down his liquor. That's how I want it. . .the truth, I mean, not the liquor!"

He laughed. But then his eyes told me he understood the seriousness of what I was sharing. He left, but didn't hop down the stairs or sing a song this time.

"See you tomorrow, big guy?"

"Yup," he said glumly, and went toward home.

I yelled out to him, "Tell your dad I said to take it easy on you. Tell him what goes around comes around. That's sort of a paraphrase from the Bible."

He stopped and turned around. I saw a big smile on his face and I knew that my sobering comments hadn't screwed up the continuation of our morning visits. I felt relieved, because I can be overbearing and overwhelming sometimes.

After Major left, I started thinking on where my interest in history began. It certainly wasn't on my "top ten list" growing up. I recalled when my church started a small private school. As a Florida certified teacher (I guess I do have a varied background!), I had the privilege of teaching a host of subjects over the years, from K to 12th grade. The history of the United States courses soon evolved into a major favorite of mine, as my young neighbor is finding out.

I'm sure most of us have long forgotten any history we learned in school, and are pretty much in the dark about our country's amazing beginning precepts and their vision for a new world, built on those precepts. Without those years of required studying, researching, and teaching this subject, I dare say I would also be in the same darkness.

Don't get me wrong, I was never a history buff, nor am I the local certified historian. Actually, I didn't do very well in high school history, often just eking by with a C or sometimes a D in the subject. But when I went for my Bachelor's in Nursing (I really do have a varied background!), I was totally enthralled in a world history class led by Dr. Liu. He was a man of Chinese origin with a very thick accent. To understand his lectures, I had to pay close attention (novel idea, heh). That was to my great advantage, though, as I developed a life-changing viewpoint about history. I soon learned that history is not just a bunch of dates and wars and conquests and long lists of ruling empires and their positive or negative impacts on the world. No, history is people; it is who we are, and what motivates our actions. And all of that is influenced by geography, heritage and the existing moral code. Dr. Liu made history come alive, but he warned of a danger with which historians have to grapple. Because the historian has not been present at the more distant historical dates, he/she then has to "reconstruct" what was going on in that era, from the artifacts and documents available. That could be like trying to describe what it was like at your great-great-grandfather's wedding. You'd only know what happened from reviewing pictures or letters and documents of the event. So, if you weren't there, would your description of the event really be that accurate? Not really. What then would make it accurate? Well, the actual documents, pictures, and comments by the people who were there, not your "guestimate" of what was said or done, which would most likely be skewed by what you know as to what constitutes a wedding today.

Another example I remembered was that of a number of years ago. One of my cousins did some monumental research into our ancestry (on my mother's side). He compiled and published his findings for all the family. As I delved into this treasure, I was delighted to find a family lineage that dated back to the end of the 1600s in this country. Our lineage included many upstanding farmers in the agrarian society of upstate New York. He even found some circuit-riding preachers in the DNA pool, so at least there's a semblance of godliness in the line!

An interesting discovery was a compilation of some of the letters my grandfather sent to my grandmother. These letters reflected his deep love for my grandmother and a little window into the mores of the time. I must show Major some of the excerpts from one dated August 5, 1904:

My Dear Alice,

It is just 9:57 p.m. by my watch. This is borrowed pen, ink and paper. Have not had time to go uptown yet to get me any.

Now please excuse me if I write fast for I am so tired and sleepy as can be. I had all the loads and pitch off. We have drawn in 15 loads so far, will have about 35 more so you see I will not get home until one week from Saturday if I do then. . . We have 20 cows and four of us to milk, we all started the same time to milk, then I milk seven or eight out of the bunch.

Say, Alice, I am keeping my promise strictly to the mark. God gave me strength to tell some young fellows I didn't care to hear any of their stories. Some of my old cronies too. . . Well, I never saw them when the Lord was so precious to me as He is now. He blesses me every day, all the time, for that matter. I wish I could see you and tell you about it. Alice, I am not surprised, for Tuesday night while praying for you, the Lord came to my heart and I felt you were going to get special help and not only that, but keep it.

> *Tomorrow might will (sic) be a hard time for me, for I will have to go to town and be among my old companions. Oh <u>my dear Alice</u>, <u>pray for me</u> as you <u>never have</u> in the past. . . Oh Alice, swing (sic) out for Jesus. Make a clean sweep. Clean up everything now. Then it will be smoother sailing later on . . . With love, Will.[3]*

In it is seen some clear details of the life of a hardworking American farmer and the deep concern and encouragement of a common man to live a godly life. Major can see the godly thread of the letter, common in many circles and forms of communication of the day, even among our government officials.

The point being, the picture painted by the historian can also be tainted by the historian. The key is going back to what the historical figure actually wrote and quoting that, not what the historian assumes the writer meant. Of course, some areas of history are not afforded that luxury, because all that is left are bits and pieces of documents, or tiny shards of clay, or puzzling artifacts. In only those cases can the burden of accuracy fall heavily on the historian.

That is not so for our country's founding era. There is ample evidence in documents that are in pristine condition, which clearly define the Christian moral principles at the start of our nation. And it was on this foundation they developed our nation and from which, to our detriment, I fear we are quickly departing. There are also ample admonitions from these same sage founders of the dangers this new form of government posed. They knew that a free society not bounded by a high moral code would be headed toward a free-for-all (are we there yet?). This detour from the route mapped out by our country's Forefathers may just lead us over the cliff. I hope we back off soon!

Those born since the 1990s only know a society saturated with sex, drugs, violence, alcohol, etc. The books, movies, magazines, and TV programs of today are very different from yesteryear, and encourage our youth to live a morally and often physically unhealthy lifestyle. . .for themselves and for our nation. Some of us old dogs even remember the old black and white TV shows where they actually showed married people sleeping in separate twin beds. . .and none of us ever thought that strange. It was a protection of the minds and hearts of our youth that I think is imperative, yet sadly lacking today. Some people may call it "brain washing," but I prefer to call it "heart washing"!

I must find that chart to give to Major that shows the differing results seen with teen life today versus our previous "Christian-based" society. There is no way to convince those of us who have lived long enough to see this slow, deleterious moral decline, that it has seriously undermined our country's ability to make the type of leadership decisions needed to successfully run a family, a community, and a nation.

The thought keeps coming to me that we are in danger of giving over our cherished freedoms either to the aforementioned free-for-all, or even worse, to a dictatorship. That is not too far-fetched, because today we actually have legislators, leaders, and judges who have looked at the founding of our country and our Constitution from the vantage point of today's altered viewpoint, and not the actual original intent. Thus, we are seeing some legislation and legislative interpretations that are egregiously far from the original intent of the framers of our constitutional foundations. Some are even saying we should scrap our current Constitution and make a new one based on a European model. Duh — I think our founders broke away to be independent of the "European" model. Hey, are we going forward or backwards here?

I must also remind Major that we are seeing many controversial opinions regarding our Constitution, especially our First Amendment rights concerning the freedom of religion, freedom of speech, the freedom of the press, the freedom to peaceably assemble and the right to redress grievances to the government.

Hmm, "the right of the people peaceably to assemble". . . the "Occupy Wall Street" groups have recently smashed cars and buildings, defecated on the flag, burned property and been arrested in droves (for their violence, not their viewpoint). Any possibility their moral code has changed since the original intent of this First Amendment Right was written. Now, some history buffs will bring up the "tar and feathering" atrocities of the early colonies, but, lest we forget, the Bill of Rights was penned not to allow violent and disruptive assembly, but allow the freedom to assemble — uh — peaceably!

Oh, how things have changed. And some historians even claim that many of the founders of our nation were not even Christians but only "deists," meaning just acknowledging the existence of a God. How they can come to that conclusion, after reading the many letters and documents from that era, including official documents of governors and early presidents, which were full of references to Jesus, Savior, or Redeemer. No Buddhist, Muslim, Transcendentalist or any other mindset but Christian was ever used by our Founding Fathers.

I'd better get some copies of the typical writings of some of our country's early leaders so Major can catch my drift on this.

"Slow down girl," I heard my brain saying. "Don't drown the kid who just comes by for a few swimming lessons."

6

*"*Hey, Dad, where are you?" shouted Major.

"Over here with this little calf."

"Dad, I'm so sorry that I left that stall door open. It doesn't help you if we don't keep our heads in the game."

Don Sr. looked up from the calf he was holding. "You see this little calf, son? It not only needs its mother, it needs us too. When I took the responsibility of caring for the momma, I took the responsibility of caring for everything that came with her. God wants us to tend to these little critters with the utmost of care."

He continued, "Do you think the momma cow is going to hate this calf because it ran out from that stall and even got a bit hurt in doing so?"

"No," Major said softly.

"Well, I'm not going to be angry with you, either. I love you, son, more than you can ever know. You are special and we are blessed that God chose to send you to us to be a part of our family. I pray every day for your safety and success. I hurt when you hurt. I laugh when you laugh. I love you so much I'd like to crawl in your pocket and go with you wherever you go."

"I know, Dad. And I love you right back, too."

"You know what's filling my heart right now?" his dad continued. "I am full to my hat brim knowing that you realized your mistake and didn't try to pin it on anyone else. You're truly sorry and I accept that. That's what God does for us, and I will continue to do that for you. That doesn't mean you're off the hook, though. Just like with God, my mercy is tempered with some justice. In order to help you remember a little better, I told Joshua that you'd be doing his chores for the next two days. That means you won't be able to visit next door for a while. Make sure you let Chaplain know so she can hold off on makin' any of her fancy pastries."

"Yes, sir," Major quickly replied.

"Oh, and tell her seven adults and Donny Jr.'s three little ones will be over for her spaghetti dinner she's puttin' on Saturday. She can make them fancy pastries then if she wants."

Major smiled that big smile again. He mused to himself, "I can stand being in the dog house for a few days, especially with that feast going down on Saturday."

As Major went in the house to start some of his extra chores, Joshua came over near him.

"Hey, at least this isn't as bad a punishment as when we were kids. Do you remember that winter when you and I had those new snowsuits?"

"Oh boy, do I. Who could ever forget that! What were we thinking?"

"Thinking. . .key word there, bro, we weren't!" he replied.

"As I recall," Major said, "It was your stupid idea in the first place."

Joshua laughed. "But it sure was fun while it lasted."

"Yeah, I remember that we were stuffed into those suits. Heck, what were we, about six and seven years old at the time?"

"About that."

"Mom specifically told us not to slide on the cement ramp leading down into the storm shelter. But oh no, my oh-so-smart older brother said if we just use a piece of old cardboard box, then our suits wouldn't get ripped up. . .such famous last words, bro!"

Joshua stood with his hands on his hips, a little offended at that statement. "Yeah and where were your brains that day, up your butt?"

"Back off," Major said, and gave a little push against Joshua.

Joshua quickly said he was sorry. He wasn't stupid, and both boys knew their dad would put the chores right back onto the perpetrator, as he had done many times before, if either one got into a shoving match.

They didn't fight too often, but Joshua could see that Major was a bit ticked off with the extra chores now on his work list. Not angry, but just a bit miffed that Joshua ended up with a gift from that mistake.

"Whoa there, little bro. I don't want to fight. I'm just remembering some of the fun we used to have when we were kids. Remember how big those ramps looked going down into the shelter?"

Major started to smile again. "Yeah, I sure do. That was funny that day. We kept sliding down the ramp over and over again. We started out fine on the icy parts, but once the cardboard piece caught the bare places, we went the rest of the way down on the cement!"

"We had a great time," Joshua continued. "Until you walked in front of me on the way back to the house, that is, and I saw that you had shredded the whole back side of the snowsuit. I looked at my rear end and saw the same damage. I panicked."

"Yeah, I know. That's when you came up with the other brilliant idea to go into the house and then turn around and walk backwards down the hall. Didn't you think that Mom would catch on when she saw two little kids with their snowsuits on, walking backwards?"

Joshua replied, "Thinking was not my strong suit back then."

Major howled with laughter and said, "And you think it's your strong suit now?"

Both boys scurried off to the barn as fast as they could, playing tag with each other as they ran. They were strong, manly men. . .with little boys still wrapped up inside of them. Their parents knew they would make fine husbands and fathers someday.

Mrs. Garrett looked out the window as her two "boys" playfully ran toward the barn. Beyond them, way out in the field, she saw her husband. The little calf was tripping around the hay mounds that he was spreading for the herd. She was glad the little thing was fully recovered from the earlier mishap. She knew her tough, soon-to-be-a-Marine son was such a tender soul inside and his heart would have been broken had anything serious happened to the calf. Her own heart was as full as her husband's was as she soaked in the love of the family she knew was hers. *What gifts*, she thought. "I am so blessed. Thank you my Lord," she softly prayed.

All of a sudden, her sun-browned face broke out in a wide, white-toothed smile. "Hmm, I don't have to make dinner Saturday night, either!"

7

I just got off the phone with young Major. He explained that he wouldn't be coming over for a couple of days. We agreed to meet up this coming Monday and continue from there.

Not a problem. As a matter of fact, that may be quite helpful, as I have to go back to the store for a few more things for Saturday's banquet, and then I can finally start my "vat" of spaghetti!

Like a gnat in my brain, I heard, "Off we go into the wild blue yonder". . .! Yikes, that's worse than the song "It's a Small World After All," running through there. Oh, why did I just think that?

I drove off humming, "It's a small, small world. . ."

As I returned home from this umpteenth shopping trip, I saw the blinking light on the home phone's message machine. Who would call me on the house phone? Everyone knows to call my cell. I figured it couldn't be that important, so I just unloaded the groceries and flopped on the couch for a well-deserved nap.

My head no sooner hit the pillow than Major came bounding up the steps again, only this time he was yelling at the top of his lungs, "Chaplain, Chaplain, come over here real fast. Johnny fell from the barn loft, he's hurt real bad."

"Slow down, slow down, buddy. Is anyone with him right now?"

"Yeah, my dad is out there."

"Did anyone call 9-1-1?"

"Yeah, my mom did. We tried to call you but you didn't answer. I finally noticed your car was back and my mom sent me to get you."

"Okay, let's hurry." I hid my concern but my stomach was churning. My heart leap-frogged back to Vietnam.

"I don't have time for a ride down memory lane; especially that one," I chided myself.

"Keep your head on straight," I mumbled as we ran across the field to the barn.

Major's dad looked up. His face was pale. Twisted beside him on the dirt and hay-strewn floor was his son, John. John's left leg was jammed up under his body, his right leg extended at an odd angle. About midway down that leg was a tear in his jeans with a small pool of dark blood that had formed underneath the battered leg.

"How long before the medics can get here, Don?" The pounding of my heart seemed so loud I thought that surely the others must have heard it.

"It will be at least another forty minutes. They are tied up about ten miles west of town with a barn that collapsed onto some workers."

The fear and apprehension was so thick in the room you could cut it with a knife.

By this time, Major, his brother Joshua, and his mom all anxiously stood around our wounded man.

"Okay, we have a bit of work to do, guys," I said authoritatively, wondering where that came from!

My nursing experiences may be long in my past but not the need to continue helping, as circumstances warrant. From somewhere deep within, the orders started flowing.

"Major, get me a pair of scissors and some long rags. Pick ones as clean as you can."

He dashed off immediately to his precious task.

I felt so sorry for the whole family, for I knew they were frightened beyond measure, but there was no time to comfort them, or myself, for that matter.

"Joshua, go get a couple of flat boards. Try to get ones about two feet long. There may be some from the shed area your dad is building."

"I will," he said with a nervously tight jaw.

"Aimee, get some cold water, a clean cloth and a blanket that you don't mind getting wrecked."

"I don't care what happens to any stupid blanket," she angrily muttered as she ran off to the house.

I leaned down beside Johnny and took his pulse. It was rapid, but he was conscious and able to speak.

"I was trying to fly like Superman," he jokingly said.

"Well, you must've forgot your cape, buddy."

He winced in pain as I tried to move a flap on his jeans.

"Yeah, I guess so. Need to review some flying lessons with my brother," he replied with a grimace.

Everyone quickly returned with all the items I requested. "Thank You, Lord," I whispered to myself.

"Let's see what we have here," I said as I cut back the jeans around the lower leg.

The family group recoiled in horror as they saw a white, stick-like piece of broken bone jutting out from the bloody, snarled mass of muscle and tissue. The blood around it was dark and I sighed with relief.

"No bright red blood squirting out from anywhere, so I don't think we have any arterial involvement," I explained to them.

"Let's go ahead and splint this thing to hold him a bit until the ambulance gets here," I said with forced calmness.

I sensed the family was feeling a bit more relieved. Joshua and Don helped me splint the leg. Johnny was in quite a bit of pain and frequently groaned. I looked over to Aimee. It might as well have been her on the floor; her agony was difficult to watch. John might be a grown man, but he was still her son.

Once the splint was in place, John was able to pull himself up ever so slowly and carefully into a sitting position, and leaned against one of the support posts in the barn. He was still pale, but a bit more settled and aware of what had just happened.

Don asked, "Can we give him something for the pain?"

"Sorry, but that won't be a good idea before the medics get here. They will check him from head to toe before they determine anything else. The best thing right now is to keep him warm, and watch for any further bleeding."

"One of you go get a flashlight, please. I need to check his pupils."

"I didn't hit my head, Chaplain. I just landed kind of funny."

"Well, we just need to make sure, honey, that's all. They will check all this again, anyways. I just want to see for myself."

I knelt down again and shined the light into each eye. His pupils were equal and reacting. This was looking better each moment that went by.

"Johnny," his mother impatiently quipped, "you are not a doctor. Listen to the Chaplain; she's seen this many times before. We don't want to make anything worse than it is."

"Mom, I'm fine, I'm fine. Don't make a big deal out of this," Johnny replied.

Major piped up, "You idiot. You almost killed yourself. You scared us all half to death! What do you mean not to make a big deal out of this? It is a big deal, you stupid dope."

"Slow down boys," Don said sternly. "I know everyone here is pretty upset and scared, and that makes it harder to stay calm. Let's just settle down and take this one step at a time. It's going to be okay."

I could tell Major felt badly about his little outburst. Mr. Tender-hearted hated to see his big, strong, older brother in such bad shape.

"I am so sorry, Johnny," he said, "I was just pretty damn scared."

Through a firmly clenched jaw, his mother loudly said, "Watch your mouth, sonny."

"I know, I know," Major said awkwardly.

Aimee gently placed the blanket over John's upper torso so we could still keep a close eye on the badly injured leg. She then gave him a few sips of water and wiped off some of the bloodied dirt and hay from his head and face. Those gentle acts of caring were probably as healing for her as they were for her son.

John was bearing the situation a little better; he was stable but everyone saw that he was still struggling with the intense pain.

I quietly said, "No further bleeding, he is conscious, rationally thinking and clearly speaking. I think my work here is done.

"May I call John's wife for you?" I hesitantly asked.

"Thanks, Chaplain. But I already called her when I called 9-1-1."

We all looked outside as the sound of a car rushing down the gravel road grabbed our attention. It was Melody. She stopped the car, jumped out, leaving the door open, and ran full speed toward us.

"Is he okay?" she worriedly screamed before reaching the barn.

She ran over and carefully knelt down beside her husband, visibly unsure if she should even touch him. Gently, she cupped his face in her hands and lightly kissed him on his forehead.

"I'm okay honey, I'm okay," John said as he tried to reassure her. It wasn't working because she broke out into tears. She just slumped over by his side with her face covered in her now-bloody hands. Aimee quietly slipped beside her, comforting her as only one woman could with another.

As I led our precious little group in prayer for help and healing, we were relieved to hear the faint wail of the siren off in the distance. Help was on the way.

The medics were quick and efficient. Both of them knew John and chided him a bit while ensuring he was stable and ready to be moved. Those few minutes seemed like hours, but now that they were here, it seemed like seconds and John was in the ambulance and off to the hospital.

All of John's family members rushed off in the big farm truck, following the ambulance. The medics let Melody ride in the back with John because she was the spouse. She was ever so grateful for their kindness. I told Don that I'd secure the animals and lock up the storage areas and the house, then meet up with them later.

A whistling sigh of relief seeped out of my mouth. I thought, barring any unforeseen circumstances, he was going to be okay. Our young farmer should be back in the saddle before we knew it.

Yikes, what a day this has been! I spent an extra few minutes alone in prayer for John and the whole crew of Garretts. These are some of the tougher parts of life, for sure. Multitudes wonder why bad things happen to good people. I have had to address that many times, with many people, in oh so many ways.

But I think it is harder for those of us born in modern times. We think a broken leg is a catastrophe. It is, to the one whose leg is broken, but not really in the scheme of things. For those living back in the earliest times of civilization, they were annihilated by diseases, eaten by lions, their children thrown into the volcanoes as sacrifices. As time went on, suffering continued with the rotted meats, worm-ridden produce, and contaminated water, certainly making living a daily challenge. Heck, if you got through all of that and lived to be thirty-five, you were old by their standards!

Today, when suffering hits, it seems people can't get past their anger towards God. At these times, they often feel betrayed or left behind by Him. They feel God is teasing them or is cruel. How can He allow starvation, terrible accidents, cancer, terrorism, or the many things that assail us today?

Upping the ante somehow works in our favor, though. In C.S. Lewis' book, *A Grief Observed,* he wrote that you never know how much you really believe anything until its truth or falsehood becomes a matter of life and death to you.

Lewis struck on such a truth. As I study the numerous sufferings of the persecuted in third world countries, I have come to the conclusion that American Christians, bloated with the abundance of our blessed country, just may have a skewed view of suffering.

When you think about it, pain can actually be a gift. It is a physical warning that something is not right, something is out of place. It sends a signal to stop what you are doing so you can prevent further injury. It is a warning to run quickly for a remedy and a cure. I think that is what "soul pain" is all about, too. Rejection, anger, relational catastrophes, broken promises, unforgiveness, bitterness. . .maybe if we recognized those pains as "gift signals" that something in our souls was broken, maybe we would run for their remedies, too.

Now don't get me wrong, I am not ever going to volunteer to suffer, but when calamity comes, I must really look deeply into my soul as to what my response will be. Just as a refiner refines gold, the Garretts are being tested in the crucible of life, and in that heated pot, the dross will rise to the top and be skimmed off by a merciful God. The result will be even purer gold!

I packed up some water and snacks for my weary and worried neighbors, and headed off to the hospital. While I rushed off, I continued to thank God that we have vehicles and paved roads to get there, and that we have a destination of a modern, well-equipped, well-staffed hospital that will take care of our young patient with the utmost of care. Suffering? I suppose so.

At the hospital, I met the family at the surgical floor's waiting room. They were a bit brightened by the doctors' assessment of

7

John's wounds. After the corrective surgery, which would include the insertion of a rod into the bone of the lower leg, followed by a cast for a number of weeks, the prognosis was excellent. We all rejoiced at the news.

I knew Melody was especially grateful, for she loved her husband dearly. He is her whole world, and for a short time, that world had come crashing down on her.

"Chaplain, could we talk for a minute, please?" she asked.

"Of course, step over into my office," I jokingly said as I pointed to two empty chairs on the other end of the room.

"I can never thank you enough for being there for John and our family."

"Whoa, stop right there," I replied. "That's what neighbors are for. It's what makes our country great. We look out for each other. Maybe the politicians don't have that tied down yet, but most of our great citizens do. I love your family and would do anything for them."

"I know, but I just want to make sure I take the time right here and now to personally tell you how grateful I am, that you knew what to do and also helped the others in doing it. And our family loves you, too. You know that we would do anything for you. You have been such a blessing to us over the years. Sort of like a sister to Don and Aimee and, how can I say this without offending you. . .like a second mom to the boys."

I laughed aloud. "Don't worry, honey. The 'mom' word is good. I always wanted to be one." But inside I thought *you'll never know how much I've wanted to hear that word lovingly spoken to me.*

After hearing me laugh, Melody seemed to feel at ease to do the same. The family looked over at what seemed a bit of an inappropriate response. I heard Major pipe up, "Oh, that's just the Chaplain cooling the heat off the situation a bit. She's pretty good at that."

Don quietly asked us all to join in with a prayer of thanksgiving. We gathered around, holding hands, heads bowed as he started reverently and humbly speaking.

"Dear God, Your mercy has been seen today with my son, John. It's as if Your hand caught him mid-air and You laid Him down gently to prevent an even worse injury. We are grateful beyond measure. I thank You for my family, our friends, and for our lives in You.

We do not take it for granted that You are in authority over us and have chosen mercy and love to be given to us while in this suffering time. Help us to have the right viewpoint in it all and may we never forget that we can do all things in You. Amen."

Hmm, it almost seemed as if Don crawled in my head and heard my thoughts about suffering! Weird!

Upon the prayer's conclusion, Don looked at the boys and said, "It will be hard for you to leave right now, but those animals and the farm still need tendin' to. I hate to ask you to go, but it's the better part of wisdom. I'll call you as soon as John gets out of surgery and you can come back up this evening." He hesitantly said, "Okay, guys?"

I was so proud of them, especially my young Major; they never even winced when they heard their father's decision.

Joshua started gathering his things and stoically said, "Dad, a man's gotta do what a man's gotta do. Major and I will take care of everything. Don't you worry one bit. If we have any questions, we'll just give you a call. Take care of Mom, we'll be fine."

Don replied, "You are two fine young men, and I love you so much. You have what it takes. Thanks for all your help."

Major eagerly said, "We got this one, Dad." And off they hustled.

I asked, "Would this be a good time for me to leave also? I think I'll go back and make some dinner for the boys before they return here, and that way you'll have some leftovers for tomorrow, too. Then Saturday night is all taken care of, if that is still on, that is."

Aimee was quick to reply, "I am going to milk this for all it's worth. Saturday spaghetti and tonight's chow, that's two dinners I don't have to make. . .I'll take it!

I smiled at her reply. I could see a bit more peace shining forth on her once saddened and worried face.

"But" she added, "If you could bring the spaghetti over to our house and we could eat it there, I'd feel a little better. I know it may sound stupid, but it would feel more like a party to me if it was at your house and I'm just not up to that right now."

"Sure, no problem, dearheart."

8

*W*ell, it surely had been a long week, but John was doing extremely well, was resting comfortably at home, getting used to crutches and a portable potty by his bed! Things were good. The farm routines seemed to be settling down, and I think the family has dodged a bullet in the battle of life.

No excuses, I had better get that coffee on. This morning Major will be coming over to continue our talks. Hmm, maybe I'll throw on some pancakes, too. . .he's an eating machine and he'll need something for the coffee to wash down.

About an hour later, as I watched him scoop up the sweet concoction, I jokingly remarked, "Well, I see you like my invention of hot pancakes, smeared with peanut butter, topped with a scoop of vanilla ice cream and dripping with warm maple syrup!"

"Oh yeah," he said through a delectable mouthful.

"With all that has gone on over the last few days, have you even had a chance to look at that list I gave you of the mess assailing our country?"

"Sure did, ma'am. My dad read it too, and said we were slowly going to hell in a hand basket."

"Seems that way sometimes, but I think we have a huge majority of people who are tired of being told that all that junk is okay. It seems that those without a high moral code have the microphone right now and are calling out the cadence. Little do they realize that so many of us are not marching to the beat of that drummer. Personally, I think all this talk of legalizing drugs, legalizing prostitution, having laws on the books about abortion on demand, allowing homosexual marriages is going to wake up a 'sleeping giant' in our country—not a giant that goes around pulverizing all those who don't meet the code, but a giant that finally stands up and decries the debauchery! A wise man once said that for evil to triumph, all that is needed is for good people to do nothing. True back then and it's still true today."

Major said with puzzlement in his voice, "Yeah, but what can you do?"

"First, finish eating your pancakes so you don't have to talk with your mouth full!"

"Oops, sorry 'bout that," he said with a grin.

"Probably the most important thing to do is to make sure you live a high moral standard yourself. Nothing falls flatter than someone saying what to do and then not doing it themselves."

Major was still eating, and I continued, "But again, it is not all about rules. What God is talking about is holy guidelines. Everything God did has deep meaning to it. . .and many things, especially in the Old Testament, were word pictures so we could see things more clearly. The whole essence of the Old Testament would come around again in the New Testament, only this time it would be a new and living way. . .not by law, but by love.

The Tabernacle in the Wilderness is a good example. God gave specific instructions on its setup, the colors to be used, the size of the structure, etc. Building it wasn't just so they would have something to do; everything about the Tabernacle was symbolic. It was a picture of what was yet to come. So much of what it means can be seen only when we look back and compare then and now."

"Like what?" he managed to mutter.

"Like, there was only one entrance to it then, telling us there is only one way to God. The first thing you saw once inside the entrance was the altar of sacrifice, and that is the first thing we have to do today to enter into God's presence. That is, give up your life; give up what you want and how you see it, so you can put on the life of Christ. Like, the Laver was there for the priests to wash up before going into the presence of God in the 'Holy of Holies,' and today we are told to wash with the water of the Word of God. Like, some

70

bread was on the table in the 'Holy Place' section of the Tabernacle, and today, Jesus is the Bread of Life that we are to 'eat,' meaning to take inside of us for strength, just as you would physical food for physical strength. Get my drift?"

"Wow, never heard that before. And let me guess. . .the Tabernacle, where God would have a meeting of sorts with His people, that symbolizes our bodies today. . .the 'Temple of the Spirit of God,' right?"

I know the shocked look on my face could not be hidden. Could this young pup have possibly understood what I just said, and to the magnitude that he got to the crescendo of understanding before I finished the rest of my statements? God must have a special plan for this guy!

"And you didn't think I was listening, did you, Chaplain?"

"I knew you were listening, but I never thought you went down that deep, kid", I responded.

Major continued, "My dad used to tell me something like that. I don't know how I know, I just do. Sometimes when he would read a passage, I would know what it meant for us today and I would share it. He would look shocked like you just did, too."

"Well, I don't mean to be shocked; it's not that you can't understand this moral and spiritual stuff, it's just that not too many young ones do."

"I'm good, I'm really good," he said with a smile.

"And humble, really humble," I said with a broader grin.

"Let's get going here, Major. Are there any pressing issues to cover, or anything bugging you about the circle of life or something?"

"Yeah, lots of things. But before we get into that, you really stirred up my curiosity about the Founding Fathers and the way things were long ago. You said people in the government actually talked about Jesus and stuff."

"Yup, actually said His name, right out loud in meetings and in speeches."

"Gee, we can't even pray at our sports activities or graduation. My oldest brother said he heard that students used to pray in school and even read a Bible verse to start the day, but not anymore. You got any more of those papers like you gave me before. I'd like to look them over."

"Sure do. I think you'd like to see the account of Gov. William Bradford. The contrast to today is stark, but it fits right in with exposing the foolishness of what some of our politicians are trying to do nowadays. Socialism and Communism only sound good on paper, honey. . .'From each according to his ability, to each according to his need'. . .so lofty, so fine!"

"Yeah, that sounds good, what's the problem?" he asked.

"Well, the problem is that it only works on paper, because when you apply it to human beings, it falls apart. Sort of like this. . .people like you and me are hard workers. You don't have to tell us twice to do something."

"Correction there, Chaplain, sometimes I have to be told a few times before I get it in gear."

"Well, that's another story. . .I think they call that 'teenage-itis'!

"Anyways, it's sort of like this. I would be out in the field picking twenty bushels of corn a day because that's just who I am. . .a worker, competitive, Type A personality, etc. And the soul next to me might be one of the 'artsy-fartsies' of life, a Type B personality. He's looking at each ear of corn and he revels about how the sun shines on it. Under Socialism and Communism, the state, to varying degrees, determines all the rules. . .the hiring, the firing, the salaries and the salary caps of all workers. So I pick twenty bushels a day, my compadre out there picks only five bushels a day, but the state has decided that we both are paid the same. . .you know, the 'fair share' junk they proclaim today. What do you think will happen after a few short weeks? Will the five bushel a day guy start picking twenty bushels?"

"Yeah, right! The twenty bushel a day guy will only pick five bushels."

"And why's that?" I asked him.

"Because if you both make the same pay, why would you work extra hard? You'd start backing down to only five bushels a day."

"Bingo, you got it! And that is why, throughout history, those types of systems have failed miserably. It's not that the twenty-bushel guy is better than the five-bushel guy. . .their difference in

8

attitude and ability is just a fact of the human existence. You have
the workers and you have the shirkers. You've seen it, even in high
school. Everyone knows the ones who always volunteer to plan and
help set up and clean up after school events.

And then there are those who show up and take full advantage
of what everyone else has done. They eat the food, have fun with all
the people, enjoy the decorations and the prizes. . .and then just go
home. I think you understand, right?"

"Roger that," he said.

"Now, with Capitalism, more correctly called 'free enterprise'. . .the scene is different. What someone like me would do
when the system offers me to be paid for every bushel I pick, I
would keep picking so I could earn even more. At some point, I
would remember that I had a bunch of brothers and sisters back
home and I would get them out there, too. Then one of my brothers
would want to invent a machine that could pick even more. Because
we had more money from all of us picking bushels like crazy, we
could build the machine and pick even more bushels.

"When the bushels start piling up, we could hire more workers
and pay them. We could build barns to store the corn and pay people
to build the barns. When the business grew, we could construct an
office building, and that's more jobs, then people could invest in the
company and we could pay them back dividends on their invest-
ment. And on and on it 'grows.'"

Major said, ever so seriously, "I guess that making money is a
good thing then."

"You bet. The point is, though, what you do with it, and that's
where the morality comes in. If you share your profits with those
who helped you make them, then everyone wins. If you have even
bigger bucks, then you turn around and help improve the community, which supports your business. The incentive is profit, and more
of it. I don't mean the greedy, crawl up your mother's back type, but
rather with the attitude that the more you have, the more you can
give and the more you can help."

"Why don't they teach that?" he asked.

"For the life of me, I don't know why. All you hear lately is the
President and others quoting the Bible where it says that to the one

whom much is given, much is required. They never seem to quote the verse that says, 'If a man doesn't provide for his family, he is worse than an infidel' or the one that says, 'If you don't work, you don't eat.'"

"Yeah, you never hear that."

"But we used to in this country. And that brings me back to old Gov. Bradford. He remembered that when the early settlers from England came to Jamestown, their charter established a communal or common store system. The system failed miserably because that broken nature of man kicked in and some worked hard while the others lived off the fruits of someone else's labor.

"Anyways, Gov. Bradford saw that this communal system only dumbed everyone down to the lowest common denominator, and practically destroyed diligence and efficiency. Some people worked hard to 'fill the barn,' while others did not, because they knew the communal system gave out equally to all, so they fell into the inevitable slacking off. Gov. Bradford fixed this dilemma by dividing the land among the families, so each family was responsible for itself. Can we say 'free enterprise,' anyone? Lo and behold, the next fall harvest brought abundance to all.

"Here, you can read this later, but look at some comments found in *Of Plymouth Plantation*:"

> *This had very good success, for it made all hands very industrious, so as much more corn was planted than otherwise would have been by any means the Governor or any other could use, and saved him a great deal of trouble, and gave far better content. The women now went willingly into the field, and took their little ones with them to set corn; which before would allege weakness and inability; whom to have compelled would have been thought great tyranny and oppression.*[4]

"My, my. . .look at that. When you give the individual the free enterprise opportunity, the industriousness of the individual is encouraged and even wanted, because it meant they could work as hard as they wanted and the blessings of their labor could be theirs.

Even the women, who before said they were too weak or unable, all of a sudden wanted to be in the field, because they could be part of providing even more for their children and family."

"Chaplain, maybe you could apply to be a history teacher again."

"Don't think so. But I do want to get a message out there. And not just about capitalism and free enterprise. It's not about money and 'stuff.' It's about living a life led by God. And that doesn't mean you'll be perfect in doing it, either. That great God of ours is not offended when we stumble about; He just looks for a willing heart. But, as I said before, if you try to live your life like God directs, but only with the broken human nature, it will never work. Graft, greed, corruption. . .all that junk will just sneak right back in there, no matter how good you try to set things up. The nature of man will always perform at the lower level. That's why it is imperative to ensure you have the God nature inside and let its perfection start coming through!"

With a sad look on his face, Major stated, "I guess we're not doing a good enough job at that in our country."

"Unfortunately, you're very right. But I am not dismayed. There is always hope, meaning a happy expectation of good. We are Americans, with a long history of a fierce desire to have individuals share the power that forms their own destiny. These desires course through our veins, unlike any other group or country. I don't say that with ignorant pride, I say that by observing the facts of our history. We have within us a deep, innate desire to have the opportunity to work and live with each other, unencumbered by the constraints of an overbearing government. And even though we are in a struggle to maintain that level of freedom today, I am a great believer that good will win out."

Major smiled and said, "You mean that God will win out!"

"Yeah, that too, Bubba. Say, while we're on the subject, let me give you a few more examples of how some of the founders of our nation thought and what they wrote. You can take these on home and look at them later. For now, you had best get back a little early. Your dad may need that extra hand on board, seeing as your brother John is going to be down for the count for a while."

"Good idea," he said. "I'll look at these before I crash tonight. And thanks again for taking the time to get this stuff to me. It's funny, at first I thought I'd be bored when you started talking about this stuff, but I really kind of like it. See you tomorrow. Hey, how about some of that famous barbequed chicken of yours sometime soon?"

"What? Who died and made me the cook?" I jokingly said.

"Oh, you love to cook. . .especially for me. . .I can tell!"

"Yeah, right, you little bozo. I'll think about it. Get on home now."

That kid cracks me up. I am blessed to be around him and his family. He has me wrapped around his little finger, and he knows it! I'll have to make sure I stay one step ahead of him.

Well, now it's time for me to get a bite to eat. Hmm, maybe I will work on that chicken. Oh, brother, that means another trip into town!

9

*A*fter a long day of working with his dad and Joshua, Major hurriedly finished his dinner and dashed off to take a shower. "Major, what's the rush?" shouted Joshua.

"I wanna finish going over some info Chaplain gave me. It's really interesting. Gotta run," he shouted back.

"What about watching the game with Dad and me tonight?" Joshua continued.

"Record it for me, will ya'? Thanks."

Joshua turned to his dad and said, "What's up with that? He always watches the game with us. Heck, it's the finals and the Celtics are winning, for crying out loud!"

"Be patient, son. Major has some soul searching to do on his journey right now. God's just using Chaplain to help put together some of the pieces. Sort of like what Pastor was talking about last Sunday at church. Remember, he told us of the 'theme' God had given him for this year; 'Transforming Lives; Putting the Pieces of Life's Puzzle Together'."

Joshua was quiet for a long time. Don broke the silence and asked, "What's up, son?"

"I don't know, Dad. I've been thinking a lot lately. Ya' know with John's accident and all. Sometimes I really doubt God and feel bad about that and then get angry with Him again. I feel like a bouncing ball sometimes about the God stuff."

Don smiled at his son. He was thinking how blessed he was to have his kids talk about the "God stuff," even in their doubts. He said to Joshua, "Wondering about God is a universal part of our humanity. You may think that people disobey God because of all the suffering and pain in this world. But you gotta remember, Adam and Eve were in a perfect world without any of that junk going on and they still chose against God. It's your own will and choices, not your surroundings that cause the doubting. That's why you have to surrender that will to God so He can fill you with His. Then the doubts fade, at least for a while.

"Remember, Satan wants you down in doubt, not firm in faith. His work to destroy you is so much harder when you stand with God; so you have to seek for God with all your heart. I think that's where Major is right now in his life. So, do you still want to insist that he watch the game with us?"

"Heck, no. I ain't jumpin' into that spiritual stuff. Let's just watch TV for now."

Don put his arm around Joshua's shoulders and they walked into the living room.

"Hey, Aimee," Don yelled, "Make a batch of your famous popcorn for us, would you please?"

"Sure honey," she replied. "I want to catch the game, too. Go, Celtics."

They all laughed.

Major was sitting at the desk in his room and heard the laughter downstairs. He smiled and tenderly said, "Bunch of nuts, but you gotta love them."

He pulled out the papers that Chaplain gave him earlier and started going over some of the quotes.

"That's some pretty interesting info. I gotta share this with Joshua, too."

He started reading again.

JOHN DICKENSON, signer of the Constitution wrote,

Rendering thanks to my Creator for my existence and station among His works, for my birth in a country enlightened by the gospel and enjoying freedom, and for all His other kindnesses, to Him, I resign myself, humbly confiding in His goodness, and in His mercy through Jesus Christ for the events of eternity.[5]

JOHN JAY, original Chief Justice of the U.S. Supreme Court wrote,

Unto Him who is the author and giver of all good, I render sincere and humble thanks for his manifold and unmerited blessings, and especially for our redemption and salvation by His beloved Son. [6]

GEORGE MASON, Father of the Bill of Rights wrote,

My soul and I resign into the hands of my Almighty Creator, whose tender mercies are all over His works, who hateth nothing He hath made, and to the justice and wisdom of whose dispensations, I willingly and cheerfully submit, humbly hoping from his unbounded mercy and benevolence, through the merits of my blessed Savior, a remission of my sins.[7]

"I never saw any of this before," he murmured. "These are smart guys, the leaders of our country, and look what they were writing to each other and to the people. I don't hear anything like that today. I guess we really have switched from a God-honoring, God-including people to a God-excluding generation. Who can I tell this to? How can I get this out there? I guess this is what Chaplain meant in seeking for and finding out the truth."

"Hey honey," his mom yelled up to him. "You want any popcorn before I start cleaning up?"

"No thanks," he yelled back. "Who won"?

"Celtics did!"

"Yes," he cheered, pulling his arms towards his chest in a victory gesture.

He finally put the papers down, crawled into bed and started dozing off to sleep.

He mumbled to himself, "It's been one hell of a long day. Holy crap, I had better start cleaning up my mouth. Can't be out there saying one thing and doing another. Man, what am I going to do in the Marines? They'll think I'm a jerk or something if I don't swear; can't worry about that right now. And besides, I have a bigger problem chewing at me inside. Oh, help me, Lord, to figure it all out. I am so afraid to tell Chaplain or my folks what I've done. They'll be so disappointed in me."

10

As I pondered life, liberty, and the pursuit of happiness, I wanted to give Major a few sides of the story here. He will need to start knowing what is true, and what is not, and he can't if he only gets one viewpoint. It is dangerous, though, to throw some of this philosophy out to our young ones. They are so new at life, so gullible. I can see why God said to bring up a child in the way in which he must go, so even when he is old he will not stray from it. I guess another old saying is just as true that if you don't stand for something, you'll fall for anything.

I can't control anyone's response to life. Heck, I have enough trouble controlling my own, but I do want my hands clean in what I tell the young ones, and for them to turn around and do the same to others.

A significantly different slant on all this is seen with the secular humanists. Paul Kurtz, in 1980, drafted up a document called, *A Secular Humanist Declaration.* That would be a good one to show Major. There are some great ideas in there, and some not so great ones. I'll report, he'll have to decide. I will pray for God's ways to win out in him.

I'll have to dig up my notes on my computer. If I remember correctly, Kurtz gives an outline of the secular humanist's basic doctrine. They say it's not, but I call it a religion really. . .it has all the tenets of a religion, it seems. . .a god they worship (the mind), a set of doctrines they follow and make their decisions upon (the Secular Humanist Manifesto), and a church they attend (life and the desires of their hearts). It all sounds so good, that is until you apply it to that problematic broken human nature. But, wait. . .Secular Humanists have fixed that problem. . .they just state there is no such thing as a broken human nature or divine interventions to redeem you from the power of that nature. Isn't that simple now! You don't like the rules of a God, so you just say there is no God and can now do what you want. Brilliant, eh? But wait. . .aren't we back to the football game without the rules situation? Oh well, I'm trying to explain something here, but sometimes people just don't listen.

"Where did I file that?" I asked myself quite loudly.

Some secular concepts are just ever so nice sounding, sweet, beguiling even. They speak freely of free inquiry, civil liberties, and diversity of opinion, and I surely can agree with that. They defend basic human rights and the pursuit of happiness. And to tell you the truth, they do not mock religion in any way and are totally against the aggressive sectarian and religious ideologies that use political parties and governments to crush dissident opinion. [8] I hope Major doesn't get the idea that I am mocking these people, but I have to bring up their tenets of belief, not to mock or revile the philosophy, just to compare it.

The problem with applying this ideology to our system today is that it leads us even further away from the original intent of our Forefathers. And that poses that sticky problem again. We have inherited a democratic republic with unheard of freedoms, but the secular humanist wants to put it solely in the hands of humanity without acknowledging any divine Intervention. As far as I can tell historically, the hands of humanity haven't done so good a job at that. Some may even say that God Himself hasn't done too good a job, either. I hope people remember though, we kicked Him out of much of the public square quite a while ago, so we can't really blame Him. Sort of like the sign that I saw the other day. "Dear God, why have You allowed so much violence in our schools? Signed, A Concerned Student. Dear Concerned Student, I am not allowed in schools. Signed, God." Kind of says it all!

Let's see, here are a few of the secular humanist viewpoints and conclusions they have regarding our moral compass and the road they feel we should travel. I'll get these run off for our meeting in the morning.

Secular Humanist Ideal #2, ". . .secular humanists believe in the principle of the separation of church and state." [9]

My, my, where have I heard this before!

Secular Humanist Ideal #4, "The secular humanist recognizes the central role of morality in human life. . .ethical judgments can be formulated independently of revealed religion, and that human beings can cultivate practical reason and wisdom and, by its application, achieve lives of virtue and excellence. . .thus, secularists deny that morality needs to be deduced from religious beliefs. . .we are opposed to absolutist morality. . .and [that] ethical values and principles may be discovered in the course of ethical deliberation." [10]

Does that seem to translate into, "We can do this better than God can"? I am eager to hear what my dear Major's response will be to all this.

If humankind is now the head of morality, what power must they exert to have people follow it? People don't obey God's commands, how do they think they will get people to obey men? Oh well, I just think too much.

And how can you have "ethical deliberations," without a common <u>truth</u> and <u>base</u> from which to work? Not just a belief system, but actual truth. For example, how can you have successful ethical deliberations when some say abortion is a woman's right, and others say continuing the life of the fetus trumps the inconvenience and discomfort of the mother? Or, how can you talk about what entails integrity if some are of the opinion that some types of lies aren't really lies? Anyone remember, "It depends on what your definition of 'is' is"!

The ethical deliberations will get pretty muddled when some say consensual sex is okay for fourteen-year-olds; yet others say sixteen-year-olds, and yet still others say not until within the boundaries of a solid, stable marriage. A marriage, by the way, which should include a decent dwelling place and mature adults who are eager and able to provide the necessities of life for any children they may procreate. I think those ethical deliberations will get really heated too when some say the federal government should be large and powerful while others say it should be small and contained. How is anyone going to come to consensus on these and many issues without a common core belief? It can't be done, as is evident from today's gridlock on every issue.

Secular Humanist Ideal #6, "We are doubtful of traditional views of God and divinity. . .and. . .reject the idea that God has intervened miraculously in history, or revealed himself to a few, or that he can save or redeem sinners." [11]

No God, no rules. . .just right! Oh, yeah!

Secular Humanist Ideal # 7, ". . .the need to embark upon a long-term program of public education and enlightenment concerning the relevance of the secular outlook to the human condition." [12]

And embark they certainly have done. Of the fifty-eight signers of this secular humanist declaration, thirty were college professors. I dare say they have achieved a huge portion of their goal to secularize our country through the educational system. And many of the "secularized" individuals who sat under their teachings are now in charge in all facets of our society.

I will make it clear to Major that I am not picking on the secular humanists. They have a right to say their piece and live accordingly. I am just using their philosophy as a contrast against the philosophy and guiding principles of the Founding Fathers and encouraging us to take a closer look at the effects of a godless, secular viewpoint on

10

a society and its people. I wonder if people really like what we have now and where we are heading.

Oh, it's late, but I'd better run off some of the vastly contrasting statements from our Founding Fathers. That way Major can do some comparative analysis. . .if he even goes that far with it. Am I going overboard with this? Not that I tend to do that. I laughed as I thought that!

JOHN ADAMS (1735 – 1828), Second President of the U.S. and the first to live in the White House, was a graduate of Harvard, signer of the Declaration of Independence, U.S. Minister to France, and author of *A Defense of the Constitutions of the Government of the United States*. This three-volume work was instrumental in influencing the American states to ratify the Constitution.[13] He wrote in a diary entry of February 22, 1756:

Suppose a nation in some distant region should take the Bible for their only law book, and every member should regulate his conduct by the precepts there exhibited! Every member would be obliged in conscience to temperance, frugality and industry; to justice, kindness and charity towards his fellow men; and to piety, love and reverence toward Almighty God. . .What a Eutopia, what a Paradise would this region be. [14]

LEWIS CASS (1782 – 1866) was an American soldier, lawyer, politician, and diplomat. He served in the war of 1812, was a United States Senator and the Secretary of State under Pres. James Buchanan. In 1848, he was the Democratic candidate for President. [15] He stated:

Independent of its connection with human destiny hereafter, the fate of republican government is indissolubly bound up with the fate of the Christian religion, and the people who reject its holy faith will find themselves the slaves of their own evil passions and of arbitrary power. [16]

Oh, I hate to say it, but right now, I'm feeling it. . ."I told you so, I told you so"!

BENJAMIN FRANKLIN (1706 – 1790), author, scientist, printer, diplomat, signer of the Declaration of Independence, the Articles of Confederation and the Constitution. He also taught himself five languages, made important discoveries in electricity, invented the lightning rod, the Franklin stove, the rocking chair, bifocal glasses and numerous scientific discoveries. He organized the first postal system, the first volunteer fire department, a circulating public library, a city police force, and even the lighting of streets.[17] He was no illiterate country bumpkin, clinging to his Bible and his guns. And in 1748, as Pennsylvania's Governor, he proposed Pennsylvania's first Fast Day, saying:

It is the duty of mankind on all suitable locations to acknowledge their dependence on the Divine Being. . .[that] Almighty God would mercifully interpose and still the rage of war among the nations. . . [and that] He would take this province under His protection, confound the designs and defeat the attempts of its enemies, and unite our hearts and strengthen our hands in every undertaking that may be for the public good and for our defence and security in this time of danger.[18]

It's late, or early, depending on how you look at it. Two o'clock in the morning and I just can't sleep! My head is spinning with all the things I wanted to share with Major. "Oh, just slow down," I scold myself.

"But I can't." Good grief, I am talking out loud to myself. I am so glad I am alone right now.

Well, I am wide-awake, so maybe I'll just run off a few more things for our morning meeting, some that are more recently dated rather than those from back in the 1700s and 1800s. Just to show that it wasn't only two hundred years ago that we had Americans thinking about God and the common moral code. It has been much more recently than that.

Then I'll slip back to bed for a little nappie. I might as well, because I still can't sleep with all this on my mind!

SCHOOL DISTRICT OF ABINGTON TOWNSHIP, PENN-SYLVANIA (prior to 1963) endorsed the following public school policy:

Each school. . . Shall be open by the reading, without comment, of a chapter in the Holy Bible. . . participation in the opening exercises. . . is voluntary. The student reading verses from the Bible may select the passages and read from any version he chooses. . . There are no prefatory statements, no questions asked or solicited, no comments or explanations made, and no interpretations given at or during the exercises. The students and parents are advised that the student may absent himself from the classroom or, should he elect to remain, not participate in exercises.[19]

Now that intelligent interpretation allows for the reference to our Christian heritage to continue without subjugating the people to its constraints. And that would have sounded extremely reasonable to someone back at the founding of our nation or even as recently as the 1960s. That is because Christian principles were acknowledged as the backbone of this nation and in previous years (as is obvious from just the few previous quotes) produced a different type of individual with a vastly different viewpoint of who we are as a people and as a nation and where we stand with the need of God as our help.

I will remind Major that some can laugh all they want at the "Beaver Cleaver" generation I came from, and the Christian ethics upon which it was built, but look at what type of problems it generated versus the challenges of today.

1940 High School Seniors' Behavior Requiring Intervention	1990 High School Seniors' Behavior Requiring Intervention
Talking out of turn	**Drug Abuse**
Chewing gum	**Alcohol Abuse**
Making noise	**Pregnancy**
Running in the halls	**Suicide**
Cutting in line	**Rape**
Dress code violations	**Robbery**
Littering	**Assault**

Figure 1[20]

To the 1990 list, add the following for today[21]. . .

- Disrespect for teachers
- Bullying
- Sexual harassment
- Gang activity
- Undesirable cult/extremist activities

This is not looking good! The "don't tell me what to do, I live in the land of freedom and can do what I want, when I want with whom I want" mentality is undeniably destroying us.

Oh great, just what I need to help me drift off to sleep. Don Sr. reminded Major that we are going to hell in a hand basket and I'm supposed to be lulled off to sleep with those happy thoughts.

I quietly prayed, "Dear Lord, help me to keep my mind fixed on You and not the ever changing details of this world. Help me to rest tonight with a peaceful heart, trusting You. Amen."

11

The clouds were hanging low overhead this morning. Funny how that affects us sometimes, sort of "hangs" over our moods too. It was damp and dreary after an evening storm and I had to fight to remain chipper. "Oh, I want my sunny, crisp, clear, blue-skied day back!" I cried.

What a spoiled brat I am!

"Sorry 'bout that, Lord," I said under my breath.

I really am so grateful for my health, for my family, friends, and so much more. I can still bike, run my marathons, and hike out on the Appalachian Trail. The hiking is a bit slower and the running is now closer to lumbering, but at least I'm still out there doing it. I'm reminded of a sign I saw that said, "I may be running slowly, but I'm lapping everyone on the couch!"

In a way, it is a good example to the ones coming up behind me. I feel good that some of my younger acquaintances have taken up the same or similar activities. God made our bodies to be used and not abused. I laugh sometimes, though, when I read in the Bible where Paul mentioned that he "buffets" his body, meaning he fights its inborn cravings. Ha — in our country today, too many must think that means to go to a buffet and eat all you can!

"Hmm—that hot coffee is going to feel good going down," I said to myself. The storm brought in a bit cooler weather and I quickly went back inside to put on a sweatshirt and delight in the wafting smell of crescent rolls that filled the kitchen. Reminded me of my childhood on winter mornings when we came inside after shoveling the often four- to eight-foot-deep snowdrifts. My mom always had hot chocolate and some homemade goodies waiting for us. The memories covered me like a warm blanket.

As I came back out on the porch, I was glad it had a roof over it. That has made it very comfortable to stay out here, even in the rain. Only the most inclement and cold weather pushes me back inside to the protection and warmth of the cabin. Must be that farmer in me, I just love the outdoors.

Speaking of farmers, Major was coming up the road. . .and can I believe my eyes, his brother John was with him!

"Good grief, you nut. What the heck are you doing over here?"

"Hey Chaplain, just had to get out of the house," John said with a happy smile.

"Well, I surely am glad to see you getting around so well with those crutches. Most people never get the hang of them."

"No problem," he said. "I have 'Garrett' blood in my veins. We just tackle it as it comes!"

"I'm going to tackle you if you do anything to damage that leg," I quickly replied.

John just laughed and said, "I hear you cook up a mean breakfast!"

Major laughed and said, "Why do you think I come over here every morning?"

With a contrived look of shock on my face, I replied, "So that's your motive, you little weasel!"

We all laughed.

"Can I help you get up these steps, John?"

"Nope, I got it down, uh, I mean 'up.'"

The chuckles resumed, but John scurried up the stairs without hesitation. Ah, youth. . .it's wasted on the young!

"Well, John, you picked a bad morning to stop by. I only have coffee and pastries today."

"Sure, I get it. My brother is just your favorite!" he jokingly countered.

I thought, *oh, if you only knew.*

"Now boys, you know I love you all the same," I countered.

90

They dove into the coffee and freshly baked frosting-topped crescent rolls.

"Mm-mm, good," said John.

"True that," said Major.

"You guys threw me off this morning. Don't know if I can handle the two of you here together."

"Oh, sure you can," Major piped up.

I grinned and handed him the copies of the statements from the Founding Fathers, the info about secular humanism, as well as some of the more recent examples of God-honoring by the leadership in our country. On a separate sheet was the comparative list of the teen problems of the 1940s as compared to that of today. That caught John's eye.

"Hmmm, do you mind if I take a look at that, Chaplain?"

"Go right ahead, it's all going home with Major anyways. You can look at it now or later."

"Whoa, I never realized the seriousness of these changes," John commented. "By putting this stuff side by side, it gives you a better idea. You know most of us, me included," he continued, "are up to our necks in just trying to do the right thing. We work hard and don't have time to study the changes around us. My brother Don has three kids, and I have my two younger brothers. How can we possibly fight this sh. . .I mean, crap? Excuse my language, Chaplain."

"No offense, John. It's not me you offended, it's Him," I said looking and pointing up to the sky. "I'm just the sales rep!"

He laughed heartily at that comment and continued, "But I am serious. How in the world can we turn this ship around?"

I took a sip of coffee and started sharing some things with them both.

"I am reminded of a dream I once shared as I was speaking to one of the classes on the Vietnam War. In that dream, I told them I saw a bridge, representing the bridge of life, over raging, shark, snake and alligator-infested waters. And on that bridge, on each side, were high brick walls. I explained that the walls represented the high moral code with which my generation grew up. Those high walls prevented us from accidentally falling into that raging river and suffering grave injury or even death. Of course, there were always some fools trying to climb that wall because they didn't want to be 'controlled' or 'fenced in,' by the wall, and little by little, over the years, all the bricks were knocked off. Because of the slow, steady removal of the brick wall, many more of today's young people were going over that bridge of life and falling into the raging waters. But there was hope in my dream, for I saw this current generation crossing that same bridge, but each one of them had a brick in their hand and each one was laying down that brick, which would eventually return the moral safety net that our Founding Fathers knew a free society would require. Will our country, as we know it, last until that wall is rebuilt? Will we even allow its rebuilding? I am prayerful we will.

"As far as I can tell, the liberal, 'don't fence me in' crowd has the microphone right now. Our only hope is that we can somehow turn their volume down. I'm not saying to take the microphone away from them; I'm just saying to turn it down a bit so other voices can be heard and people will be able to make an informed choice."

Major jumped into the conversation. "I have been reading over all that information you gave me, Chaplain. And one thing seems to bug me. Why do we keep repeating the same mistakes? Don't we learn from history?"

Shaking my head, I said, "Unfortunately, history teaches us that history doesn't teach us! Wait here, I have something to show you."

I ran back inside and shuffled through my ton of research items. I was so glad I brought this boatload of stuff up here. I thought I was going to start writing my next book while here in the peace and quiet, but God must have had another plan for my time. . .and for these materials. Now where was that pile of historical commentaries? Pressure, pressure! Slow down and just keep looking. "Ah, I found it," I yelled.

Back outside, I continued. "I hate to read anything to you, but I haven't run off any copies of these. I tend to be a visual learner, and being read to doesn't help me much if I don't have a copy in front of me. Hope you can follow along. I will get some copies of this off to Major, and he can share it."

I jokingly added, "That is, if he wants to."

Major puffed up his chest, stuck his thumbs under his armpits, jutted out his lower jaw and said, "We'll have to see about that. I am sure I can work out an appropriate price for it all, bro."

"Yeah, right," chimed in John. "That'll be the day, you little jerk!"

"Listen to this," I said. "I think it surely proves that we don't learn from history. Rosalie Slater, a prolific Christian writer and thinker wrote:"

> *We maintained our Christian character as a nation. Then began our period of "falling away" when we worshipped the "effect" of our great success – and forgot the "cause." This vacuum was readily filled with man centered philosophies, which replaced the internal battles of conscience with the social, economic and political struggles of society.*
>
> *We veered from a period when, even our governmental proclamations were filled with the language of salvation and the recognition that Christ alone could change the hearts of men, to a preoccupation with educational, social, economic, and eventually political arrangements, which claim to ensure progress and improvement for society and hence for man.[22]*

"And here's another one, from a Dr. Jedidiah Morse, often called the Father of Geography. He wrote:"

> *To the kindly influence of Christianity, we owe that degree of civil freedom, and political and social happiness which mankind now enjoys. In proportion as the genuine effects of Christianity are diminished in any nation, either through unbelief or the corruption of its doctrine, or the neglect of its institutions; in the same proportion will the people of that nation recede from the blessings of genuine freedom, and approximate the miseries of complete despotism. I hold this to be a truth confirmed by experience. If so, it follows that all efforts made to destroy the foundations of our holy religion, ultimately tend to the subversion of our political freedom and happiness. Whenever the pillars of Christianity shall be overthrown, our present republican forms of government and all the blessings which flow from them must fall with them.[23]*

Both John and Major stared at me in disbelief. "Sounds pretty dire to me!" said John.

Major continued staring.

I started to speak and Major said, "Chaplain, I am going to make sure that for the rest of my life, I will honor God in all I say and do and will share that with whoever will listen. I don't want this great country of ours to be wasted. I want a great place to live in and a place to eventually get married in and bring up my kids."

"Glad to hear that," I continued. "It will be difficult to swim against the tide, but you're strong and can do this. John already has a great start and is doing his part, as are your mom and dad, your sister and older brothers. You two are really blessed to be in a family that understands these things. The key is going to be to continue to let God rule in your lives and let Him take care of the rest of this mess."

The coffee and pastries were gone, but my eager listeners weren't, so I continued.

"These apparently prophetic statements have not been heeded. It seems we just do not learn. The effects of such deep moral changes aren't just for discussion's sake—they are important because they change the basics from which we govern ourselves.

"A very liberal, revisionist philosophy of life is now flooding our homes, schools and government. This is significantly changed from our Forefathers' idea of life, liberty, and the pursuit of happiness. As a result, we are faced with the challenging, heck, dare I say 'screwy,' legal decisions of late.

"Let me read a few of them. Hang on, you won't believe these."

> *"When a student addresses an assembly of his peers, he effectively becomes a government representative; it is therefore unconstitutional for that student to engage in prayer."*[24]

"Here's some more, you be the judge of whether we've inadvertently given in to a decadent moral code, and even worse, have given to the government the power to actually legislate a religious belief. . .that of non-religion! Do you remember the wording of the beginning of the First Amendment? 'Congress shall make no law respecting an establishment of religion, or <u>prohibiting</u> the free exercise thereof. . .'

"Here's another interpretation, far from what was initiated by our Founders."

> *"A verbal prayer offered in the school is unconstitutional, even if that prayer is both voluntary and denominationally neutral."* [25]

> *"Freedoms of speech and press are guaranteed to students and teachers—unless the topic is religious, at which time such speech becomes unconstitutional."* [26]

"Here's another real goody". . .

> *"It is unconstitutional for students to see the Ten Commandments since they might read, meditate upon, respect, or obey them."* [27]

"Ya' think!" said Major.
John just shook his head.

> *"If a student prays over his lunch, it is unconstitutional for him to pray aloud."* [28]

"You can scream the vilest, most demeaning things toward the teachers and students, but you can't pray out loud!" said Major with a bit of irritation.

"Oh, but there's more," I said.

> *"It is unconstitutional for a public cemetery to have a planter in the shape of a cross, for if someone were to view that cross, it could cause 'emotional distress' and thus constitute an 'injury-in-fact'"* [29]

"Makes me want to injure something right about now too," blurted Major again.

"Hold on, big boy. I am not telling you this to incense you, but to inform you. If you go barreling out of here in the heat of anger, then you're going to be part of the problem and not the solution."

"But I feel like the country and all we stand for is being ripped away right under our noses," Major cried out.

With all the love I could muster, I calmly said to him, "Honey, that's just what happened to Jesus. His 'bride,' meaning us, was ripped right out of His hands by what Adam did. And what did He do? He turned right around again, not in anger, but gently put the offer back on the table and again asked us to come away and follow Him. He calls us His beloved, and we either do it or not; it's our choice to say yes or no to Him."

"So, what do you mean by that, Chaplain?" John asked.

"I mean that our response to these horrible moral changes must be the same as Jesus. Instead of wanting some militant takeover of those who have fallen for the lies, we have to woo them with love; kindness for unkindness, forgiveness in the face of unforgiveness and so on."

"But that is so 'girly,'" said Major.

"Hey, I resemble that remark," I quipped.

"I don't mean that, you know what I mean, Chaplain."

"You're right buddy, I do. But what I'm saying is that we have to depend more on the power of God. His power will convict the people who do not understand His truth about who He is. The old devil has been very active in using deception, right from the beginning, with Adam and Eve, for crying out loud! Satan's job is to rob, kill, and destroy us down here, and he's been very good at it. He's so good that people don't even shake their fists at him for all the evil they see; they shake their fist at God, who is their only rescue!"

"Yeah, I guess you're right," Major sighed.

"What do you mean, you guess she's right? She's the Chaplain, for Christ's sake," John said with a raised voice. "Oops, my bad."

"Let's get something straight right now, guys. I am not right because I am a chaplain or a pastor. If I am sharing what God has said is right, then it's right. I am no different than you are."

Major laughed and said, "Yeah, right."

"No, it's true. Just because I teach people what God says, doesn't make me 'holier than thou.' If anything, it makes me more responsible, but not holier. I have the same broken nature and have to fight it off in order to obey God too. I want His nature to rule in me because that is where the best counsel, decisions, actions, and help come from. I often tell people, your best day with me is when I'm not me!"

They both laughed.

"Well, can we wrap up here?" I asked. "I have just a couple more of these legislative rulings to read to you and then you can go and munch on them the rest of the day. Chores are waiting, you know!

"Here goes."

"It is unconstitutional for a classroom library to contain books which deal with Christianity, or for a teacher to be seen with a personal copy of the Bible at school." [30]

"But a book with graphic photos of men performing homosexual acts is okay to have in schools!" said John with obvious disagreement.

"And another that you will like. . ."

"It is unconstitutional for a kindergarten class to ask whose birthday is celebrated by Christmas." [31]

Major just rolled his eyes!

"In a high school class in Dickson, Tennessee students were required to write a research paper using at least four sources. Despite the fact that the students were allowed to write about reincarnation, witchcraft, and the occult, because student Brittney Settle chose to write her paper about the life of Jesus Christ, she was given a zero by her teacher." [32]

"And the corker of them all is. . ."

> *"In DeFuniak Springs, Florida, a judge ordered the courthouse copy of the Ten Commandments to be covered during a murder trial for fear that jurors would be prejudiced against the defendant if they saw the command, "Do not kill."*[33]

"Heck, maybe the defendant should have read it first!" said Major.

I tapped my papers on the table to arrange them in a neat pile again and said, "Granted, some of this legislation has been challenged, but many of them, and items like them still remain on the books. I am not picking on any one person, county or school district; I am just noting the changes unfolding in our country that are ever so different from what it was like way back when and what it is like now.

"I even heard on the radio the other day that some teachers wanted to change St. Patrick's Day to O'Green Day! Just the word, 'Saint' was considered inflammatory in the public square!" I exclaimed.

"Dang, where is common sense?" John said.

"I know," said Major. "It's not so common." There was a big grin on his face.

I rolled my eyes and shook my head. Major kept on grinning.

"Go ahead, Chaplain, continue."

"Well, thanks for the permission," I answered with a wry smile. "When you realize in the study of the demise of the Greek or Roman Empire or Hitler or Saddam Hussein, or Osama bin Laden, or their ilk, that their demise was not for their moral excellence, it was for their moral decadence. Whether village or villain, the moral code leads either to devastation and destruction or to success and prosperity. Which way are we going? And no, Major, you don't have to answer that question either!"

"I am glad of that cuz you sure have had some tough questions lately!" he cried out.

"It's just that I want to remind us that the Founding Fathers were not divided nor puzzled as to which moral direction they wanted our country to head. They, being men of faith, would certainly not have set up a system with policies that would limit that faith. They did not exclude but rather included God and His wisdom from the Scriptures in all phases of their existence.

"That does not mean they walked on water. . .far be it! They were men, with that same broken nature we spoke about earlier. They were prone to bribery, lies, and corruption just as we are today, but that 'moral wall' they fiercely clung to helped them greatly to keep from falling off into the raging waters of destruction as frequently and as furiously as we are today."

"I don't know where you get this, Chaplain, but I am glad I decided to talk to you each day. This is much more 'stuff' than I was thinking about, but I like it."

I proceeded, knowing I had to wrap this up. These guys had to get back; John needed to rest and Major had to get to work.

"I could give you example after example to make the point, but I'm in hopes that you've gotten it. Many laws we see today, whether through the legislative process or executive orders, along with the educational vision being promoted, the economic policies proposed and the principles upon which these things are based, are drastically different from the mission, vision, and purposes outlined in our founding roots. And this is a difference, I dare say, that has not promoted the common good and is the main reason we are in the social, economic, and political turmoil of the current time.

Our varied problems should direct us to new solutions, not a new 'updated' morality! Our Founding Fathers kept reiterating their basic tenet that the free society they espoused could not survive without a high moral wall securing it. Our current responses, whether regarding the war on poverty or the war on terrorism, seem to be based on an eroding moral foundation that is only creating more problems than it is solving.

"Just as originally said, history teaches us that history doesn't teach us."

John then said, "Well, I'd better get rollin'. It sure has been a great visit. You've got my brain running around inside my head, for sure. I have a lot to think about. Thanks again, and for the coffee too."

"Okay, guys. See you tomorrow, Major?"

"Yup, sure thing, ma'am. Big breakfast, by any chance?"

"I'll think about it," I replied with a smile. "Tomorrow, let's talk about what's good about America. This conversation hasn't been too encouraging lately, ya' think?" I asked.

They grinned again and simultaneously echoed, "Ya' think!"

Carefully they descended the porch stairs, being cautious with the crutches. Major gently helped his brother — well, as much as an older brother would let him!

They hobbled on down the road and across the field to the house. I was sure they were both exhausted, in body and brain. "Oh God, let my words be few and Your work complete," I prayed as I cleaned up the dishes.

What a nice surprise today when John came over with Major, I mused as I finished tidying up then started my day of studies and that much-needed rest I thought I came up here for! *Hmm, in regards to what is right about America, I have a couple of special poems I need to find. They too are buried in my "pile" of knowledge somewhere. . .let me see, just where are they?"*

I shuffled through the myriad of materials I lugged up here. Ah yes, here they are, "I Hear America Singing," by Walt Whitman and Sir Walter Scott's, "My Native Land." These are two of my favorite poems because they seem to shout out the very essence of the greatness of our country. I will run them off for him too. Let me read them again. . .

I Hear America Singing — Walt Whitman

I hear America singing, the varied carols I hear,
Those of mechanics — each one singing his, as it should be, blithe and strong.
The carpenter singing his, as he measures his plank or beam,
The mason singing his, as he makes ready for work, or leaves off work;
The boatman singing what belongs to him and his boat – the deck-hand singing on the steamboat deck;
The shoemaker singing as he sits on his bench – the hatter singing as he stands;
The woodcutter's song – the ploughboy's, on his way in the morning, or at the noon intermission, or at sundown;
The delicious singing of the mother – or of the young wife at work – or of the girl sewing or washing – Each singing what belongs to her and to none else;
The day what belongs to the day – At night, the party of young fellows, robust, friendly,
Singing with open mouths, their strong melodious songs.

My Native Land — Sir Walter Scott

Breathes there the man, with soul so dead,
Who never to himself hath said,
This is my own, my native land!
Whose heart hath ne'er within him burn'd,
As home his footsteps he has turn'd
From wandering on a foreign strand!
If such there breathe, go, mark him well,
For him no Minstrel raptures swell,
High though his titles, proud his name,
Boundless his wealth as wish can claim;
Despite those titles, power, and pelf,
The wretch, concentered all in self,
Living, shall forfeit fair renown,

> And, doubly dying, shall go down
> To the vile dust from whence he sprung,
> Unwept, unhonour'd, and unsung.
> (http://www.poemhunter.com)

I pondered over those words and thought, *"And doubly dying shall go down to the vile dust from whence he sprung, unwept, unhonored and unsung"! Growing up, that verse was what most of us felt described people who did not love this country and did not have a burning desire within their heart for her.*

Our country celebrated a tremendous victory in World War II, where most of the world was extremely grateful for the hard work and huge sacrifices our country made to make that happen. We not only maintained our own freedom but also brought a semblance of such to many others when the horrors of German Nazism, Japanese Imperialism and Italian Fascism were finally brought to an end. For years, our country was applauded for that, at least until those who were never rescued by our valiant effort came to the forefront of time.

Being born after WW II, I grew up in a country that saw the goodness of its people, honored God throughout the culture, and was extremely optimistic about our future, and the future of the world. It was a much safer place back then, not just in a dreamy type remembrance but also in actuality. I could and did walk safely to school by myself. . .and that was at age five on the way to kindergarten! And I did that in the big city of Boston; well, just outside of it in 'Dawchestah.' Yeah, and I lived in the Projects, to boot! Try that today without a police escort! Wait until I tell Major that story!

My mind wandered again. . .America is great for a combination of reasons. Mainly, we are great because its people are great. . .er, I mean, they used to be, that is. Naw, I think we still are. We live in an awesome country, blessed not only with the freedoms insisted upon by our forefathers but we are also blessed with a unique geographical location, all of which have prominently helped us achieve our greatness.

11

We have rich soil in vast plains, multiple mountain ranges with ample snow to feed our streams, massive rivers, whose location mid-country and north to south opened up endless shipping and commerce variations for life-sustaining supplies. We were sheltered by gigantic oceans on both sides, which protected our fledgling country from the foreign invasions that so disrupted the expansion and strength of many other countries.

All of this, along with that wonderful, inborn American "pioneer spirit" and the daring bravado that comes with the wind of freedom blowing through your hair, have given us the expansion of liberty and wealth we enjoy today. We are blessed with tremendous natural resources in great abundance, for which we have a sacred responsibility to use with wisdom and resourcefulness.

The freedoms to which we have access have allowed our people to embark on new horizons in research, discovery, and unimaginably creative technological advances. We have been able to expand our businesses freely and to invent products for use all over the world. No wonder Walt Whitman could pen that poem he heard "America singing." What an awesome place we have!

Yes, the magnificence of our country is found in its individuals. . .and that means every citizen! Our people, bathed in the myriad of choices and opportunities that only a free society can offer, have stepped up to the plate generation after generation. Our Declaration of Independence clearly stated our desire to come out from under the shackles of a monarchy, which was a form of government that chose its next leader by the birth line and not the ballot. Our founding nation screamed out, "F-R-E-E-D-O-M." I can hear their voices loudly echoing throughout the towns, bellowing that word, just as Mel Gibson did in the movie "Braveheart."

The principle of the individual having God-given rights, separate from what the government may bestow, was so strongly set in the hearts and minds of our forefathers that they even went to war to keep it. I pray that desire for individual freedom, securely wrapped in moral excellence, will still course through the blood of today's Americans. It is necessary because freedom is not free and must be fiercely fought for and guarded. Hmm, but a country not worth living in is a country not worth dying for. . .oh, so much to share with my young friend. I hope we'll be able to continue to bask in what is so awesome about our people and our nation and still shout, "God bless America, land that I love!"

Well, I might as well get a few more items to share. Have to make sure we have some comparative analysis here. It seems lately that only the liberal thought process is covered out there today; need to give some other examples, and then Major and everyone else will have to decide for themselves. I will certainly keep praying they tie themselves to the truth and make all their decisions from there.

I would prefer that we would look at all perspectives to make an informed decision based on our moral code. Geesh, that sounds like the freedom that our founders were talking about. Propaganda or true principles, upon which shall we build our future? Hmm, maybe it's not ignorance about God, so much as it's <u>ignoring</u> what God has already said. And that has surely gotten us into so much trouble!

12

Up the walk came Major. He was carrying a large box, what could that be?

"Good morning, this fine day, how's the battle going?"

"Just fine, ma'am, just fine. I have a little surprise for you today," he said with that Hollywood smile.

"Well, what's the special occasion, kid?" I asked.

He noted the puzzled look on my face. "I think you'll really like this. I picked it out myself; here, go ahead, look inside," he eagerly said.

Slowly and carefully, I unwrapped the unexpected package. As I peered into the box, I saw the edge of a figurine.

"Oh my gosh," I blurted out. "You didn't!"

"Yes I certainly did! Me and my family all pitched in and got this for you as a thank you for all you've done. Not just for us lately, but for your service to our country and your continued service in the ministry."

Major fidgeted and shuffled his feet. Even though he seemed a little uneasy as he saw the tears flow freely down my cheeks, he gently placed his hand on my arm as I looked in amazement at this precious gift. It was a moment of kindness that I will always cherish.

I peered into the box and ever so gently picked up the rough-hewn bronze replica of the Women's Memorial statue, like the one located near the Vietnam Wall Memorial in Washington, DC. This thing is almost sacred to me. How did they know?

It depicts a nurse, sitting on a wall of sandbags, cradling a wounded soldier. Behind her is another nurse, hand on her shoulder, watching toward the sky, as if to look out for the medical evacuation helicopter. Behind all three figures is another female soldier, kneeling on both knees, head bowed as if in prayer, holding the soldier's helmet.

Speechless, I stared at this precious prize, cradling it in my hands for what seemed like forever. Tears continued to flow over my cheeks. I was present, but not present, standing there, awash with a flood of memories.

Major was patiently watching me, and out of the corner of my tear-blurred eyes, I could see him slowly lift his index finger up toward his cheek. I've always called tears "liquid love," and at that moment, he was furtively trying to wipe away his.

Vivid pictures from my tours in Vietnam raced across the movie screen of my mind. . .like the young Marine with three limbs amputated; compounded with massive abdominal wounds that had to be held together with additional mid-section bandages. His testicles were blown off; he was blind and in pain. Black dots of shrapnel peppered the left side of his face. He called out for help. As I gently held his newly scarred face in my hands I asked what he wanted, his question floored me: "Nurse, will my girlfriend still love me when I get home?" I told him, "Sure, she will love you all the more because you're going home a hero."

At that moment, looking at that young man, it took every ounce of strength in me to hold back the emotions welling up inside. I wanted to scream. . .no more wounded, no more war, somebody turn this faucet off! This young soldier had done so much, given so much and yet, with his question, he displayed the innocence of youth still alive in his being. I thought of JFK's words and knew the power of America had always been displayed in the willingness of its people to pay any price, bear any burden and face any hardship to ensure the survival and success of our liberty. And I was holding such a hero.

Little did I know that back home, America was in such turmoil. This brave young man would return to our golden shores only to bear curses and disgust; be accosted by uninformed, often spoiled, selfish people, who rarely had to suffer for their daily bread; to a country falling off the cliff of morality and greatness. . .and taking out their confusion on America's finest.

Still clutching the statue to my bosom, my mind wandered off to the Phu Mi orphanage near Saigon. It was run by the French nuns, who were saints in living color. Abandoned and orphaned children filled the rooms and sprawled on the floors, often crying, not for lack of attention or food, but for being the unlucky offspring of those caught in war.

I continued staring at the statue. My senses recalled the smell of burning flesh—a stench that is etched forever in my brain. I remembered staring in horror at the site of the freshly bombed-out dental clinic behind my sleeping quarters at Tan Son Nhut. That same fear flooded my soul as I lay trembling under my bed during an early morning attack at DaNang. Wafting through this wave of pain was the remembrance of a young two-year-old girl we evacuated with our soldiers. Her face was horribly disfigured, a result of some sort of explosion. At two, she definitely was not the enemy, but suffered as greatly as if she were. Her face was only half there, the upper part of her mouth was gone and one eye was just a shriveled up empty socket. I had to use a 50cc syringe and rubber tubing to feed her. And deep in the back of my mind that day was the pride I had in our soldiers, who, in spite of the fact that they were grievously wounded by a likely relative of this little girl, continued to smile at her and make the goofy noises and gestures that grown-ups do when around young kids.

"Chaplain, Chaplain, this is Bravo 1. . .come in Chaplain," shouted Major, as if he were trying to reach me by military radio.

"I'm still here. Just a bit lost in thought," I softly replied.

The awkwardness of the moment was so thick you could have cut it with a knife. Major didn't know whether to hold me, or to fold it and run home. He chose the better of the two and just gave me the sweetest gentlest hug. It was comforting and I guess I needed it by then. His face mirrored his compassion for me.

It was a struggle to speak, but I said, "Major, you and your family can never know the value of what you've just done. I will absolutely treasure this memento forever. Just looking at it will help the healing of my heart from those difficult times and it will always be a reminder of the love and care your family has for me. This is just unbelievably awesome! I can't thank you all enough."

Major just quietly said, "Well, I guess we called it right on this one."

"You surely did, you surely did," I said just as quietly.

We both stood for a moment, speechless, letting the wave of emotions pass from this sobering occasion.

"Well, now that I have my breath and my composure back, how about a nice cup of coffee. . .and. . .that nice big breakfast you asked about?" I said with a bit more of a smile on my face.

"Wow—you're the best, Chaplain," he yelled out as we walked into the kitchen.

We gathered our breakfast feast and brought it out on the porch.

"Chaplain, I didn't know that our gift would make you cry. We didn't plan on that happening," he said sadly.

"I didn't plan on it either, but that's okay, honey. It's just that the experiences you have in a combat zone never leave you. They go deep into your soul and sometimes they are stuck. Let me tell you a little story about that, okay?"

"Sure," he said eagerly. "I could listen to your stories all day."

"But first, I want to say something about your fast approaching dive into the military. That means you are going to write out a check, so to speak, and make it out to the United States, payable up to and including your life. It takes a very special type of person to do that. Some do it from a deep patriotic sense, some do it for a thousand other reasons. . .but the point is that they do it. And our country needs to be extremely grateful for you and all who have served."

"Roger that," he quipped.

I continued, "The trials and difficulties of war weigh heavily on those who have returned from such a ghastly adventure. My recent work in the Army National Guard chaplaincy circumstantially forced me to face my own nightmares as well as assist others in facing and correctly filing theirs. I have been asked tough questions a number of times by soldiers who have had to face the brutality and killing characteristics of war. They questioned their own morality in trying to justify being someone who loves God, values life, and yet has been called upon to kill another human being."

"How can you answer a question like that, Chaplain? Does it even have an answer?"

"It doesn't have an easy answer, and certainly not a black and white, right or wrong type answer, either."

"So what do you tell them?"

"I tell them that their question is one asked over the ages, and remind them that the fact they are even asking the question shows their high level of moral care and excellence. I then go on to tell them that I don't have the most satisfactory answer, and that the finality of it all will be wrapped up between them and God. But, and this is a big but. . .I ask them to reflect on something very important. Our country's biggest and baddest warriors struggle with having to kill someone. They often return home ridden with guilt and shame; with confusion and doubt often wrecking them the rest of their lives. But I remind them again, that it is better to come from a society in which even its strongest warriors suffer after having to kill someone in war, than to come from a society that freely encourages its soldiers to kill everyone and anyone who is not like them. I repeat over and over that we have often been asked to fight against people who have strapped explosives to their own wives and children in order to carry out their violent expressions; enemies who would think nothing of cutting off your head, skinning you alive, or raping your young child in front of your very eyes. We are not like that, so in that context, many of them find some semblance of comfort and relief."

Major looked so serious right now and with furrowed brow, he continued to listen to my comments.

"As I was saying, it is a huge responsibility for the military because it is the military that is charged with the defense of our nation, and, as has been the case for most of our country's history, the defense of many others. Because of that, we are ever in need of our best, brightest, and most morally sound people to serve in our various military components. We are not a nation of brigands and mercenaries. We have a well-trained, well-outfitted, morally sound military. Some voices out there rail against the veracity of that statement, but I venture to say, they have never, ever served in a combat zone!"

Major nodded in agreement. "You got that right, ma'am. But don't forget your story."

"Thanks for the reminder. . .I do get off on those pesky tangents sometimes, don't I? Ah, don't you dare answer that, young man."

Major laughed. "I ain't that stu-u-u-u-u-u-pid," he said exaggeratedly.

"As I was saying, the dogs of war keep barking at you long after you come home. When I first got back from Vietnam, I was upset at all the crap, excuse my French, that I kept seeing on TV about our 'gentle giants' being baby killers and dope heads. That was so far from the truth, as you have heard in some of the situations I related earlier. I was angry, and unknown to me at the time, I hadn't properly mourned all the death and dying that had gone on all around me. I felt inadequate, felt like I hadn't done enough because so many of the wounded just didn't make it."

With a response full of wisdom, Major interrupted me and said, "I guess you forgot the rules of war you taught me. . .Rule #1-Men die in war and Rule #2-the medics can't change Rule #1!"

"Yeah, I didn't know that back then. All I knew was that an awful lot of good young men were being seriously wounded and killed. In the fall of 1968, we were evacuating about 10,000 wounded a month. All totaled, over 58,000 Americans were killed in that brutal war. If you average that out over the length of the Vietnam War, that's about 322 dead Americans every month, every year, for FIFTEEN YEARS!"

"Wow, when you put it like that, it really starts to paint a bad picture, Chaplain."

"Yes, a picture that is forever etched in your heart and mind. One that can make you better or bitter. . .and the key difference is the 'I.' I suffered silently a very long time. Tried to drink a lot of that pain away, party it right out of town, go on one adventure after another to chase those demons away but somehow the sadness never left; only the difficulty in pushing it back down remained and ever increased."

"What did you do?" he asked ever so delicately.

"Well, what looked like coincidences at the time, but you know how God works in mysterious ways. . .I had the opportunity to participate in a few research studies that were evaluating the effects of war on females. They had a ton of them regarding the men, but none involving just the women. A friend of mine from nursing school was doing some work on her doctoral dissertation. She contacted me and asked if I would like to come along for the ride.

"Of course, at that time, I figured I was untouched by the war, so I thought. I was doing just fine; working as a nurse full-time, coordinating Air Evac missions for the Air Force, and flying all over the world. My life was under control. I told her I would be glad to be involved, especially since it meant an all-expense-paid trip up to my hometown in Boston. When she met me at the airport, we had a brief conversation while waiting for transportation to the research center. She just asked the simple question of why I went to Vietnam. I started telling her that, as a surgical nurse at Boston City Hospital, I felt I had adequate training regarding multiple trauma patients. With the plethora of gunshot wounds and car accidents that we cared for, I knew I was up to the job of helping our wounded men. In addition, I was already a Second Lieutenant Flight Nurse in the Air Force Reserves. After sharing those mundane details, I went on to tell her that I volunteered for Vietnam because I 'thought I could help.'

"As soon as those words came out of my mouth, they were like iron letters dangling from a crane right in front of my eyes and without any warning, a torrent of tears and uncontrolled weeping and crying began. My friend looked on with a helpless expression. Moved to tears herself, but dumbfounded and shocked, she was at a loss as to what to do."

Major was on the edge of his seat, leaning over on his elbows and not saying a word, just listening.

I continued. "It was only at that moment, that I finally came to realize my lofty reason to serve our wounded warriors was shattered in the reality of young men dying by the thousands, even though all our medical teams did their best with what we had. In the midst of that uncontrolled bereaving, I finally came to understand that the war had blown a cannon ball into that innocent, youthful goal and continued to pierce straight into my heart with guilt and shame.

"What could I do, except continue with the program's activities and meetings? I completed all their questions and tests that weekend and actually, was glad I did. It forced me, for the first time since Vietnam, to take that fire-breathing dragon out and stare it in the face. Somehow, my name got around the research circuit and I participated in two or three other studies, each time digging down deeper into the issues that had eaten away at my soul, and each time coming out with a cleaner and clearer understanding of what had happened ever so long ago.

"And the best part was during the last research study. We had been hooked up to biometric gadgets and had been tested for responses to bomb sounds, pain stimuli, etc., as well as asked to dig down deep and answer questions regarding the best and the worst scenarios from our war time experiences. And, yes again, the tears were flowing. But in my final interview with the psych doc, I got an answer that would settle my issues and allow me to go on in life without the burdens of guilt and sadness ever lingering at my door.

"I told her that I was a bit disheartened and was still very sad after so many years removed from the war's experiences. In expressing those feelings to her, I indicated that I thought I was 'fixed' and asked why I was still crying. Her response buoyed me up like a nuke flying off of a submarine!"

"What in the world did she say, Chaplain?"

Did I see some tears welling up in his eyes as I was relating all this to him? I think so, but I won't mention it to a future Marine who may even go on and become a Navy Seal!

"She told me that because I was crying, I *was* fixed. She went on to say that the ones they can't reach are the ones who have stopped feeling. They never cry, they just zone out on drugs and alcohol to dull the pain, but all they dull is a chance at a great life. It really hit me like a ton of bricks. It was okay to cry and feel bad about all that loss and mayhem. I was having a normal reaction to an abnormal situation. I wasn't crazy after all."

Major blurted out with a smile, "Try to tell that to your family and friends!"

"Ha-ha, funny boy," I continued, glad for a break in this somber conversation.

12

"After those research experiences, I started to realize that some of us had to come out from that smoke and fire to tell the truth of what really happened there. From that moment on, I knew that I had done my best; we all had done our very best with what we had. We made sure as many of them as possible made it back home. And you know what, we did a good job, no, I take that back, we did a great job. I am blessed today to be able to continue to help many veterans who also have struggled with their combat experiences. I can tell them with assurance that there was a divine reason they made it home and some of their dearest friends did not. I remind them they now have a sacred duty to live their lives twice as well, because in doing so they continue to honor those who did not make it back."

Major just nodded in agreement; not a word left his lips.

"It was quite a revelation when I realized I could actually 'file' some of this stuff in my heart, so I could pull it up when I wanted to, instead of it just having a free reign in my life and memory. It was so liberating and I can honestly say I am glad, not ashamed to have been involved with the gallant effort to help the Vietnamese people come out from under the shackles of Communism and the invasion from the North. Even though ignorance, coupled with the 'politically correct' decisions that were ultimately made by our country, rendered our efforts unsuccessful in Vietnam, we at least tried. I had hoped for, at a minimum, the same results as we had in Korea, but the changing moral climate in our country would have nothing to do with the perseverance it would take to prevail in Vietnam. The pursuit of comfort instead of courage was slowly creeping into the lifestyle of America."

"I am exhausted just listening to all this. I don't think I could ever do what you and all those brave guys did back then," Major said, slowly and deliberately.

"Of course you could, you could do that and more. Your good and godly attitude and sound moral foundation will take you through every decision and circumstance you may face. You're solid in the knowledge that freedom is not free and must be fiercely guarded and fought for, at all costs. Just like President John F. Kennedy once said, 'Let every nation know, whether it wishes us well or ill, that we will pay any price, bear any burden, meet any hardship, support any friend, oppose any foe, in order to assure the survival and success of liberty.' You have that in you, Major, and I am mighty glad of it and ever so proud of you."

"I don't know what to say to that," he mumbled.

"I don't want you to think I am a war monger or anything. It's just that I love this country so much. I have seen its greatness and been blessed with its treasures. I have seen the mud and the blood and those who've died to keep us free; and that does something to a person. I guess the old saying that 'Freedom has a flavor the protected will never know' is still very accurate.

But I love freedom more than I hate war, so I guess I'll always be willing to lay my life down for our country. And you have the same feelings in you, Major, so the legacy goes on. But my deepest concern is for some of the changes I see in our country because, as I've said before, a country not worth living in is a country not worth dying for. Sometimes I call it the 'curse of the blessings' that we have nowadays."

"Hmm, what does that mean?" Major asked with that furrowed brow again.

"It means that we have so much in this country that we are getting soft and spoiled. Instead of appreciating our blessings, we have often come to take them for granted. Heck, two-thirds of the world doesn't live like we live and yet we still have so many in our country who think they are deprived! They often have TVs, a car, a computer, X-boxes, computer games, bikes, cell phones, and refrigerators. They have microwaves, the list goes on and on — and that is in the homes of our poor!

"In so many other places on the planet, there is no electricity, no running water, no paved roads, no solidly built housing, no medical care, no computers, iPads or iPhones, no indoor plumbing, heck, no plumbing at all. . .and that list goes on and on too. We have all that and more. And we have it, not because it dropped down from the sky somehow. We have it because good, hardworking people applied themselves in a free society and succeeded. Don't ever get the idea that success and making money is bad. . .it is good. No homeless, penniless person ever gave someone a job or built a factory or a company that provides needed goods and services. Nor have they ever had enough money to donate toward building an orphanage, or a school or a hospital and the like. No, only someone *with* money can be so productive and helpful. Our goal should be to offer the opportunity to make money, not just hand it out.

"Ah, but I digress. . .greatly. Let's stop here, buddy, before your eyes glaze over!"

"Chaplain, I told you, I like hearing what you have to say. I have a lot of life to live and I want to get as many of the tools as I can to build a good one. Let's just say you're adding to my tool chest, one screwdriver at a time!"

He laughed. His eyes danced with mischief. Rather makes me jealous that he is just starting out. Oh, if I only had the strength to go through Basic Training again. . .wait, what am I thinking. . .I must be nuts!

I waved at him as he scurried home. What a great kid. I am so thankful to have a part in his life; maybe someday I can tell him the truth of who I really am. I continually pray for his success. . .well deserved, so well deserved, after all his hard work at school and in the community.

Well, I feel a nap coming on. So nice to be on somewhat of a sabbatical!

13

A warm breeze blew through the open window beside my bed. It felt like heaven on earth. Oh, I am so enjoying an extended break from the rat race. I stared at the ceiling, reflecting on my life's numerous adventures with its many twists and turns. The daily chats with Major are stirring up the 'bottom of the pond,' and a lot is going through my mind. Mostly good, some uncomfortable, some terrifying remembrances, but it's okay, because I am in charge of the file system now. Thank You, Lord.

My floating menagerie of thoughts was interrupted by a knock on the door. Who in the world could that be?

"Be right there, just a minute," I yelled.

As I threw my clothes back on, I looked out through the porch window. Oh, it's Pastor Jeffries. He's from the church I go to while I'm up here. It is a growing church, a church with a heart for the youth in the community and a young pastor with a heart for Jesus. Just my kind of place!

"Pastor Jeffries, it's so good to see you," I said as I answered the door. "Come on in, please."

"You always call me that," he said. "Please, feel free to call me Jackson or Jack will do."

"Sorry about that. Formalities stick out so much in an informal world. Heck, all my uncles' first names are still 'Uncle' to me!"

We both laughed.

I started to tell him my reason for staying a bit formal, especially with my male acquaintances.

"As a single woman, I just want to keep everything above board, you know; can't leave any room for misunderstanding and error."

"No need to explain. Actually, I respect that. It is far too infrequent, I'm afraid," he said in total agreement.

"What can I 'do you for,' as my dad always used to say."

"Chaplain, I know you are on one of your breaks up here, but I would really appreciate it if you would consider being the guest speaker at our Fourth of July celebration at the church. It happens to fall on a Sunday this year, so we'll have our Sunday service in the morning and then put on a big, old-fashioned barbeque afterwards. The church grounds can hold a ton of people. We're doing it up big this year and have even hired this company out of Sevierville, Tennessee called 'Days Gone By.' It's a family-run group, which comes to events and sets up all the old time games of yesteryear. They have greased pig races, walking on stilts, beanbag tossing, and all sorts of games, face painting and the like. The owners are wonderful people who have brought a lot of joy for many groups over the years. I met them at an event at another church last year and couldn't wait to have them come here and bring us some good clean fun."

"Sounds like a great time. I would be delighted to speak at your church. My favorite thing in the whole world is to tell people of the awesome and wonderful God we serve; a God who loves us and longs for us to love Him right back. It still blows my mind to know that God doesn't *need* us, He actually *wants* us."

"Looks like you're writing your sermon already," he said, laughing.

"I get carried away when I start talking about God. It's just a shame that so many have such a warped view of who He is. They think He's some sort of rich uncle in the sky who is supposed to dole out the goodies to them; or they think He is some mean ogre up there just waiting to pounce on their every error. I guess there will always be this huge chasm between a perfect God and our fatally flawed humanity while we're on this side of heaven."

"I know," said Jack ruefully. "It's a shame that untruths and deception have such a hold on so many good people."

"So many wasted lives out there," I continued. "They are trying to fill that gap with a bunch of good works, as if God was going to weigh those works on some big cosmic scale at the Pearly Gates to determine their eligibility for entrance."

"I hear ya," he said. "God didn't fill that gap with good works; instead He filled it with Himself. God actually came in the flesh as Jesus, and then led Him to be sacrificed, once, for all; not religious mythology, but a true plan of rescue. With that sacrifice, He put the knockout blow to sin, hell and the grave. Jesus is sort of like the 'knight in shining armor' who came back to rescue his stolen love."

"I just love how you think; we're on the same page, Pastor Jack," I smilingly added.

"Some people wonder what pastors talk about. . .well, this is it!" he quipped.

I responded, "When you think of it, though, Satan actually thought he won by killing Jesus. What an idiot! It was planned for Jesus to take the punishment for our crimes and that was just the beginning of God's plan of conquest and rescue from man's downfall because of Adam's bad choices. It's just a shame that people let a justifiable fear of God discount His ever-abounding love. I guess our work is cut out for us to wade through the sea of lies and help people to the shore of truth."

"Oh, that's deep," he said seriously. "You'd better write it down!"

"Well, if it was coming from me," I explained, "I'd take lots of credit for it. But I think we both know that any wisdom or understanding we have of the heavenly things, comes from the Maker of heaven."

"It certainly makes our conversation smoother when we have the same family line, Chaplain."

"Couldn't agree more. Oh, and what time will the services begin on July 4th?"

"We'll start at 10:30 that morning with some worship time, and then you can start sharing around 11:00. After you finish, we'll head out to the barbeque."

"Oh, great! You're going to have all those 'hungry, eager to get going to the fun and games' people just sitting on the edges of their seats, praying I hurry up and finish my sermon. You'll probably have that song, *Let My Words Be Few*, wafting in the background."

"Spoken like a true pastor." He continued to laugh as he walked back toward the front door. "See you then, if not before. God bless you and thank you so much, Chaplain."

"God bless you, too."

Well, well, thank You, Lord, for the opportunity to do a little teaching while I'm up here too.

Pastor Jack is a good man. He lives a simple life up here in this laid-back community. . .Uh oh, I feel the jealousy buttons being pushed with that bucolic thought! I just smile wistfully. During a previous visit a few years back, he told me why he worked so hard at what the world would call a dead end job that seemed so fruitless. He said he was greatly influenced to spend his life caring for the poor and those in need when he read a quote from Margaret Mead, the cultural anthropologist. She said, "Never believe that a few caring people can't change the world. For, indeed, that's all who ever have."

I like that.

When Major came by the next day, I told him about the speaking engagement at the church service and the barbeque to follow. He expressed an eagerness to be there.

"I'll let Mom and Dad and Joshua know. And if John is feeling up to it, he and his wife can go too. I don't think Don will be back from his overseas flights yet, but I'm sure his wife and kids will be there, too. Poor Rebecca lives way out West and misses so much here. Oh, well. And my mom will just love it that she doesn't have to make lunch for us after church."

"I can appreciate that, for sure," I noted.

We settled down with our coffee, listened to the sounds of the breezes whispering through the surrounding trees and just relaxed a few minutes.

Major started, "Chaplain, I really appreciate being able to stop by here so often. I know I've said it before, but I mean it. I know you are supposed to be on vacation or something and yet you still let me come by each day. And on top of all of that, you research and run off all those copies. I hope I haven't been a pain in the. . ." he paused, "neck."

I chuckled, "No, you haven't been a pain in the. . ." I paused, "neck."

We both laughed and enjoyed the view and the brew — coffee, that is!

"The other day when I was telling you how much I love this country and how very great it is, I didn't get to another piece of the puzzle. You are going out into a world that sometimes doesn't appreciate who we are as a country. They consider us brash and full of hubris."

"Uh, don't know that word, Chaplain. What's hubris?"

"Look it up when you get home, kiddo."

"Really, you're just like my teacher used to be!"

"Good, you need to do more on your own and not have everything handed to you."

Major rolled his eyes, "Now you sound like my dad! Do you guys all go to the same school?" he asked, with increasing boldness in his voice.

"Yeah. We all went to the School of Hard Knocks and finished up at the University of Adversity!" I smartly replied.

"True, that," he said, smiling.

"True what? Anyhoo, as I was saying, you may not always be appreciated as an American. That's because there is a lot of disinformation and opinions out there. But I think there is a good amount of jealousy, too. As I always say, though, if you want what we have, you have to do what we've done. And that means a lot of sacrifice, hard work, individual determination, achievement and pride in what you've done and who you are and, most importantly, you have to have a small, non-infringing type government working with a highly moral citizenry. We *had* that, to a great extent; but it is leaking a bit right now from our core. It seems to me that so often those who have benefited so much from our country are at the forefront of the mob berating it. At least, that's my observation.

"We are growing as a country, and it seems the larger and more unruly the crowd gets, the more controls the government assumes it needs to impose. Just think if we had a majority of highly, and I mean highly, virtuous people, there would be no need for so many rules and regulations. It seems if we went back to teaching some of the principles of what is morally correct instead of what is politically correct, we would be able to bring back self-discipline initiated from the individual instead of coerced behavior from the government. The stifling of individual freedoms and rights for the benefit of order is a bad combination! I often have asked myself if we are heading toward personal freedom or political serfdom!"

Major interrupted and said, "There's nothing wrong with having pride in doing a good job or wanting to do your best. There's nothing wrong with competition; it actually brings the best out in you. If you see someone running faster or reading better. . .whatever. . .it makes you want to do that yourself, doesn't it?"

"Not if the benefits of doing better are stifled by stupid rules," I replied. "Like the one that says you can't keep score in a baseball game because some of the kids' feelings might get hurt if they lose! Or you keep promoting kids in school even if they don't meet the standard, saying they'll just get it 'someday'! Why work doubly hard at doing your best and improving if everyone gets the same trophy, so to speak. My head is going to burst when I keep hearing about all that 'fair share' crap. Oops, I'm getting too excited, sorry 'bout that language, there!

"As I was saying, all that lowering the bar will do is produce a lazy, dependent generation of 'feel good' morons! Uh oh, I think I need that duct tape from your dad. My head is going to explode as I think on these things!"

Major howled in laughter by this time. "Chaplain, you are so funny. You talk really fast and are so passionate about this country, but I am encouraged, not discouraged. I just wish you'd go to every school around here and tell them what you're telling me."

"Well, that's some vacation you have planned for me," I answered with a pretend growl.

"Don't get me wrong now," I continued. "All this bragging about America doesn't mean we are a perfect country or that we have always done everything correctly. But we cannot just throw away the beauty, the awesome opportunity to thrive and succeed, and the wonder of our nation and our history because of the relatively few, though grossly negative, negligent or incorrect seasons of our past.

"We are a great people in a great nation. Remember, we have what I called that 'curse of the blessings.' We are so bloated with the blessings of freedom that we get sloppy and are way too tempted to become lazy with a 'let the other guy do it' mentality. Caution is needed so we don't abuse our gifts, and accidentally take advantage of our country. . .a warning given to us by our Forefathers. I want this warning of the past to stay right in the front of our eyes. If we are not careful, our quickly eroding moral base will lead us to the very enslavement we originally fled!"

"Yeah, that is so right," Major said pensively.

"I'm sorry, I think I'm repeating myself here," I interjected.

"It's okay, ma'am. Remember, you told me that repetition is one of the pillars of learning and the successful use it as a building tool to construct their kingdoms."

"I said that? Well, I must be smarter than a fifth grader!"

Major just smiled as he shook his head and rolled those blue eyes of his.

I continued and asked him, "Do we really think we can garner the same booming results of the past if we erode the traditional values that catapulted us to achieve them? If we enlarge governmental control and limit free enterprise through crippling regulation and further government intrusion, we take away the instrument of success. . .a free individual who can keep the fruits of his labor! Or, suffer lack if he cannot! If the free individual is not morally strong, hard-working, honest, generous, diligent, and vigorously desiring self-sufficiency. . .we lose!"

"Easy there, Chaplain, with the big words again. I haven't yet learned that fifty dollar vocabulary!"

"You 'quack me up,' kid."

We both enjoyed the silly humor.

"You got time to hear me out on this, Mr. Wonderful?"

"Wait a minute, wait a minute," he quickly said.

He pulled out his phone and pulled up a website.

"You'll bite your lip off, you're so intense in what you're doing," I joked.

"Hold on, I have an answer for you." He looked at his phone screen and said, "You asked me if I had time to hear you out and my answer is. . .I am all 'auricular orifices'."

"Oh, brother, do you mean, 'I am *all ears*'?" I incredulously asked.

"Yup, how's that for fifty dollar words!" he smugly retorted.

"You're one sick puppy; must be why we get along so well! Now, where in the heck was I?"

"You were talking about losing our nation's greatness," he quickly summarized.

"Whoa. . .you are a good student, grasshoppa!" I joked.

"As I was saying, today some people, even some of our own citizens, decry our nation as an imperialistic and aggressive country. Stop and think about those words. Imperialist, aggressive. . . those are some serious charges here!

"I would like to ask them, once we were an established nation, which country did we invade and take over and where did we plant our flag and forcibly put that country under our laws? If we were really imperialists, wouldn't we already own Canada and Mexico? Wouldn't Japan, Italy and Germany be part of the U.S.A?

"Yes, we still have troops in Europe and the Far East, heck, even the Middle East. And though WWII ended almost seventy years ago, Vietnam almost forty years ago, and Iraq, and Afghanistan finishing up, as we speak, not one of those countries has been taken over by our government and forced to come under our structure of law or our way of life. So how can we be imperialists?

"We do fight wars; but our war machine, so to speak, <u>leaves</u> eventually. We pour bazillions of dollars into repairing what the ravages of war have destroyed. What other country has done as much to rebuild the roads, the hospitals, the schools and businesses of the people and places unfortunate enough to be caught in the crossfire of war? And not just once, but we have continued these acts as part of our history. We even helped rebuild Germany, Italy, and Japan, who were our sworn enemies during World War II! We helped rebuild England and a huge portion of Europe in areas we didn't even bomb, but rather were bombed by the Germans.

"Our people are hardworking, thrifty, innovative, and determined to succeed. Because we are a democratic republic, we get to vote for who will lead us and make our laws. We are not forever under the powerful rule of despots to which we have a forced allegiance. If we don't like who's in charge, we can remove them by voting them out.

"But I want to shout out, 'What a country. Why are people complaining?' It's a funny thing. It seems to me that if so many people hate our country and we're such a bad place, then why are so many people, some even risking their lives, to get here? Ever think of that?

"Son, someone said you know the value and greatness of a country not by how many are trying to get in, but rather how many are trying to get out!

"We surely don't have the problem of people trying to leave the U.S. en masse! Did you ever wonder why anyone who doesn't love this country and who is not willing to help us achieve excellence here, why they don't feel compelled to just drop what they're doing and head on out of a country that they hate so much!"

"I'm sure it's because there isn't as good a one as ours to go to," Major replied.

"You are one smart cookie, kid."

Major just smiled that great smile and continued to listen quietly as I continued commenting.

"Actually, we have a problem with unauthorized masses just pouring across our borders. Not only is that a security risk, but a health and economic risk. Those who are calling for open borders, I wonder if they practice what they preach? As an example, do they lock the doors to their own homes, or do they just let anyone come in for dinner and the use of their home, without their permission, or vetting, or reimbursement? Yet that is what they are asking our country to do! Then I'd ask them, what if they come into your house and start asking to be put on your health care plan too, at your expense? That would be fair, right? C'mon, they're already there, shouldn't you put them on your health care plan; and oh, yeah, pay for their college tuition too. . .yeah, that's good too."

"Chaplain, now Chaplain. . .you're getting politically 'incorrect' here!" he chided.

13

"Maybe we need a little more of that kind of prompting and challenge, instead of just walking around like zombies or sticking our heads in the sand. America cannot continue in greatness and the ability to help others if we let unbridled altruism throw out common sense! To bankrupt and destroy your own home helping another to gain sufficiency in theirs would be irrational. The object should not be to take from those who have and give to those who don't; the object should be to teach those who don't have how to be one of those who do have! If we diligently did that, instead of just haphazardly giving to someone who does not have, then there would be ample resources left to help those who *really* and *desperately* require our help, such as the disabled, the elderly and children.

"Our country was founded on individual freedom, granted by God, not the state. Those gifts from God were called 'unalienable rights,' and were named specifically to be life, liberty, and the pursuit of happiness. The government cannot 'give' us these things, they are rightly ours; the government can only take them away.

"The more we let any form of government do for us, the less people will do for themselves. In our rush for 'free stuff' from the government, we are trampling on the fruits of our labor in our garden of plenty! Just throwing money at the problems and not addressing the immorality behind it is only opening up more opportunities for the morally corrupt to invent even more fraudulent schemes."

"I don't like the sounds of that, Chaplain"

"Neither do I," I said with sadness. "Neither do I."

"Well, Chaplain, have to get going. I have a long day working with Dad and Joshua in the field. John is just itching to get back out there, but he's not going to be able to for quite a while. He's still busy, though, while he's laid up, cuz he's doing the paperwork part of the business on his computer. Mom said it was a 'blessing in disguise,' cuz now John is catching up on all sorts of projects he could never get to while doing so much of the actual labor part. He is setting up PowerPoint presentations for the milk sales; putting lots of figures into Excel; getting the files organized so he can get them onto the computer. . .you know about that stuff."

"Sure do," I said. "In the military we had the old adage, 'The job ain't done til the paperwork's finished.' Still true today."

"Let's see," Major said. "I have about six words to look up for their meanings. All this work; you're bustin' my. . ." He hesitated a moment then said, "Bustin' my butt, Chaplain."

I heartily laughed. "You think I'm bustin' your. . ." I hesitated, and then said, "your butt. . .just wait 'til those Marine Drill Instructors get a hold of it!"

He jumped off the porch again, only this time singing, "From the halls of Montezuma to the shores of Tripoli. We will fight our country's battles on the land and on the sea. . ."

He has no idea what awaits him at Parris Island, but he'll be fine, he'll be fine.

14

*M*ajor hadn't been able to get by for a few days. They had been busy with all the summertime chores that consume a farmer's life. I'm glad, though, because this short hiatus gave me time to relax, and do some research to prepare for that church service this Sunday.

While musing alone out on the porch, I thought of a poster idea. Maybe I could hang them around my church back home; maybe even Pastor Jack would want some for his youth group classes too. Hmm, maybe we could even post them out around the community or something.

I started drawing out a rough sketch. It was a bar with shelves of liquor bottles in the background and one huge close-up of a large shot glass in the foreground. The lettering over top of that was in white and said:

If you drink from the cup of immorality, you'll suffer the hangover of:

- Disease
- Divorce
- Unwanted pregnancy
- Abortions
- Broken relationships
- Prison
- Perversions of all kinds

I stopped in the middle of my drawing and was reminded of the stupidity of trying to do that. . .heck, the list would be so long that the poster would have to hang from the Empire State Building! I laughed and crumpled up the paper.

"Back to that sermon," I commanded myself, while thinking that writing sermons and doing more church services wasn't exactly my idea of a break.

The rest of the week flew by as it always seemed to up here in God's country; it was Sunday morning already and I headed off to church. While driving, I thought of something that Oswald Chambers wrote in his devotional, *My Utmost for His Highest*. He said that a saint's life was like an arrow in the archer's hand. That is so true. I came up here for what I thought was going to be an extended vacation, but God had some other thoughts on that. What's that old saying? "If you want to make God laugh, tell Him your plans." I guess He's having a sidesplitting time now. Better make sure I write any future blueprints in pencil!

As I pulled up to the church, I saw there were hordes of people buzzing around, more than usual. Cars were slowly entering the grassy parking lot; children were squealing and running off ahead of parents, who were trying to call them back to walk together; the sun was shining, even a bit warm already. There was a neighboring dog or two barking at all the commotion. Reminded me of a Norman Rockwell painting. . .life is good.

Pastor Jack started the service with prayer; a deep and fervent call to repentance for a fallen nation. He sees the reality of the changes that are burdening our society and longs for a halt to its certain destruction. Gotta love the guy.

The worship team's songs and music were uplifting and honoring to the Lord; I felt boosted and refreshed in it all. I spent a few minutes in quiet prayer in the midst of the boisterous gaiety that worship often brings upon His children.

Pastor Jack got up and said, "And now I would like to ask our visiting pastor, affectionately known to many as 'Chaplain,' to come up and share some thoughts and comments with us today. As you know, she is a passionate patriot. Her years of military experience and teaching history have given her what I think is an informed vantage point from which to express the character and accomplishments of our country.

"She told me she is convinced the United States has a God-given, sacred mission to uphold freedom and justice at home and in the world. And I think many of us here today can heartily agree with that. Please welcome Dr. Jeanne Fontana. "

As I walked up the steps onto the elevated stage, I felt a peace in my heart and the presence of God surrounding our gathering. Pastor Jack nodded and smiled as I walked past him at his seat on the far left of the platform. I looked out over the audience while placing both hands on either side of the oak podium and began to speak.

"Thank you so very much, Pastor Jack. Good morning to you all on this warm and wonderful weekend. It is good to see so many of you here today. I would like to take this opportunity to honor our God by honoring our country—a country He founded and wanted as His own. But we cannot honor our country without also honoring those who have given a portion of their lives to defend this great nation. Would all those who have served in the military or are currently serving in the military please stand? Now, would all those near them please go and shake their hands or give them a hug and tell them thanks and show them the heart of a grateful nation?"

A number of the congregation stood. They were greeted with the sweetness of love shining on the faces of those surrounding them. A stir of momentary conversation blanketed the assembly, and hugs and handshakes warmed the hearts of the seasoned veterans, many of whom had borne the horrors and scars of war.

"Thank you for your kindness in that wonderful show of gratitude," I continued.

The sound of my voice signaled the end of the well-deserved greeting for the veterans. I waited a moment until all were seated and settled and a quiet hush returned to the room.

I continued, "July 4th is a great celebration of the birth of a great nation. This greatness isn't just rhetoric or empty nationalism of which I speak. It is a REALITY that our country has a history of growth, generosity, and industry, which we have shared with the world.

"We celebrate our technologically and morally superior troops, during all the ages of our country, but especially we salute the young, brave military members in harm's way in the Middle East, even as we gather here today.

"Some may dispute or take issue with portions of what I just said about our great country and our great troops. Some of our own citizens are even disputing the greatness of our country. I challenge them to open their eyes to a broader vision and I challenge you here today to reflect a moment on who we really are as Americans. We are a God honoring and Christianity-based nation."

A round of applause broke out.

I smiled, and then continued. "Take a look up at the screen at the list I have posted."

All eyes were drawn to the screen above my head and to the right of the podium.

"Did you know that:

♦ As you walk up the steps to the U.S. Supreme Court building, you can see, near the top of the building, a row of the world's lawgivers, each facing a central figure. That figure is of Moses holding the Ten Commandments

♦ As you enter the U.S. Supreme Court's courtroom, the two huge oak doors have the Ten Commandments engraved on each door

♦ As you sit inside the courtroom, you can see on the wall, right above where the Supreme Court judges sit, a display of the Ten Commandments

♦ James Madison, the fourth president of the U.S. said that our country staked the whole idea of self-government upon the capacity of us ". . .to control ourselves, to sustain ourselves according to the Ten Commandments of God."

♦ Patrick Henry, patriot and one of the Founding Fathers of our nation said '. . .this great nation was founded not by religion- ists but by Christians, not on religions but on the gospel of Jesus Christ.'

- Every session of Congress begins with a prayer by a paid preacher, whose salary has been paid by the taxpayer since 1777
- John Jay, the very first Supreme Court Justice said, 'Americans should select and prefer Christians as their rulers.'
- President Harry Truman in the 1950s, said, 'We all can pray. We all should pray. We should ask the fulfillment of God's will. We should ask for courage, wisdom, for the quietness of soul which comes alone to them who place their lives in His hands.'
- President John F. Kennedy in the 1960s, said, 'With a good conscience our only sure reward, with history the final judge of our deeds, let us go forth to lead the land we love, asking His blessing and His help, but knowing that here on earth God's work must truly be our own.'
- President Ronald Reagan in the 1980s said, 'America was founded by people who believed that God was their rock of safety. I recognize we must be cautious in claiming that God is on our side but I think it's all right to keep asking if we're on His side.'
- The U.S. House and Senate declared 1983 the year of the Bible by a joint resolution that said, 'Renewing our knowledge of and faith in God through Holy Scripture can strengthen us as a nation and a people.'"

There was a quiet rustle throughout the audience. Some were leaning in towards each other and whispering in agreement, some in shock at the facts just presented.

I waited just a brief moment until it was again quiet and said, "How then have we gotten to the point that everything we have done for 237 years in this country is now suddenly wrong and unconstitutional?

"I believe there is an answer to that. I believe that what Edmund Burke said back in the 1700s has come true. He said, 'All that is needed for evil to triumph is for good men to do nothing.' And this next quote is certainly one to meditate on. He also said, 'By gnawing through a dike, even a rat can drown a nation.' Let's take a short journey of reflection on the times we did do something to defeat the evil gnawing at our nation.

♦ In the start of our nation's discovery, even though some of the European merchants took advantage of Indian lands and people, many Christians paid for the land in their development of the original colonies

♦ As slavery enveloped the South, we fought our first and ONLY Civil War to end it. Over 600,000 white men died to free those African slaves, preventing secession of the South and preserving the Union of our states

♦ In the early years of the Industrial Revolution of the late 1800s and early 1900s, we saw child labor abuses and worker suffering and we developed ways to outlaw those evils while other countries still agonize under their despotism today

♦ As we saw Europe suffer from tyranny — we sent out our military to defend and liberate them, not once but twice in World War I and II

♦ As Communism spread throughout the Far East and Eastern Europe, we made brave attempts to stop its devastating reach from extending not only to us but also to South Korea and South Vietnam. Korea was successful and Vietnam ripped the soul out of America

"Things got tough. We got soft. We did what was expedient or politically correct and stopped doing what was right."

Heads nodded in agreement and a few "Amens" came forth with those statements.

"I believe that was the beginning of good men starting to do nothing."

"For example:

1979- Iran, U.S. Embassy hostages taken. . .we did nothing
1983-Beirut, Lebanon, U.S. Embassy attack. . .we did nothing
1983-Beirut, Lebanon, Marine barracks bombing. . .we did nothing
1988-Lockerbie, Scotland, Pan Am flight to NY blown up. . .we did nothing

1993-first World Trade Center bombing. . .we did nothing
1996-Dhahran, Saudi Arabia Khobar Towers military complex bombing. . .we did nothing
1998-Nairobi, Kenya U.S. Embassy bombing. . .we did nothing
1998-Dar Es Salaam, Tanzania U.S. Embassy bombing. . .we did nothing
Pre-election 2000-Aden, Yemen USS Cole bombing. . .we did nothing
Sep. 11, 2001-World Trade Center and Pentagon attacks. . .WE FINALLY DID SOMETHING!
Good men DID SOMETHING.

Many detractors said President Bush was wrong and our actions against the Islamic extremists and those who harbored them were wrong, unnecessary, unfounded, pre-meditated, and personal. That's up to you to judge—I'm not going there today. The point is made that evil WILL triumph and continue, if good men do nothing."

I looked over the crowd and was encouraged as I noticed that everyone was still wide-awake!

"So, where are we MORALLY today? Let's look at a few more slides with some information from a great book, *Original Intent*, by David Barton. He has enumerated some of the judicial interpretations that I think demonstrate a moral decline.

1962-*Engel v. Vitale* — the Supreme Court struck down school prayer in public schools (The prayer was: "Almighty God, we acknowledge our dependence upon Thee, and beg Thy blessing upon us, our parents, our teachers and our country.") . . .we did nothing
1963-*Murray v. Curlett* — the Supreme Court banned Bible reading in public schools. . .we did nothing
1965-*Reed v. Van Hoven* — a lower court decided if a student prays over his lunch, it is unconstitutional for him to pray aloud. . .we did nothing
1973-*Roe v. Wade* — the Supreme Court said abortion is legal and not a crime. . .we did nothing

1976-*Ohio v Whisner* — a lower court decided it is unconstitutional for a Board of Education to use or refer to the word "God" in any of its official writings. . .we did nothing

1979-*Florey v. Sioux Falls School District* — *it* is unconstitutional for a kindergarten class to ask whose birthday is celebrated on Christmas. . .we did nothing

1980-*Stone v. Graham* — the Supreme Court removed the Ten Commandments from view of students in public schools because they might "read, meditate upon, respect or obey them". . .we did nothing

1981-*Collins v. Chandler Unified School District* — a lower court declared that freedom of speech and the press is guaranteed to students unless the topic is religious at which time such speech becomes unconstitutional. . .we did nothing

1986-*Kay v. Douglas School District* — the Supreme Court removed all benedictions and invocations from all public school activities. . .we did nothing

1990-*Warsaw v. Tehachapi* — it is unconstitutional for a public cemetery to have a planter in the shape of a cross, for if someone were to view that cross, it would cause 'emotional distress' and thus constitutes an 'injury-in-fact'. . .we did nothing

1990-*Roberts v. Madigan* — it is unconstitutional for a classroom library to contain books that deal with Christianity or for a teacher to be seen with a personal copy of the Bible at school. . .we did nothing

2003-*Lawrence v. Texas* — sodomy is legal and is not a crime. . .we did nothing

2003-some Christian denominations accept homosexual bishops as leaders in their congregations. . .we did nothing

2003-*Goodridge v. Department of Health* — the Supreme Court in Massachusetts says it is legal for homosexual marriage in their state. . .we did nothing

2004-homosexual couples legally marry in Massachusetts. . .we did nothing

2010-President Obama rescinds the "don't ask, don't tell" policy from the Clinton era and allows openly homosexual individuals to apply for or remain in the military. . .we did nothing.

"How much longer will our good people stand by and do nothing? Is the 'rat' gnawing at the dike? Have any of you ever gone to a meeting regarding these issues, or written a letter or made a phone call to your elected representatives? Have any of you started a prayer meeting in your home to seek God's guidance as to what we *can* or *should* do?"

A few heads were shaking as if to indicate a 'no' answer to that question.

I smiled and said, "These are rhetorical questions, folks, there won't be any exam at the end of my sermon."

Laughter rippled through group.

I continued, "This is a Christian country; honoring the one, true God who sent Himself, in the form of His Son Jesus, for our rescue from sin and into salvation and life everlasting. Our nation was supposed to be a beacon of light, presenting the principles of Christ in family, education, business, medicine, science, government, and every part of the American fabric.

"Will you be an American who stands by and does nothing while evil triumphs or will you be an American who stands up and does something so good will flourish in this country again?

"The problems we have created for ourselves by doing nothing can be solved. The official unfriendly stand taken against God must be corrected and the religious principles and moral teachings must be restored and made available to individuals in the public arena.

"This is a great country, with great people. Our Declaration of Independence, our Constitution, our history, character and overall morality are the finest doctrines, dogmas, and demeanor in the world; but they are eroding into a spineless, unbounded, anything goes mentality that is often the curse of the overly blessed.

"God has blessed this nation for a reason — and that is to share and show His blessings to a sin-sick world. We must strive to keep our nation under God. Stop acting like the heathen. If Christians are no different from non-believers. . .there is no holy message there!"

Again, many nodded in agreement.

"Will you join with me today and covenant with God to keep this nation morally healthy and spiritually strong? Let us not stand by any longer and have evil flourish. . .let us do something today.

"The next slide covers a list of things we can do. Do them and teach them to your kids!

- ◆ **Pray** for our leaders and legislators
- ◆ **Teach** your children how to pray
- ◆ **Find out** the truth about issues and teach that to others
- ◆ **Become** a voter and vote
- ◆ **Investigate** the candidates (Christian Coalition helps with those listings)
- ◆ **Communicate** with the candidates, especially on the moral issues that are now being dragged into the "civil rights" arena
- ◆ **Be active** in your community — bring the light of Christ everywhere
- ◆ **Develop** a long-term, resolute spirit. . .this will be a long and difficult battle

"And when you pray for our leaders, pray that God will root out the wicked from office and will raise up righteous individuals to replace them, as is instructed in 1 Timothy 2:1.

"Voluntary prayer in school is severely restricted, but that doesn't mean children should not be trained to pray daily. Pray with your kids each day before they go to school. Pray specifically for students, families, schools, and the nation. Train the children in the importance of prayer. Read over Proverbs 15:18, 1 Thessalonians 5:17, and Colossians 4:2 to confirm what I just said. Your kids can even meet voluntarily in the schoolyard area and pray with others kids before school starts. And there is no law against that. They may have taken prayer out of the schoolroom, but they can't take it out of the students!"

Another round of applause arose.

"Let me continue. The first casualty of war is the truth—and that is true in the war for the minds and hearts of your children. Currently our kids receive little accurate information from their schools or public institutions about the historic role of Christians and Christianity in the formation of and present operation of our nation. Help them obtain correct information and realize that there is *NO* mention of "separation of church and state" in any of our founding docu-

136

ments. The "Doctrine of Separation" is hostile toward Christianity, is unfounded, and is wrong. Or, if you don't have kids, then educate those around you.

"The realm of politics used to be dominated by Christians. So if it has evolved into politicians eliminating religious activities and the public acknowledgment of God, then the politicians can restore those same precepts. We have been led to believe that Christianity is a minority vote—it is not—anywhere from 80-90 percent of the nation indicates they believe in God and the vast majority of those people are Christians. And most of those approve of voluntary prayer in school, oppose abortion on demand, and do not see a need for further legislation of any special rights for homosexuals, as they have the same basic rights under the Constitution as any other citizen. Making up 'new rights' not previously delineated in our Constitution opens a Pandora's box that future generations will revile. So, we can believe a lie and do nothing—or use the political system and vote to make changes. If we want different national policies, it is up to *us*, the citizens, not up to *them*, the leaders. Many men and women who stand for returning godly principles to public affairs are not soundly beaten in many elections—and if they do lose, it is often only by a handful of votes. Godly candidates are most often defeated, not by activists and radicals, but by *inactive Christians*! Exodus 18:21 states to let it be impressed on your mind that God commands you to choose as rulers, just and good men who will rule in the fear of God."

I continued, "Charles Finney, in the early 1800s, said, '. . .God cannot sustain this free and blessed country which we love and pray for unless the Church will take right ground.'

"Christians are not a minority — we are a majority in this country! It is time to declare at the ballot box that we will no longer allow officials, who embrace the values of the few, to take away the rights of the many. Your vote does count.

"If God has established that we have the responsibility to choose godly leaders, then before any election we must find out more than just the professional qualifications of the candidates. Find out the private life and personal beliefs as is best possible before voting them into office. Jesus said in Matthew 7:16-20, and Luke 6:43-44, that bad roots will produce bad fruit. A candidate's moral and religious 'roots' should be investigated. A candidate who is producing bad fruit in private *will* produce bad fruit in public.

"Help the godly candidate as much as you can, with your finances, campaign help, and prayer. Learn to look beyond your political party—you might have been born a Democrat; you might have been born a Republican—that doesn't matter because you have been reborn a Christian. . .now you are a 'Christocrat' or 'Christican'!

"Use direct contact with your Congress. Many of them say that just fifty letters on an issue makes it a hot item and can cause those in office to reverse his/her stand! Call them, write them, and express your concerns on the moral as well as the civil issues of the day.

"Spread the truth. Write to your local newspapers and "Letters to the Editor" sections. Express a God-based truth or moral stand on important current issues.

"Know that involvement in civil government *is* a legitimate ministry. Romans 13:4 states that civil leaders are ministers of God."

I stopped, chuckled a bit, and said, "Hang on now, this isn't a history class, I'm getting ready to land this thing."

Soft laughter echoed in the sanctuary.

"Finally, we must develop an attitude that is patient, long-suffering, unswayable and steadfast in these pursuits. We must avoid the short-term, microwave mentality sweeping the nation. Change takes time and we must change for the good. Do not give up. If laws change to allow immoral actions, then work hard to reverse them to laws of moral excellence. Galatians 6:9 promises that we will reap the benefits if we just hang in there long enough. To retake lost ground will require a courageous, little by little mentality.

"It is fitting to end with something Ronald Reagan said that expresses the sentiments I feel this wondrous July 4th: 'The time has come to turn to God and reassert our trust in Him for the healing of America. Our country is in need of and ready for a spiritual renewal.'

"May we be instrumental in keeping that dream alive and continue as one nation under God. May we always have the courage to do what is right, not just convenient, and may our lives reflect Christ to tell the world what is so good about our awesome nation.

14

"God bless you all, happy 4th of July, and God bless the United States of America."

A surprise round of applause thundered through the church in place of the normally muted sounds of rustling Bible pages and of people gathering their belongings in preparation to depart the completed service.

"Lord, you have touched their hearts in a very special way," I quietly prayed. "Seal it, Lord, and make it evident in their lives."

I left the podium and joined Pastor Jack in walking down the side aisle to the back of the church in order to greet the people as they filed out. We both were ebullient with the spiritual energy God had just released. People were happy and laughing and hugging each other. I sensed a feeling of hope rising in their hearts.

For so long, many of these people were downtrodden with the overabundance of ungodly and depressing news reports, along with the vile changes they have seen in the country they love and have served so well.

They now were stirred to pray as never before and to live their lives as beacons of righteousness and light in a very dark world. I will pray this lasts long enough in them to make the changes needed to continue in strength and courage to recapture our beloved land.

As I pondered the message and the people's response to it, I was happy in the knowledge that God is in charge and we are His workers. May His mercy pour out upon us.

"Chaplain, Chaplain." I recognized Major's voice emanating from the crowd that was now heading to the church back lot where the festivities were about to begin.

"Yes, over here, buddy. Well, was my sermon too long for you?" I joked.

"Just right," he said, laughing. "But one more minute of smelling that chicken grilling out back and I would have had to bolt!"

I laughed at that remark, too.

As I looked up, I saw the rest of the Garretts headed my way.

"So glad to see you all here today," I said with a big smile.

They are like family to me, and I am so welcomed in their lives. I noticed that the whole gang made it. And lo and behold, the headmaster himself, Don Jr., was in town after all.

"Don, Don, Don. . .you old dog," I said as I gave him a bear hug. He returned the same.

"Chaplain, I don't get home too often and it's so very good to see you. You are looking well. Heard there was quite a bit of excitement here while I was away."

"Yes, John was practicing his flying routine, but didn't do too well at it!" I quipped.

John was standing just a few feet away with his family.

"I heard that, Chaplain," he said with a broad grin.

All those within earshot laughed heartily. It was good to see the levity because a relatively short time ago they were in fear and dread at the horrifying accident that had befallen him. Still laughing, we headed off to the "trough."

It seemed everyone had come ready to put a dent into the fantastic bounty prepared by some of the best cooks in the whole state. What a feast. We chowed down on grilled steaks and chicken, corn on the cob, potato salad, mixed veggie salad and beans. The food kept on coming; they even had grilled veggies and veggie burgers for the few vegetarians in the group. Casseroles were lined up one after the other on long tables that seemed to go on for a mile! Soups, chili, baked sweet potatoes. . .no one's on a diet here, for sure.

I didn't even go near the dessert table. Apple, blueberry, peach, and pecan pies added such a delicious scent in the air. I think I absorbed calories just by breathing! And of course, the old home-made ice cream machine was busy, with all the children squealing for more. Brownies, cookies, tarts, cinnamon buns, bowls of candy and mints. . .you'd think this was the "Last Supper". . .and I mean the last!

Those who finished eating, or more likely just taking a break before going back for more, retreated momentarily to the "Days Gone By" fun fest and were engulfed in competition at the bean bag board or trying their skills at walking on stilts. I hoped that no one pulled a "Johnny" trick and that all the bones, in all the bodies, stayed intact.

We continued until dusk; food flowing, patriotic songs playing, people dancing and singing, lemonade spilled on most tables. Then, as if a silent signal had been given, pretty much everyone started to clean up and put away all the music gear, the tables and chairs went back into the church storage shed, and the leftover food was wrapped and distributed.

I spent a long time reminiscing with Don Jr. and his family, and joking with Don and Aimee and their boys. John and his wife left a bit early. He was feeling that pain creep up on him again and made a wise decision to fold it up and go home to rest. I knew that he was anxious to get back to work on the farm and wasn't going to do anything that would delay that return.

I could see Major taking this all in; he laughed, danced, and joked around. Just having a blast; but he was pensive at times. I knew he was soaking it all in because he starkly realized that in a short time he would be far away from his family and everything in his comfort zone. He was embarking on a new adventure that held so many unknowns; he probably wanted this celebration to last forever.

"Hey Chaplain," he called out to me.

"Yes, sir," I replied.

"Uh, I think you have that backwards, Chaplain. That's my line."

"You tawkin' ta' me?" I taunted back.

"Yes, ma'am," he said with a faked military bearing.

"You nut, what is it, dearheart?" I asked.

"I am looking forward to meeting with you tomorrow morning. Just didn't want you to think I was going to be too tired to show up."

"Hmm, more likely too full," I said with a long chuckle. "You ate enough to feed a small village in Cambodia!"

"Well, you didn't do too bad either, Chaplain. Just don't know how you can survive on your vegetarian 'wabbit' food.

"Get 'hopping' along there yourself, kid. See you at 10."

All the remaining Garretts piled into their trucks and cars and headed on home. It had been a long and remarkable day. I was full and tired. . .unlike my young friend who would probably play a few hoops with Joshua, followed by a snack of the leftover goodies before he goes to bed.

I chuckled under my breath, "Youth, it's wasted on the young."

As I started up my car, the radio came on. I was open eyed and staring at the dumb thing as it blared out, ". . .we are proud to claim the title of United States Marines." Hmm, I think that just might be confirmation that all will be well with our upcoming "grunt."

As I pulled onto the driveway and up to the front of the house, the warm glow of the living room's light in the dark of the early evening reminded me of the many cherished evenings of my childhood. A warm and fuzzy feeling enveloped me as I entered the house. Sweet memories of winter nights, birthday parties and piles of Christmas gifts swirled in my head; those memories made a grand pillow on which to fall asleep. I was out like a light in minutes.

15

A loud crashing noise abruptly awakened me from my comfortable slumber. The sound of breaking glass is distinct and I wondered, "What the heck was that?"

I grabbed my Glock and prayed that I didn't have to use it. I turned on the lights and searched the house, noting there was nothing disturbed and no one in sight. I encountered a different scene in the front living room. A huge rock had been thrown through the window. Glass was shattered all over the wooden floor, and on one end table. Bits and pieces of shiny glass adorned the arm of the sofa like little zirconium gems.

"What a mess!" I exclaimed. "Who in the world would throw a rock through my window. . .better still *why* would anyone throw a rock through my window?"

The police arrived shortly after my 3 am call. They asked if I had touched anything or moved anything. I indicated that I had not. They took pictures, dusted for fingerprints and handed me a note that was attached to the rock.

"You better take a look at this, Chaplain. It's addressed to you," the lieutenant said. "Here, put on these gloves while you hold the note, so you won't disturb any evidence."

"Addressed to me? Why in the world was it sent on a *rock* and through the window?"

I slowly unfolded the piece of paper. Roughly written in what was obviously a forced scribble were the words, "You better shut your mouth. All your God talk is screwing up the heads of the folks around here. Religion is the opiate of the people. We need freedom from religion. Death to you, and all like you."

A shiver of fear ran down my neck. From very deep within, I heard a voice saying to me, "Fear not, for I am with you. I will bring you through the flood and the flame. You are My child and I am your God."

I took a deep breath and asked what all of this meant and what was I to do next.

The lieutenant calmly said, "It's probably just a teenage prank, but I don't want to take any chances. I am going to station a squad car here overnight, just as a precaution. We will be back at daylight to search for more clues. You okay, Ma'am?"

"Yes, I'll be fine. Just want you to know, Lieutenant, that I am armed and if I feel my life is threatened, I may have to take some drastic action."

"Understood," he said slowly. "Just don't get antsy. I'll tell my outside detail that bit of information so they won't make any unfounded moves."

"I'm not that antsy. I'm still a good shot and won't do anything foolish. I never shoot at anything unless I know what I'm facing and have a clear shot."

Just then, Don Sr., Joshua and Major burst in through the door. The officer took a crouching stance and drew his weapon, shouting, "Stop where you are."

He might not have taken that action, if Don wasn't brandishing a shotgun.

"Oh, it's you, Don," said the lieutenant, lowering and holstering his weapon. "You know better than to run on into a place with police all around. I almost took a shot at you cuz I saw the gun first!"

Don apologetically said, "Me and the boys were awakened by the commotion and all the police cars flying up here. I brought the weapon just in case we ran into any unsavory characters on the way. In today's world you never know what you're gonna run into."

The lieutenant looked over the place one more time.

"Well, we've done all we can here tonight, Chaplain. We'll see you again at first light," said the lieutenant, looking unhappily at Don and his sons.

"Thank you so much. I appreciate your kindness," I said wearily.

Don piped up and said, "Chaplain, you probably will object, but I'm going to insist that one of my sons stay here to pull watch for you tonight. I already decided I wasn't going to take no for an answer. I'll leave my shotgun here with Major. And don't worry, he's very skilled in its use. Joshua will help clean up and put a board on that window until you can get it fixed. And that's an order, if I may be so bold to say, Ma'am."

"Don, I won't fight you on any of that tonight. I really appreciate the extra troops in light of this mystery. If this nut decides to come back, I'll need the bigger platoon to help me."

Just then, the lieutenant spoke up and said, "Hate to interrupt, but you won't be able to clean up any of this until after I finish some further investigation, and that won't be until tomorrow. It may be a bit inconvenient, but you'll just have to leave everything just like it is until then. Sorry."

I looked over at my rescuers. I knew their hearts were a bit heavy that someone had done this to me; especially something that could be perceived as a death threat.

Joshua gently said to me, "Are you okay? If you are, I'm going to head on home with my dad. We'll be back here in a minute if you need us, though. Major will stay here with the shotgun; he thinks he's a Marine already, so he is eager to pull guard duty for you."

"I'm fine, really. A bit shocked by the weirdness of it all, but I'll be fine. Thanks."

Don and Joshua headed back to their house. They knew the police officer in the squad car and stopped to talk for a few moments. I watched from the porch until they faded off into the dark night.

"Well, I am not too sure I can get back to sleep after all of that," I exclaimed.

"I am wide awake myself," Major replied.

"I'm going to put some coffee on, would you like some?"

"Yeah, that sounds good right about now," he said as he yawned.

"I feel safe with the police car out there, but they can't stay here forever. This is one of those times I'll have to dig in deep to the Lord to fight any fear, to make sure I act in wisdom and not in haste," I numbly stated.

"This is a pretty strange situation. I don't know anyone who hates you," Major said with puzzlement in his voice. "In my mind I'm running through the names of everyone I know at the high school, in town, at church, in my sports. . .I am just coming up blank with anyone who might want to do this."

"I'm not a stranger to you and your family because I am a long-time seasonal neighbor. But some people up here may not know me at all. It's a puzzle to me, too."

We were both on the second cup of coffee, and after a long period of sitting in silence just staring into the mugs, Major started talking.

"Chaplain, I do have questions for you still. If you're not too tired after all this mess, I'd like to bring something up right now. It's really been eating away at me."

"Too tired, are you kidding? I'm totally wired right now and couldn't sleep if I wanted to!"

My mind thought that this was as good a time as any for a serious conversation.

Major started telling me the story of his girlfriend from last semester.

"Well, I really liked one of the girls on the track team at school. She's so pretty, I know her family real well, and we have a lot in common. We went out on a few dates, but a lot of guys at school liked her and dated her too."

He went on and told me of their growing tender relationship. He also noted, with a bit of anger in his voice, that he started to get jealous that other guys were still dating her. I wondered if this subject was the true reason he wanted to get together for our meetings. So many times, he talked about her; did I miss those earlier clues? *Too late now,* I thought.

I nodded at his comments and said, "So, you were feeling jealous, or impatient maybe?"

"Well, we were getting kind of serious there for a while and. . ." He paused, shifting his gaze away from me.

His face was red; his feet were shifting back and forth. He kept taking deep breaths as if starting to speak but nothing came out.

I thought, *Oh boy, here it comes.*

He took another deep breath and after a long pause looked at me and said, "Well, one night we snuck into the barn loft. I brought a blanket to put down over the hay so we'd be comfortable. We were just going to lie down and look up at the stars through the little loft door. We held hands; well, my hands were shaking really. But I felt on top of the world. We started kissing and things got pretty hot and heavy. It just seemed like we couldn't stop. I guess I didn't really want to at that point. And before I could even think. . ." He paused, put his head down, slowly shaking it back and forth, then looked up again and blurted out, "I had sex with her." His head sank again onto his chest.

He looked up at me and winced as if I might smack him.

"Go on," I said quietly.

"And now, it's really bad. . .because. . .because. . .she's. . .pregnant. She said she doesn't want to get an abortion, and is really confused cuz she doesn't know who the father is either. She had sex with one other boy around the same time as she was with me. What can I do? I'm getting ready to go off into the military. I haven't told my mom or dad about this. I'm screwed. What a jerk I am, I hate myself and even worse, I feel so rotten to have let God down, and to let my girlfriend down. I should have been stronger and been in more control of myself. I know for sure God won't forgive me. I get sick every time I wake up and have to face another day. That is why I wanted to come over and talk to you, but it just wouldn't ever come out."

He continued in a barrage of emotions and comments. "You were telling me about the changes in our country and the immoral waterfall we were going over in a barrel and how my generation was the one to take it back. . .I felt so ashamed, I just couldn't tell you!"

I took a deep breath, waited a moment or two and then said, "Major, in no way do I mean to give you excuse here, but you and your generation have been asked to swim in a moral and sexual sewer, and yet are expected to come up with some 'clean' ideas about love, fidelity, sex, marriage, and parenting! And yes, it was a stupid move that can have some damaging effects on some of your dreams for the immediate future; repercussions you are going to have to face head-on. And yes, you need to tell your mom and dad about all this."

Major had a dark and sad look on his face with that comment. He remained very, very quiet, so I continued.

"But I want you to seriously think about some things. First, you're not screwed. Second, you're not a jerk. And third, I really hope you don't travel down the self-hate and self-loathing road. No one can force you to understand these things; only you can make some of these choices on what you need to do and on what you let yourself think. God will not throw you away because you sinned. He knows you and that all of us are born with a 'handicapped' nature. But most of all, you have to remember He wants to help us all get through it with the least amount of damage. He doesn't give excuses for your sins, but He does offer forgiveness and a much better way. He will even show you how best to remedy this mess."

"I know, I know," he said slowly and with remorse. "I will tell my mom and dad, and tell them soon. I will take responsibility if the kid is mine and I will make the right decisions, I hope," he said forlornly. "I really need some help, Chaplain. What am I supposed to do, where do I start?"

"I want to apologize to you, Major."

"What?" he said incredulously.

"Yes, I have to apologize for yakking so much when you came over each day. I am a terrible listener. I seem to always lean toward teaching everywhere I go and I need to be a much better listener. Oh, and I will be, but it's going to take a great work of God in me. I am so sorry I didn't pick up on your need to let you speak."

"It's not your fault, Chaplain, it was me. . .I was just stalling every time I came over. In light of all the good things you were telling me, I felt worse each time and it got harder and harder for me to bring it up."

I looked directly at him and firmly said, "Major, you have to understand something very important right now. I *do not* think any less of you. I *do not* think you're stupid, nor do I think you are a jerk. God has loved me through all of my sins and has *never* thrown me away. With all my heart, I shall do the same to you, and someday, you will turn around and do that to others who have also sinned against God.

"Eventually this will work out, and if you stick with the Lord, it will all work out for good. Remember that scripture that says, 'And we know that God causes all things to work together for good to those who love God and are called according to His purpose.' Check that out in Romans, chapter eight; a great chapter that tells us about our victory in Christ. But I want you to look a bit closer when you study that next time. Notice that it does not just say that all things work together for good. . .it clarifies it. . .all things work together for good to those who *love* God <u>and</u> are *called according to His purpose.*

"I'm not going to give you a 'listen up lecture.' God has you in His 'crucible' for sure, and that is painful enough right now. You are a good man who has made a bad decision. God will forgive you, I forgive you, your parents will forgive you. . .but will you forgive yourself? Only you and God can work that out. Some of the suffering we go through in life isn't what God put on us, it is what we put on ourselves, and this is one of those times. But if you remain attentive to God and seek His forgiveness, He will work this out.

"Many young people in this same situation just panic; the young man runs off, having nothing to do with the pregnant girl; the girl often opts for an abortion; an abortion which is all too frequently sought as the answer. But it's a bad answer, one that rips away a little baby's chance to have an opportunity to make it in this life. Abortion is an answer that often dooms the would-be-mother to a broken, guilt-ridden heart. That just doesn't make any sense, not in the physical or the emotional world."

Sheepishly Major interjected, "I know, Chaplain. And I am glad my girlfriend, I mean my former girlfriend, decided to have the baby and give it up for adoption. I agreed to that, too, if it's mine, that is. But all this is killing me inside. I might have to go through the rest of my life knowing that there is a kid of mine out there and I am not there loving, protecting, and providing for it. I feel so rotten right now; I am just sick over this."

I answered, "I am really glad you told me. I would like to be there for you in all this. I'll even go with you to tell your parents if you'd like, just let me know. I won't do anything until you ask."

"Thanks, Chaplain. I really needed to get that off my chest. I was choking on that secret and didn't know what to do. I still don't, but will you pray with me?"

"Sure, let's take a minute now, okay? Do you want to start, or shall I?" I asked.

"I don't think I have any words right now, Chaplain. Could you say something for me?"

"Sure," I softly replied.

"Dear God, we come before You right now. I can't speak for Major, but I know he is ever so sorry for his disobedience to Your commands. You made it so that a man and woman should come together physically, and that is right and holy. But you also placed that union inside a specific set of circumstances, not because you are a Providential Prude, but because Your wisdom is far beyond what we have here on earth. Your directives help diminish our problems, not our pleasures.

"We are bound by time and physical sensualities, which often override any wisdom in our decisions. Lack, loss, or rejection in our inner hearts often has us seek solace in that which is only temporary, fleeting, and always leads to more pain and confusion. We ask Your forgiveness for everything that does not meet Your measure; a measure that is born in majestic understanding and wrought in the fire of Your love.

"In no way do we take these things lightly, so we come to You to ask for Your mercy on all who are involved in this situation. You said You would never leave us nor forsake us, and right now, we get to practice living in that promise and with that hope.

"We ask for Your intervention, for Your answer as to the final resolve and to set in motion the beginnings of the great change You have for Major. I ask that You establish the route You have planned for his life and that any evil intended for him would be turned around for good. We ask You this in Jesus' name. Amen."

Quietly, Major said, "Amen."

He continued, "Chaplain, I can't believe I dropped all this on you, especially when so much scary stuff has happened to you tonight. I came here to help you and you ended up helping me. . .again."

"I know, dearheart, I know. But I think God may have been more involved in arranging our meeting than we think."

"What?" he exclaimed. "God wanted that rock to come through your window?"

I laughed a little. "No, that's not what I mean. It's just that we assume so much is just coincidence or just the happenings of the world, but they are really things that are orchestrated by God, controlled by God, or allowed by God."

"You gotta be kidding me. Why would God allow some jerk to throw a rock through your window, tell you to stop talking about Him and that you should die?"

I took another deep breath. "It's not that God wants my window broken or my life threatened; this is all about what He is going to do with the seriousness of the situation. Did He get your attention through this?"

"You bet He did!" he replied.

In an effort to encourage my hurting young fellow, I said, "And yes, God will use our health, our wallets, fear. . .anything that will bring us to a closer walk with Him and expose some crack in us that might weaken us later on. God is in the business of *construction* not *destruction*."

Major quickly added, "It sure doesn't feel that way. Sometimes it seems as if God is far away or doesn't care or is really trying to hurt us."

"A lot of people feel that way. But stop and think of when you learned the most and changed the most. Was it while you were lounging at the lake with your friends, having a great time, or was it during some of your greatest trials and tribulations?"

I continued, "You learn anything from that calf drama you just went through? You learning anything from this tough challenge you are facing right now?"

"I see your point, Chaplain."

Out of the corner of my eye, I noticed the sun was starting to peek through the partially drawn blinds on the porch door.

"Wow, that was a short night," I said wearily.

"Yeah, but a good one. Thanks, Chaplain. I don't have all the answers and I sure have a lot of thinking to do on this mess. And oh, yeah, I think I want to talk to my parents by myself. I am a man, not a kid anymore, and I want to hear what they have to say. This will be hard for them, and I hope they won't be too disappointed in me."

After a pause, he continued. "I really understand now how just a moment of pleasure can cause a lifetime of pain. Maybe that's why God tells us to experience a moment of pain in doing things the right way, so you can have a lifetime of pleasure afterwards. That is a wisdom that is far greater than ours is, for sure. And I want that kind of wisdom."

I smiled at his remarks. "You really do have much in front of you that is destined to bring you joy and security. Go get right with God, with this girl, with yourself, and then it will be all right with others."

Major looked out the window, "Boy, the lieutenant wasn't kidding. There's a bunch of officers out there heading right up to your porch. Well, I guess my job here is done. Mom will be getting up soon to make breakfast. I don't think she'll mind if I take a nap this morning, seeing as I think we've already had our morning meeting. I hope you get one, too, but it doesn't look like it will be any time soon."

I answered, "I'll be fine. I'm still curious about all this. Let's see what happens. Tell your dad and Joshua I said thanks again for coming over and helping."

"Yep, I will. Pray for me to have good timing on telling all this to my mom and dad. Well, really, my whole family.

"Will do," I answered quickly.

"But I think I'll tell them one at a time rather than the whole gang being there at once. I'd really be embarrassed."

"You'll figure it out. I bet your dad will have some words of wisdom for you."

Major went out the front door, pausing to look at the front window. He turned to me, but didn't say anything else. He just shook his head in lingering disbelief and headed on home.

The officer greeted Major as he left to go back home.

"Thanks, son, for pulling guard duty. That was real nice of you."

"No problem. Felt good to do it for her."

He just smiled and said, "Be careful with that shotgun, son. Don't want any more challenges around here. Tell your dad I'll stop by if I have any questions for him."

"Sure will. Hope you catch whoever did this," Major said solemnly.

"Me, too."

The young officer then walked towards me. He was tall, in a sharp looking uniform, reminding me of my earlier days in the military. I looked at his nametag, "Sgt Greene".

"Good morning Sgt Greene, thanks for coming back out here."

He smiled and tipped the bill of his hat as he greeted me. "Good morning Ma'am. We'll be here for a few hours. Hate to inconvenience you, but we'll need to take another look around, inside as well as out. The forensics guys like to scour the whole scene."

"Sure," I said. "Can I get you guys some coffee? Breakfast, maybe?"

"No, Ma'am. These boys already put on the feedbag down at the café. They are pretty focused on their work right now. Thanks anyways." He turned and went back outside.

"Whew, what a night," I mumbled. "Hope Major gets all his thoughts in order, but I hope I do too!"

Slowly I gathered my glasses, pens, Bible, journal and other reading materials and trekked on over to my comfy "prayer chair." The view of the mountains was always so calming for me and I certainly could use that right now. As I slowed down to seek God in all this mess, my eyes just seemed to close on their own. Exhaustion won out over the nagging curiosity and the ever-encroaching fear; in minutes, I fell fast asleep.

A knock at the door woke me suddenly. Oh, bless her little heart. It was Aimee with a boatload of food. Whoa, one o'clock already. I must have crashed!

"Well," Aimee declared. "You have had your share of excitement lately, for sure!"

I sleepily nodded my head in agreement.

"Didn't mean to wake you, but thought you could use a little something to eat. I know that at times like these, my mind isn't thinking on making any meals and I thought it might be the same with you."

"Thanks so much, Aimee. I am still tired, but hungry too. This is perfectly timed," I exclaimed.

We set the table so I could have a bite to eat. I marveled at the care and love this woman has for those in need. She makes it all look so easy. But then, she has a heart tested in the fire of life and has proven to be one of God's finest.

The brunch fare was delicious. I thoroughly enjoyed it and the accompanying small talk. For a brief few moments, my mind was removed from the seriousness of the situation. As I finished eating, Aimee started to clean up.

I protested. "No, no, don't you dare even think about doing these dishes."

Aimee just smiled and continued with the task.

"Well, to tell you the truth, I wanted to talk a little, if we could," she said hesitantly. "It seems my family has taken up a lot of your time lately, and I didn't want to intrude any further, but I have a few things on my heart, uh, if you have a minute that is."

Sounded like Major. I smiled and told her, "Hey, I'm on vacation. . .got plenty of time!"

"Some vacation. . .you could write a book about it!"

"Just may someday," I laughingly retorted.

She continued, "Major is a great son, a great kid, and a great help to his dad. We love him so very much. So, it was really hard to hear what he had to say about his girlfriend. I had to fight back such disappointment in my heart. Not so much at what he did, although I was shocked and probably angry at that, but disappointment at what this could do to his plans. I don't mean to exclude the girl in my thoughts, but Major is my son and he has worked so hard and my heart is just broken."

She was sobbing by now. Quietly, I stepped over to where she was working at the sink, and gently put a hand on her shoulder. If tears could spell, they would be writing out fear, anger, guilt, and a host of other words in the letter of her heart.

My feeble attempt at consolation began. "Aimee, you do have a fine son and you are a fine mother. The pain that is being experienced all around is real and will last for some time, but in due time, this will all work out, and work out for good as you look to the Lord. You are strong people who have close ties to each other and will figure out what is best for all concerned. It's the not knowing what will happen that makes this so tough. One mistake does not change who a person is. It may grievously affect what happens, but you and Major are still the same strong, independent, hardworking, God-loving persons that you were before this went down. You may sometimes hear otherwise, but condemnation and rejection are not of God. He's in the rehab business and helps us get stronger, not weaker."

Aimee slowly spoke through her tears. "I know, thanks for the reminder. It's just that with John's accident, the vandalism at your house, and now Major having to face this situation. . .it is so overwhelming. But you're right, we will find a way and go on from here. And I don't mean I'm brushing any of this under the rug. Major has to face what he's done and come up with the wisest route, and we're there with him for the long haul. I do trust God to lead us and guide us. It's just pretty hard."

I nodded in agreement, as we both finished the dishes.

"Thanks again, Aimee. Everything was just perfect. . .the timing as well as the food."

She looked at me and said, "Even though my heart is heavy in all this, I hope and pray that 'perfect' will be used to describe our outcome."

"Ditto," I said in agreement.

Aimee wiped her tears with the back of her hand, stood up a bit straighter, put a smile on her face and said, "I've done all the damage I can do for today. I'll be heading on home now."

As she was going out the door, Officer Greene was coming in again.

"Chaplain, we've finished our investigation outside, and if you don't mind, we'll have a look inside now too."

"Sure, Officer. Do I need to step outside, or go in the other room?"

"No, you're fine. If you could just stay close by in case we have any questions, that would be good."

He and his men stayed another two hours, measuring trajectory estimates, taking more pictures, writing notes with many hand drawn references.

"Ma'am, we've finished looking inside. I do have a few questions for you though. Has any stranger been around here lately?

"No."

"Have you had any run-ins with anyone in town, like road rage or accusations of hitting a parked car or anything along those lines?"

"No, nothing like that," I answered quickly.

"Have you had any uncomfortable interactions with anyone or has anyone seemed to follow you or to unexpectedly and repeatedly show up where you are?"

"Nope. . .nothing."

"Okay, we're done then. You can feel free to clean this up any time. We don't need anything else from the scene. And, I think it's safe to remove the squad car too. But, if you need anything, just give me a call," he said, handing me his card.

"Thanks, Officer. I appreciate all your time on this."

He smiled and said, "We're just doing our jobs, Ma'am. Goodbye and have a nice day."

He tipped his hat again and left.

I sat in the kitchen for a long while, thinking, praying and thinking some more. I was just getting up to start cleaning this mess, when something caught my eye. Major and Joshua were coming up the road, pushing a wheelbarrow full of tools and pieces of wood. They were talking and smiling and that made me smile, too.

They came up on the porch and just barged right in.

Joshua bellowed, "Now, we know you're going to tell us that 'you got this', and we know you do, but we would really like to help in cleaning up. So, if you don't mind, just make yourself busy and we'll let you know when we're done."

Major chimed in, "That's an order, uh, Ma'am," he said with a broad grin plastered on his face.

I slowly said, "All right. . .I'm not going to fight city hall. Let me get you the broom and vacuum, and let's see. . .a big trash container should do it up right."

15

They were busy with their thorough clean-up. I was impressed. Aimee had done well by her sons. They took the wood pieces and boarded up the broken window, too.

"There," said Major. "That should hold you until you can get the glass replaced. Mr. Clauser at the hardware store called my dad when he heard what happened and told him to tell you that he'll get a man out here Monday to replace the window. He said he wants to do it and he won't take any money for it. He told my dad to stress that part. So I'm just sayin'."

"Well, I. . .I just don't know what to say." At that moment, I crumpled down onto the sofa, put my head into my hands and began crying. My body was trembling and I felt I had no control over this response, nor did I even have the inclination to do so. I guess the pressures of all my bottled up emotions had just built up, not able to stay inside anymore. I felt a little foolish, but couldn't seem to stop crying.

I looked up through teary eyes and saw my two heroes just standing there wide-eyed. They kept looking at each other and then back at me. I took a deep breath, re-established some composure, and then said, "Look at the two of you. Haven't you ever seen a woman cry before? And what are you going to do, just stand there?"

Major haltingly said, "Uh-uh-uh, what can we do?

Joshua seemed to return to his senses first and said, "Let me get you a Kleenex or something." He ran out to the kitchen and returned saying, "Here, here's some water, too. Want me to call my mom?"

"No, no, I'm good. It's just a 'girl thing' sometimes. A nice cry does a body good! And for two young guys, you did fine while all the snot was flying around!"

I could hear my voice. It sounded like I had a cold, but it was just stuffiness from all the crying.

Major added, "I know about crying, I've done a lot of it since we had our talk last night." Joshua looked surprised when he said that.

"What the heck is the Marine dude crying about? You gotta be kidding. I haven't seen you cry since you got really bad hurt during one of our ballgames. You turnin' soft or somethin'?"

"No," Major said with a cringe.

I could tell Major realized he let the cat out of the bag a bit early. So far, he'd only told his mom and dad about the pregnancy situation. He knew his brother might badger him about it, so he wanted to tell him last. Joshua seemed quite puzzled with his comment and was getting ready to say something else.

In an effort to change the subject, I interjected, "Time out. . .crying is good, men or women, sort of washes out the soul, if you know what I mean."

Joshua responded with a thoughtful nodding of his head and said, "I think there's been a lot of tension over a whole lot of things lately. Everyone reacts differently, but we're all in this together."

He has no idea of the truth of that response, I thought, "but he soon shall."

"Well, guys, it's been a long day, for sure. I am grateful for your coming by last night and again today. I am going to wrap up a few things here and then I think I'll lay low for a few days. It's the weekend and I'm takin' it off!"

They both laughed at the same time. "I think that's a good idea. Can we tell our dad you suggested that for us, too?" asked Major.

"Yeah, right. You can try!" I continued to laugh with them. "Better get going and see if he has any chores for you. He's a blessed man to have you as sons; he may even consider the suggestion!"

"In a million years," said Joshua. "Bye."

"Tell your folks I appreciate them lending you guys out to me today. God bless."

"Thanks, Chaplain," they said, echoing one another. They meandered on home, laughing and talking loudly all the way.

It was early evening still, the sky was brilliantly clothed in its goodnight colors, and I was enjoying sitting on the porch, finally by myself. There had been so much going on in a seemingly very short time, but it was all going to be okay. Time has always proven out the truths of our God. In recollecting how long it has taken me to understand that, I was reminded of the need to be more patient with others who are limping along the road of life too.

As I hooked up my iPod to my earphones, I looked over toward the trees. Their gentle swaying in the breeze was rocking me like a newborn in the arms of its mother. I thought out loud, "Did you set this up, Lord? Wouldn't be surprised if you did. You have an ever-lasting uniqueness that covers every situation just perfectly. Thank You, thank You, thank You Lord."

As I turned on my music, I stopped and looked up with awe and wonder, because the song that started playing was, "Thank You Lord, I just wanna thank You Lord." You are something else, Lord. You always make me smile.

Without warning, I suddenly heard a loud cracking, then a thumping noise. "Oh no, now what?" I yelped. I jumped up quickly and looked around, wishing I had brought my handgun out with me. It was then I realized the breeze had knocked off a large dead branch from the tree out in front of the house and it had landed on the porch roof. I checked around but no damage was evident. After such a long day, I was not about to climb up there and get it. That can wait until tomorrow.

"I am just too jumpy to be out here tonight," I proclaimed to the woods. My mind wandered to one of my niece's favorite childhood books, and in an effort to feel better I jokingly yelled out, "Good-night moon, goodnight stars, goodnight air, and goodnight noises everywhere."

I'm done in for sure, I thought, and went inside, making sure all of the doors and windows were locked securely. But wait, I thought about the window with the plywood cover. . .it'd have to be okay; nothing I could do about it, anyways. This is when the trusting God part comes in. I've done everything on my part to ensure safety; now I have to give the rest of it to God to do His part.

As I trailed off into a deep, well-needed sleep, I softly whispered, "Goodnight Lord."

16

The weekend had passed without any incidents, and I quickly prepared for another morning session with Major. And a beautiful day it was, with warm and gentle breezes seemingly blowing away the cares of the moment.

My ringing cell phone interrupted the quiet interlude.

I picked up the phone and someone asked if I was Dr. Fontana. "Yes, this is she," I answered. It was the lieutenant. He explained they had picked up the young man who broke my window. He asked if I could be at the station at two o'clock.

I replied, "Oh, yes, Lieutenant, sure, I can be there. See you then."

"Hmm," I said as I pondered the call. They caught the rock thrower. Found a paper with my address on it out by the woods where he had waited before tossing his note-wrapped missile. This condemning piece of evidence was a scrap from a school paper he had written and it actually had part of his name on the backside. Well, at least this kid is no professional!

"Lord, help me to approach this with utmost wisdom, compassion, and mercy. Put the words in my mouth that will be pleasing to You," I quickly prayed.

Just then, I heard Major coming up the driveway.

"Hey Chaplain," he said as he came onto the porch. He blurted out, "The paternity tests came back and. . ."

At that moment, my home phone rang. Ordinarily I wouldn't answer it, but with everything going on, I figured I had better take the call.

"Hold that thought," I said to him with a clenched jaw and growling sound, a sound that is often partnered with my ever-present battle against the ogre of impatience. I answered the phone and quite curtly responded to the questions being asked. It was a reporter I had met at the church barbeque asking to speak to me at some point in the near future. I finished the conversation once we coordinated a time corresponding to my visit at the police station today. I hung up without saying goodbye.

"Ouch." I winced. "That was a bit terse."

"There you go with the fancy vocab again, Chaplain."

Major excitedly continued, "Was that the police station? Did they find the stupid creep?"

"No, that was the local newspaper; they wanted to interview me on what happened last week. The reporter was doing some research on troubled kids and wanted to get the info on the rock incident.

"The police called earlier and they want me downtown this afternoon. They picked up a young man, a teen-aged kid. The Lieutenant said he recognized him but didn't really know him. He's been picked up before for loitering and missing school. He's been in foster care a few times because he was a victim of domestic violence. Seems his dad's an alcoholic who also struggled with drug use. This kid is sure carrying around a bag of trouble. Now, what about that test?"

"It came back negative for me, but positive for the other guy. I am not the father after all. But I still feel kinda funny. I think it's guilt I'm feeling; I still can't shake it."

I listened quietly. He continued.

"I'm glad it's not me, but what about the girl and the other guy? How does God work all that out?"

Major was really struggling with all of this, as well he should. I finally began to speak.

"The Lord is a gentle Spirit. He is not a wrathful Master waiting to torture us in a chamber of horrors. He sees those two precious individuals in a different light than anyone else on earth sees them. He knows their weaknesses; He knows their suffering and the unkindness that has cut into their hearts. He knows the many rejections that have pierced their young souls and knows that they were probably just looking for love in all the wrong places, or just a moment of pleasure. . .just like you. God doesn't have mercy on some and not on others, and there are no favorites in His perfect plan. He loves them, and you, just as you are. But the newsflash is that He doesn't want anyone to stay that way.

"He has continually told mankind that He does not want that anyone should perish but that all should come to everlasting life. The sad truth, though, is that many people scoff at those sayings. On the other hand, 'religious' people often give excuses for their own sins, and yet want hurting young people like these two kids to hang from the nearest tree. That is not God's thinking and not God's will. What He plans to do with them is not known at this stage. They will have some extremely difficult times, decisions in front of them, and will need all the love, help, and encouragement they can get. Just like you would have wanted, if it had turned out to be you."

Major was tearing up again. He is really a softhearted person under that tough exterior, and he asked, "But what will happen now? What can I do?" He paused reflectively. "If anything!"

"Well," I continued, "most people don't care one bit. As long as they're off the hook, they go sailing on as if nothing happened. It really is a good thing that you are concerned over this and have a heavy heart. What you did was wrong, totally, no-stupid-excuses wrong! By your sin, you have 'grieved' God's Spirit. You have 'defiled' the temple of your body. Because God is in you, your own spirit actually hurts too because of that."

A sigh slowly emitted from Major's slack jaw and he said, "I was just thinking about the Tabernacle in the Wilderness teachings that we spoke of a while ago. I was so quick to catch on to the word picture God was giving us that with Jesus inside us, we then became the holy place, like the Tabernacle. God even said that where we stand is holy ground. It's not that we're holy, but what is in us is holy. How can I have had such a great spiritual understanding and still screwed up so royally?"

"Because, dearheart, like those two kids, we are all weak, have been terribly hurt by others, live in a world that more and more does not acknowledge God and thusly, even though we love God and have chosen to serve Him, that old Adam nature comes up to smack us in the head now and again. And every time that we don't smack it back and let God's nature rule in us, then sin abides. That is what happened to you. It doesn't mean you lost your salvation, or that you aren't saved. It means you sinned and need to repent and be cleaned up. . .and then go on. Every time you fell when you were learning to walk as a toddler, did your mom and dad beat you up and throw you out?"

"Of course not," he snapped incredulously. "They loved me and helped me get back up. I even remember my dad held out some mini-marshmallows for me to try to walk to. He swears I was too young to remember, but I do remember that!"

"Well, if mankind can do that, then how much more can a perfect God? God will not throw you or those other young people away because of their wrongdoing. He picks us up when we fall down and even throws in some marshmallows along the way to entice and encourage us to get up and 'walk the walk' with Him. Religious, self-righteous people don't understand that. They live in a 'bad deed gets an automatic punishment and suffering' mode. . .religious legalism often leads to religious fascism! God does not want that for His people."

"So what can I do?" lamented Major.

"First, we need to pray for these two young ones. Pray for their restoration with the Lord and for their wisdom as to what they need to do. Getting married at such a young age is not often the best route. Making the relationship 'legal' in man's eyes is often just an unthinking, automatic reaction, and not a well thought out approach. Another thing you could do is be available to encourage them, not shun them. Offer to drive them when they need a ride; ask them to hang out with you. Especially as her pregnancy becomes more obvious, because when that happens, many of her friends will just drop by the wayside, or, as is often the case, she just physically can't do the same things her friends are doing. Not wise for a pregnant teenager to go bungee jumping, motorcycling, or on an all-night dance-a-thon! They both will need your love and care. All the things we are talking about, maybe you can share with them, too."

"Yeah, right," he zinged back. "I could never talk like you talk about this stuff."

"God doesn't expect you to do what I do. . .He expects you to do what He has called you to do. . .and do that with all your heart."

"And when do I find out what He wants me to do?" he asked a bit sarcastically.

"You find that out as you go, sweet pea. You find that out as you go."

We spent a few moments in prayer, with Major pouring out his heart to the Lord and praying one of the most sincere, mature, loving prayers and requests for the well-being of the young couple.

Ah, yes, I thought. *You are doing some big time work in all this, Lord. Big time.*

"Chaplain," Major said, "You know, I feel somewhat better. It's kind of funny how when you quiet down, look to Jesus and let Him speak to you, it actually does settle down all the racing inside your head and heart. Thanks."

"Yeah, I found that out too, and you only get that with a relationship in Him, not in religion about Him! Gotta run. Have to get some lunch and then head down to the police station and see what's going on with the rock-throwing fellow they caught."

"Have fun," he slyly said.

"Oh sure. . .really looking forward to this!"

"Seriously," he chimed in, "I'll be praying for you. . .uh. . .and him."

"Thanks," I replied. "We both need it."

As I drove off to meet with the lieutenant, my mind was filled with a hundred scenarios of meeting this kid. . . .criminal, miscreant, stupid waif. Will I even have to speak to him? Do I even want to speak to him? Well, there's no sense in trying to set up the situation ahead of time. Vain imaginations are just that. . .vain.

The drive in town was almost thirty-five minutes. The police station was not one of my frequent stops; and a few U-turns and dead-ends were added to the trip. Upon arrival, it looked like something out of an old movie. Red brick walls, flat roof, blue and white sign out front, and large, old windows without curtains, which exposed a myriad of stacked boxes, piles of papers and long-forgotten misplaced ceramic coffee cups. I shuddered to think of the large, dead roaches that might have taken their last jump into those java death traps.

Parking was simple and non-metered. . .what a nice change from the big city! I laughed at the thought of "Barney Fife" greeting me at the door. Well, I guess it's not *that* much in the country.

The officer at the front desk directed me to a room behind a glass-walled area to his right. There were about a dozen desks in there, all covered with files and papers. And more coffee cups, with all but two desks vacant. While passing the first unmanned desk, I carefully peered into one of those cups, looking for a hapless roach. Gladly not seeing any, I proceeded to meet the Lieutenant. He was located at the desk area furthest from the door. It looked like there used to be a wooden or even a glass partition there to give him a separate office, but it was long gone. I stepped over the former threshold and into his workspace. He seemed unruffled that his 'walls' were rows of filing cabinets. An empty seat to his left was reserved for visitors.

He stood as I entered his 'office.' "Please forgive the looks of this hole in the wall. They have been promising to build a new police station for the past ten years. I'll probably be retired, heck, I'll probably be dead before they get it budgeted and built!" he said with a hearty laugh.

I sat in the old and worn chair. As I leaned back to relax a bit from the tension of the moment, the timeworn relic plunged all the way back, tipping over, causing my feet to go flying up in the air. Red-faced, peering through the V formation of my airborne legs, with my jeans-covered butt fully facing his gaze, I hung suspended for one brief moment; then, kerplunk! With hands grasping the arm-rests and a wild-eyed look of surprise on my face, I continued my less than graceful swan dive onto the floor. My head hit like a water-melon falling off a truck.

"Medic, get the medics in here quickly," he shouted with panic in his voice. He jumped up as if he had been tazered in his rear.

At this point, I howled more with laughter and embarrassment than with pain. The two officers who were formerly seated in the entrance workstations rushed in to help. I had a nasty lump on my head and an even nastier bump to my pride. They insisted I stay seated on the floor until help arrived. After all the commotion, the medics came and left, concurring that the only serious injury was to my pride. The ice pack felt good, I regained my composure, and finished my greeting to one seriously distressed lieutenant.

"Chaplain, I just don't know where to begin. I am so sorry about that stupid chair. Are you sure you don't want to go to the hospital? Do you want us to get a doctor over here? What can I do for you?"

I chuckled and finally said, "I am fine. Stop worrying, really. It's just a bump on my head. . .that's the hardest part of my body, according to some!"

At that comment, he relaxed a little bit. I wanted to get this over with so I quickly suggested, "Let's get on with the business at hand and hope and pray the rest of our meeting goes a bit more in my favor."

He grinned sheepishly and then continued. "We have been inter- rogating our young suspect for four hours. He has admitted that he wrote the note and threw the rock. He seems quite unrepentant and what I thought was a bit flippant about the whole thing. I contacted his father and asked him to come down here, but he said to let the little brat rot in jail for all he cared. He told me he was eighteen now and that he wasn't going to clean up after him anymore. He said that his kid was all ours, and to do with him what we wanted."

I waited for a moment before responding.

"That ought to build up this kid's sense of value in our world, eh? I'm sorry, Lieutenant. That was a pretty snarky remark. I don't want to feel too sorry for the kid, but don't want to throw him to the lions, either. He's probably had a lot of problems that have given him a shaky start in life."

"He's eighteen now. This doesn't go to juvie. . .he falls under the adult statutes. I think we could get him on malicious destruction of property and suspicion of attempted bodily harm to an individual. It all depends on what charges you agree to, ma'am."

I asked hesitantly, "Is there any way I could meet with him first? Maybe find out what's going on in his head and heart?"

He replied, "I'll have an officer stay in the interrogation room with you, if you'd like. FYI — He's in handcuffs, which are attached to the table, so he's not going anywhere any time soon."

"Is there a two-way mirror thing in the room?"

"Yes, ma'am, there is."

"I think I want to go in by myself, as long as there is someone close by looking in on us in case he gets a bit agitated. Oh yeah, and what's his name?"

"Okay by me if you want to go in by yourself, but I'm also going to cuff his ankles to the chair when you do. I'll come back out here and get you when that's done. Um, his name is Jason Westfield. He lives in a trailer over in the Hollow. We've been out there dozens of times for domestic violence calls. It's a dump of a place, a real mess inside and out. Not fit for an animal to live there; we called in social services when he was younger and they said they would start a file, but they never really did anything about the violence against him or his mother. She died about four years ago from a drug overdose and this kid has only gotten worse since then."

"Thanks for the info. I'll just wait here in my cozy chair 'till you get back!"

I think he wanted to laugh, but didn't. He just left his pseudo-office and headed toward a metal door at the end of the multi-desked room.

A few minutes later, he returned and escorted me down a long hallway lined with small, empty cells. At the end was a lone, beaten up metallic door that resembled something from the medieval ages. To the right of the door, in the little corridor that formed an "L" shape off the main hall, was the viewing window that allowed us a look inside.

Lieutenant stood for a moment before he slid back a huge silver latch that kept that sucker locked tighter than a pair of jogging pants on an overweight woman. He waited as I watched the figure in the room. Then, an unexpected loud clanging noise sounded when he quite forcefully yanked at the door; it caused me to jump and gave me the creeps, as if I was in a dungeon or something. Before he fully opened the door he said, "You okay? You still want to do this?"

"Yes," I whispered.

I didn't really know what to expect, but was a little surprised at the sight of a slightly built young man with tousled, blond hair. He was wearing a white T-shirt and dirty blue jeans. Both upper arms brandished tattoos, partially hidden by his shirt, but visible enough to see they were rough-hewn and most likely attempted by a budding 'artist of the ink.'

As I observed this young man, there was something about him. Even though he was a bit rough around the edges, there was just something about his eyes. They were of a pale blue hue, and seemed much gentler than this situation warranted. He was furtively looking around the room, as if trying to figure a way to escape, but that was pointless with the presence of the restricting cuffs and constant guard. It was when he looked over at what would be a mirror to him and a see-through glass to those outside, that I saw it. His face and his eyes looked sad when he caught a glimpse of his own image.

What is it? I pondered. *Hmm, Mr. Tough Guy just might not be so tough after all!*

The lieutenant made sure I was seated across the table from the young offender and reminded me that the guard was just outside the door, should I need anything. He left the room and slammed the door with the same clanging sound. I jumped again and thought, *I wish I hadn't done that; I don't want this kid to think I am scared.*

We both just stared at each other for what seemed like an eternity. He finally broke the silence.

"Whatchu lookin' at?" he said with disgust.

"You tell me," I sternly replied. "I'm trying to think from where I might know you. Were you ever in any of the youth classes I spoke to over at Pastor Jefferies' church?

"Yeah, what's it to you? I got turned off to that religious crap a long time ago," he said with disdain.

He continued in a tone full of hatred and vitriol, "You and your kind are messing up our world. You talk about some f'ing God and yet the world is full of wars, babies dying, jerked up dads. . .you're an idiot. I hate you and your God!"

While listening to this hurting young soul, I thought on previous times in my life when I have heard similar comments. My first reaction was always to defend God and His goodness. I would get angry with the one to whom I was speaking, because they were berating the Love of my life; I would go on and on trying to convince their heads that they were wrong. That, of course, would always go nowhere.

One time in prayer, God spoke to my heart and told me that He loved me too, but that I didn't need to "defend" Him to others. My job was not to "convince" anyone; it was His job to convict their hearts. My job was to live my life remaining full of His Spirit, so that His power and words could flow through my somewhat broken vessel as unhindered as possible in the moment. It was all a "God thing," and I am grateful to have learned that lesson.

So, as I worked at quieting myself before God to most appropriately answer and possibly be of help to this young fellow, he looked up at me and sneered, "So what the f— do you have to say about that, you sorry piece of religious sh—!"

"Sorry you feel that way, but I wanted to meet with you before any decisions are made as to what they do about the rock throwing thing the other night."

"What's it to you?" he angrily replied.

"It's a lot to me. I'd like to help you, if you'll let me."

"What the f— can you do to help me? You have no idea what my life's like, or how I live, or anything. You rich religious people have no idea what real life is like. You live in your fairy tale Bible world of angels on clouds in heaven. You're no good to me."

I smiled at his comments.

"What the f— are you laughing at?" he smugly snapped.

At that moment, the officer who was watching through the window burst in through the door.

"Hey, buddy, quit your filthy mouth when you talk to the Chaplain here. If it weren't for her, your sorry ass would be in the can right now, waiting for God knows what. Knock it off. . .you understand that, or I'll end this meeting right now!"

I interrupted the well-meaning officer, "Thanks Officer, but we're doing just fine. He was just trying to express some of his feelings to me, that's all. We're good here."

When the officer left, Jason looked at me with a puzzled look on his face.

He started to speak and said, with great hesitation, "No one ever stuck up for me before. Why the f—, err, I mean, why did you just do that? Trying to get me to believe like you do or something?"

I just looked right in Jason's face and said, "I said that because you are worth it."

To my great surprise, Jason closed his eyes, put his head down in his cuffed hands and started crying. I knew he was trying to hide a deep sadness, and the more he tried, the more he cried. Oh, the pressures he must've been under to hold it all in.

"Lieutenant, hurry up, get back here," said the guarding officer as he shoved open the corridor door into the mostly empty workroom. "You're not going to believe this."

Both men ran down the hallway and stood gawking through the one-way mirror. The chaplain was sitting across from the young criminal, her hand gently touching his bowed head as he wept.

"I never thought I'd see the day," said the guard.

"I did," said the lieutenant. "There's something different about Chaplain. God has given her a way with the young ones that gets out what's deep inside, even when they think they don't want to. Keep an eye on things and keep me posted."

"How long should I let their meeting continue?" asked the guard.

"As long as the Chaplain wants it to," Lieutenant replied, and returned to his office.

The guard remained at his post, and listened intently to the conversation. He turned up the room volume so he could hear what was being said. Without realizing it, his own heart was softening and his viewpoint was quickly changing concerning this young miscreant.

In a soft voice, I started speaking again. "Jason, I grew up in a large family. I'm the oldest of nine kids and lived in the Projects before we ever got a house for all of us. My dad was an alcoholic and it was very hard growing up, listening to him tell us we were the problem. I thought I'd die a thousand deaths when he said I would never make it as a nurse. My mom was always telling us not to listen to him cuz it was just the booze talking. It hurt a lot, though.

"My dad never, ever hit us, except for a well-deserved spanking or two, but his words were constant swords to our hearts. He never meant it to be that way; he was just stuck in his own brokenness. Years went by and I was finally able to love him again, and he loved me dearly, just how I dreamed of when I was a kid. But I was a grown woman before that ever happened. I prayed and prayed and got very disappointed in myself because I loved God with all my heart, but hated my dad and knew that was so wrong. God and God alone helped my dad and me to get it right. It took a long time for both of us because we were both so broken. But, just like God said, it would work if we kept coming to Him."

Jason lifted up his face, the remnants of tears still visible and said, "I hate my dad and my mom and I don't think God can help me with that. It's so unfair; I've been so ripped off."

He then put his head back down onto his hands.

This kid is hurting and is on a personal vendetta to ensure others hurt as much. *Oh, God, please manifest a miracle with this young man,* I prayed inside.

"Jason," I said softly. "Lots of times hurting people hurt people. In speaking to the lieutenant, he told me that your little sister had been killed. I can't even imagine what kind of pain your mom went through when that happened, especially her knowing that she caused the accident. Your mom did what many people do; she tried to anesthetize that pain with drugs and alcohol. But that doesn't work; and I'm sure you had a front row seat to how much more pain the drinking and drugs caused than they relieved.

"And your dad, as captain of the ship, must have felt as if it was the *Titanic*. The love of his life was collapsing into a shriveled heap and his whole life and family were slipping through his hands like sand. It all must've been a whirlwind of pain and confusion for everybody. No wonder you're angry.

"I'm not going to give you a sermon here, Jason, but I can tell you that God gives us a great release for that anger in two special ways. The first is when we can forgive, and that is really a difficult thing for anyone to do when there is so much agony and suffering. But forgiveness is possible and probably the most healing thing you can ever do. The second is some wisdom He shares with us when He says to be slow to anger, slow to speak, yet quick to listen. We slow the whole process down by doing those three things; sort of like putting a bit of cold water on a fire. Only then can we see a little more clearly the direction we need to take, without the heat of the moment crushing our every move."

Then Jason, with his head still down on one hand, made the other into a fist that kept hitting the table with a quiet, repetitious bang, bang, bang. For a moment, a little tingle of fear ran through me that made the hairs stand up on the back of my neck. I brushed it off, praying quietly, "I can do all things through Christ Who strengthens me; I can do all things through Christ Who strengthens me."

Jason kept hitting the table and in rhythm to the fist banging repeated, "I can't, I can't, I can't do this. I'm all alone. I'm so scared." With head still down, but fist unclenched, he quietly sobbed, "Oh God, I miss my mom and my little sister so much."

His voice had a different tone to it, almost penitent. He looked up at me, face still wet with tears and eyes forlorn with pain, and continued, "Is there any hope for me, like what happened to you? I really used to like my dad. I remember I loved all my family when I was little. Dad played ball with me; we went to the lake and did a lot of fishing. He kind of hung around a lot with me. He loved my little sister, too, and used to tickle her to make her giggle. We would all laugh when she did that. But she was killed when she was only three. My mom was backing out from the front yard and accidentally ran over her. That's when all the bad stuff started happening."

Standing outside that room, hearing every word, was that big, tough guard, wiping away his own tears with those large, rough hands.Jason sat thoughtfully before continuing. "My mom just stopped loving me; it was like I reminded her of my sister and she just kept getting more sad. Pretty soon, she quit cooking and cleaning and my dad and I were like on our own. She started sleeping a lot and was always out of it. She popped pills all day, and sometimes drank, too. She never had done that before. One time I came home from school, she had passed out and had crapped in her pants, right there on the couch; she was still lying in it. I was really scared and called 911, but my dad got really mad when I did that and told me not to get the police involved if it ever happened again.

"Right after that, my dad started staying out later and later each night. Sometimes he didn't even come home, but when he did, I could smell alcohol on his breath. He often got very angry with me. He'd come home and start throwing things around and cursing. He started drinking at home a lot, too. In the morning, he'd put whiskey in his coffee and tell me it was cough medicine. He must've thought I was stupid or something. He hit me a lot when he got angry, and he got angry over nothin' most times. I prayed and prayed to God that he would stop. God never answered me. And then, on top of that, my mom died, right in a pile of her own vomit. It was disgusting. I hated God even more then. What kind of a creepy God would allow that to happen to a little kid? Huh? Can you explain that, huh?"

I could hear the disdain and anger coming back into his voice. This poor kid had suffered so much, what could I possibly say? But I began.

"Your heart has been so torn in so many ways by so many people; often the very people who were supposed to hold you, love you, and make things right; the very people who were supposed to lead you and guide you. I think the sword seems to go in deeper when it is thrust in by those who are the closest to us. You've been ripped off and shortchanged in the family area, for sure. But you don't have to be like what you came from. . .and you certainly don't have to head in the same direction. One of your biggest hurdles on the way to healing your broken heart and your life is going to be forgiving those who have hurt you the most."

I could see Jason squirming in his seat. His jaw tightened; his hands became fists again.

Jason quickly interrupted me and sternly said, "I will never forgive my mom or my dad; they don't deserve it!"

Tenderly I continued, "Well, if 'deserving' forgiveness were part of the equation, none of us ever would be forgiven. I don't think any of us 'deserve' it, but the awesome part of forgiveness is that you can get it. For instance, I forgive you for what you did to me at my house; and not because it is a law or anything, but because it is the right thing to do. I struggle with forgiveness, too, because I have a broken inner nature, but I fight that nature and refuse to have it rule me. I fight it because with that nature, it is almost impossible to do the right thing for the tough hurts in life. You see, the human nature can only handle the little things that bug us, but the 'God nature' can handle it all. With God's nature ruling inside me, I can actually love the unlovable and forgive the people who caused the deepest hurts and sins against me. And it's there for you, too, if you want it."

Jason just stared at me, more like glared at me. I just looked right back at him. When I did, I felt such a compassion swell up inside me for this broken young man. It must have showed on my face because the longer I just quietly looked at him, the more his face lost its tension and his mouth and jaw relaxed, finally. He seemed lost in his thoughts and put his head in his hands again. A long time went by. I just reached out and softly patted his hair a couple of times. He raised his head.

Much to my surprise, this precious young man asked more about Jesus. He asked what he had to do to ask Him into his heart. I shared briefly that it only took a moment to do that and he could do it anywhere, not just in a church. Before I could say anything else, Jason just closed his eyes and prayed out loud.

"Dear God, I am so sorry I got mad at you. I guess I was just so sad and felt so lost. I don't want to be lost anymore. I don't want to be alone anymore and I don't want to hate my dad anymore. Please, Jesus, forgive me and come inside me and be my boss."

A much calmer Jason then said, "Am I supposed to say 'Amen' or something?"

I smiled a big smile and said, "No rules on the praying part, just speak your heart to God. But saying amen is fine, though."

It was sweet to watch this precious, downtrodden young man humble himself enough to let God start on a journey with him. I was rejoicing inside and could hardly contain myself. Not from a religious standpoint, but from one of joy, knowing that Jason is going to be fine over time. I knew my life had changed so drastically and wonderfully with Jesus as a real part of my life, and I knew Jason was about to experience that also. But I had to admit that these "foxhole" conversions are often entered into on weak grounds and Jason, as a "newborn" with Christ will need some long-term and intensive mentoring and teaching. Hmm, I have an idea that maybe, just maybe will work out.

At that point, Jason sat up straight, his tears had stopped flowing, and it seemed as if his whole body was asking, "What's next?"

Even though I still had a lump in my throat and tears in my eyes, I managed to say, "Jason, you have just begun your journey with Christ in your life. You'll need to learn many new things, things that God tells us in the Bible. Maybe finding a good Christian youth group would be helpful. Hanging out with good people encourages us to keep heading in God's direction. Don't expect everything to be fixed and perfect in a few days. . .this is a lifetime journey you're on."

Jason nodded his head in agreement.

"You're in a police station right now because you damaged some of my property and threatened my life. We still have to work that out. You also need a safe place to go home to, and have some sort of livelihood to pay your way. There are lots of things to iron out, son."

He looked intently at me as I spoke then he said, "I know, but I haven't a clue as to how to make anything better. But I do know that for the longest time, there was something like a dark thing or something that felt heavy on me; and it's weird, but it's gone now. Am I insane or something?"

I looked at him with tender concern and said, "Jason, you're saner now than you've ever been. You asked God inside you and He ain't goin' nowhere," I replied facetiously. "You can put Him in a box and never let Him be your guide, your friend, your mentor; or you can develop the best friendship you'll ever have in your life. It's really up to you."

Jason's face looked different from just a few hours ago; he seemed brighter, more lively. . .I just couldn't put my finger on it, except he just didn't look forlorn anymore. He was still a bit weary looking and disheveled, but not forlorn. I pray, dear God that You will protect him and get him off to a great start with You.

He looked up and said, "But where do I begin?"

"Well, don't be in a hurry and rush off into anything, but if you'd like, I'll get a Bible to you. Read one Psalm every day and read the Proverbs that is the calendar date of the week. Kapeesh?"

"Ka—what?" he said.

I smiled and astonishingly, he smiled right back. I said, "Oh, never mind. . .that's dinosaur talk for 'do you understand?'"

"I think I do," he said. "I need to read the Proverbs of the current date, like Proverbs 1 on the first of the month and so on. But how many of those Psalm things are there?"

"There are 150 of them. . .so plenty to do, a little at a time. Well, let me go talk to the lieutenant and see what happens next."

Very slowly, with eyes looking down, staring at his shackled hands, he said, "Do you think they'd let me come home with you?"

"Honey, I'd like to tuck you in my pocket and take you away, then let you out when all of this is straightened out, but it doesn't work that way. I do have an idea, though, that you may like. It will involve a lot of hard work, but if you are willing to work with your hands and sweat your head off, this could be our remedy. I have to make some calls and coordinate a few things. All of which have to be okayed by the judge or whoever does these things. I'll get back with you."

I pushed away from the table just as Jason tried to lift his hands to touch my arm. He had forgotten about the handcuffs, as had I. The clank of the chains hitting the metal table reminded us both of the seriousness of the situation. I don't know if it was authorized or not, or even wise to do so, but I walked around Jason's side of the table and patted him on the back. With my other hand on his head, I prayed. "Dearest Lord, we come into Your presence to ask for a miracle. Your young man Jason here has need of a new home, a new heart and a new way of living. I ask that you swiftly grant our plea; and I ask that you fill his heart with humility instead of hate, with responsibility instead of remorse, with grace instead of guilt, with revelation instead of revenge, and with joy instead of junk. I ask this Lord, in Jesus' name. Amen."

Jason said nothing except a quiet "Amen" at the end of the prayer. He just watched as I left the room.

The guard had already rushed to open the door when he saw that I had gone around to the other side of the table. Graciously he stopped and stood inside the room, with the door still open, while I finished my prayer. I think he was just as dumbfounded as I was that this had all taken place and that Jason was truly a changed, young man.

"Chaplain," he said hesitantly. "I've seen these guys 'come to Jesus' a hundred times. They are just telling you what you want to hear. Pay it no mind."

16

I just smiled and whispered, "Yeah, lots of times these things are genuine and sometimes not. But I sensed something different here, a real repentance. We'll see, we'll see."

I walked back out to the lieutenant's office. He was on the phone, so I waited a moment until he finished. When he hung up, he said, "Come in, Ma'am, come in."

I just stood in the doorway, not wanting to chance another "ride" in the infamous chair.

"I know this is a pretty strange request and I don't usually do this," I said slowly and articulately, "but I'd like to see if there is any way to have the pending charges against Jason dropped."

"Chaplain," he said very slowly, "I know you have good intentions in that good heart of yours, but we do have damage to your property and a threat against you that he has admitted to. But, as the victim, you do have a sayso in all this. I could speak to the judge, tell her the situation, and see if she could just drop it to a misdemeanor mischief charge. But I don't recommend him getting off totally free. Maybe he could be required to do some community service or something; I could recommend that."

I put my finger to my chin and started tapping it. "I have an idea, Lieutenant; yes, I have an idea that just might work. I have to make some phone calls first and then I'll get back to you. But what do we do with our young fellow back there for now?"

"Well, I'll get him something to eat and drink, and keep him here overnight. I can do that because his father refused to take him back home and we don't have a determination of his case yet. But I can only hold him for seventy-two hours and then there needs to be direction determined for the next step," he replied, seemingly a bit relieved that there might be a more positive solution in the wind.

He went on with a bit of apprehension in his voice and said, "Are you sure you're calling this one right, Chaplain? I mean, is this kid pulling your leg or something?"

"I have to trust that inner tug that I sensed. If it's not God, it will be manifest soon enough. God has never let me down and He sure as heck isn't going to let me run off a cliff with this thing; been praying my head off over it. I'll be back first thing in the morning and will call you before then and let you know if my idea is feasible."

"Sounds good, Chaplain. Well, it's a remedy at least for a day."

As I turned to leave, I looked back and said, "Could you tell Jason I said this will all work out for him somehow? And ask him to keep praying. Oh, and one more thing. You wouldn't happen to have a Bible here, would you?"

"Just so happens I do. It's mine. I read it at lunch. But I have another one. We had this circuit riding preacher come through a few years ago; old guy, pretty gruff for a preacher. He was drunk one night and got into a fight. We kept him in one of our cells to sleep it off. He left it in his cell cuz he said he wouldn't need it anymore. Said he had made his peace with God and was going home. We found him dead by the railroad tracks a few days later. No foul play or anything. . .just looks like he had laid down and died. But anyway, it's here in my desk.

As he went to reach for it, I said, "Could you give that to Jason? I think he's ready to make peace with God too. . .just don't let him go near the railroad tracks!" We both laughed.

"Are you sure this kid will want this?"

"Pretty sure, Lieutenant, pretty sure."

I left the police station as quickly as I could and rode straight over to the Garretts' place.

17

As I drove up to Don's farm, I remembered I had told that reporter to meet me at the police station. Yikes, that just slipped my mind. I called the lieutenant and told him I had forgotten that a reporter was supposed to meet me at his office today. Fortunately for me, the reporter had just called him and said he was delayed with an unplanned assignment.

"I told him you'd be back tomorrow and he could try then."

"Thanks, Lieutenant, you're a life saver!"

As I finished the call, Don drove up beside me. He was on his John Deere tractor. He and his boys are always so competitive about things and he frequently joked about their big farm machines and my "midget" car.

"Hey, get that sardine can outta my way," he joked.

"Don't have to tell me twice," I joked back.

He pulled the tractor on into the barn and came back over to the house.

"Chaplain, what brings you over here? You have time to stay for dinner. Aimee just put it on the table; hot and ready to go."

"How could I resist that invitation? I do have something I want to run by you; this would be a great time. Thanks. Let me run home and wash up, then I'll be right back."

"Don't even go through all that bother. We do have soap, water, and even some clean towels you know. . .it's a farmhouse, not a frat house," he joked again.

"That's good; didn't want to impose, but that will save me some time and you won't have your dinner get cold."

"Good, it's a deal," he said.

I followed him inside. The house was inviting; filled with the aroma of home-cooked fare, so much so, I could smell what was on the menu! Homemade bread would start off our meal, we would then dive into the roast beef and finish it all off with her famous apple pie. Yum.

As we finished some small talk during dinner, the boys left to wrap up the nighttime chores so their mom and dad could finish the conversation with me.

Aimee spoke first and said, "It's so nice to have you here tonight, especially not in conjunction with an emergency."

"It's so nice to be here. Your dinner was absolutely delicious. I'd weigh three hundred pounds if I lived with you."

Don piped up. "No you wouldn't; she'd work your fingers to the bone. A real slave driver, she is," he humorously said.

Aimee snapped him with the dishtowel she had in her lap.

"Hey, I'm callin' the police," he said, still laughing.

"Funny you should mention the police," I said. "I was at the station for quite a while today, talking to the young man who threw the rock into my living room."

"Yes, Major told us you were going. We prayed for you this morning after he came back home from meeting with you."

"I greatly appreciate that. You won't believe what happened!"

I related the story to them. They listened with joyful surprise.

"And that brings us to the point of discussing an idea I had. This kid is one hurting little puppy. His aggression and misery are off-shoots of his painful family situation. He was miraculously changed in that room today. I can't explain it and don't intend to; I just know that God did something really awesome in there and I want to follow up on it."

"Sure, what's your idea? Something about the kid?"

"Yes," I said. "His name is Jason Westfield."

"Don't recognize the name," Don said.

"I do," said Aimee. "His name came up in a Woman's Prayer group one time, quite a while ago. Mrs. Westfield was a friend of one of the ladies at the group and we prayed for her. We had heard of her drug use and drinking after that awful accident where she inadvertently ran over her little girl."

"Oh, that family. I do remember now; the news covered it quite a bit at the time."

Don became very pensive and quiet.

"Honey, what's the matter?" Aimee asked with concern.

Don kept his head down and said, "Gee, I didn't ever do anything at the time; never called the family even after the death of the wife. Never asked if there was anything I could do. . .you know, man to man. I feel so bad now. I should've stepped up to the plate to see if they needed any help or something. That poor family fell apart; they must have felt all alone. Did the church do anything, Aimee?"

"At the time, we made some meals and tried to visit, but Mr. Westfield just wouldn't have anything to do with us. We only did it a few times. Some of the women felt so badly about the situation but felt our hands were tied because he wouldn't let us help him. Everything just seemed to fade into the background after that."

I waited a moment and then said, "Well, there is something you could do to help now."

"Oh, please; I'd certainly be willing to help in any way I can," said Don. Aimee nodded in agreement.

"I don't even know if this is possible, but I wanted to run it by you first, before I made the suggestion. What I was thinking was if Jason could be charged with a lesser charge and has his punishment be community service, could he then serve that time working for you on your farm?"

Don looked at Aimee; then they both smiled.

"Nothing like ten hours in a hot field or a barn to build some character in a young man," Don said with that sly smile continuing as he spoke. "I would like to make one suggestion, though. It would be better if he could actually stay here with us on the farm. We have plenty of room; he can bunk with the boys. That would be a lot easier than trying to wrestle with his dad to get him here every day."

"Uh — that was one of the problems," I continued. "You see, his dad doesn't want him back after this last episode. I was hoping to ask you the hugest favor if he could actually live with you for the length of the community service. But you have already come up with that remedy."

"Well," Don said. "It looks like we're all on the same page."

"This is better than I even imagined. Young Jason can learn a lot from being in a family that is much more stable than his current situation. But, like I said, I don't even know if this is feasible. I have to meet with the lieutenant again tomorrow morning."

"Chaplain, we'll be praying for this to all work out in Jason's favor. He needs a better break than he's been getting. I'm willing to give it all I've got, and so is Aimee. I'm sure the boys will go along with it too. I'll talk to them when they get back from the barn."

My heart soared. I can only hope and pray that Jason won't screw this up and throw away such a great deal. If we get it, that is.

"I am so grateful to you both," I said with noticeable joy in my voice.

"And we're grateful to you too, Chaplain," Aimee said. "I see this as a second chance for that kid. You know, to help right a wrong."

"Ditto," said Don, "And a second chance for us to help."

While driving back to my place, my mind and heart were soaring. There was no guarantee all this would work, but what a great opportunity for Jason. "Yahoo," I screamed at the top of my lungs. "Thank You, Lord, what a miracle!"

I called the lieutenant as soon as I got inside.

"Sorry to bother you, sir, but I have a suggestion that may help in the Jason Westfield case. I don't know if it's even possible, but I'm going to run it by you."

The lieutenant listened to the plan and was very interested. He put me on hold and when he returned to the phone, he indicated that the judge was willing to cooperate with the logistics. He couldn't see my grin, but he must have heard it in my voice.

"Minor problem though," he said. My heart sank.

"Like what kind of problem," I said very slowly.

"Oh, not to worry, Chaplain; I just mean Jason has to stay at the station overnight. We can't get anything done till the morning. Can you come down here around eleven o'clock so I can officially release him to you and the Garretts? The judge has said that she will charge him with misdemeanor mischief. She also said she would consider what Jason wrote on the note as a fallacious threat. To keep things just, she wants there to be a lengthy community service, like a year's worth."

I replied, "Whoa, that seems like a long sentence for this, don't you think?"

"Ordinarily that would be the case", he said." But Jason has gotten in trouble many times before. They kept making his sentences more severe and longer each time. The last one even involved three months in juvenile detention".

"Oh", I said. "I guess you have pay the fiddler if you want to dance,"

The lieutenant laughed and said, "I haven't heard that saying in forever!"

We both laughed again.

"Well sir that should do it. I'll be here early, how about at ten o'clock and I'll bring the coffee and donuts."

"Now you're talkin', ma'am," he said enthusiastically.

As I hung up the phone, I thought about my morning meeting with Major. "Oh, where are my brains?" I lamented. "I told the lieutenant I'd be there at ten, let's see, I'll have to add in another thirty minutes to the travel time so I can swing over to the café. Brainstorm, I'll just have Major meet me there!"

"I'm brilliant," I said to myself.

That next morning, Major was more than happy to meet me. We shared coffee, breakfast sandwiches, and then he scarfed down an apple fritter too. What an appetite!

"This one's on me," I said.

"Chaplain, no way, you're not going to pay this time. You have been making my breakfast for over a month now and it's my turn. That's an order," he said with that big fat grin on his face.

"Okay, champ, it's all yours. By the way, have you heard any more from that ex-girlfriend of yours?"

"Funny you should ask. She started coming back to church and got involved in our youth group again. She said she and that other guy, who is the father of her baby, were at church that day you spoke and they both were really touched by what you said. They want to clean up their lives and get back on the road to moral excellence. It was kinda neat hearing them talk like that. They said they had kind of forgotten about the Christian heritage of our nation and they didn't just want to stand around and do nothin' anymore, either. They want to get involved in helping other teens understand the same things. I was really surprised, but they asked me to pray with them for God's direction in what they were supposed to do."

"Well, did you?"

"Now Chaplain, you know I did! It felt pretty good, too; felt sort of like what I was supposed to do. It didn't feel strange at all, as a matter of fact; I liked praying with them. . .I liked it a lot."

"Hmm," I said to myself. This young man is so special. I think God just may have a deeper call on his life after all.

I answered him, "Wow, that's different, to say the least. Something is going on here. That young man, Jason, now these kids too. God is stirring up the pot; I'm excited at the prospects, Major. We just may have some sort of revival going on in this town!"

"You gonna set up a tent or something?" he asked.

I laughed. "Not that kind of revival. No, one that God is stirring up. . .in the hearts. I've read many stories about whole towns changing overnight after people let Jesus into their hearts. Bars closed up, families got back together, porn stores left town; a whole bunch of things happened all at once after someone started preaching God's truth, not religion, but God's truth. And they started praying and praying and praying for the whole town. . .and bingo. . .the whole town changed!"

"I didn't know that; whole towns?"

"Yup, whole towns," I repeated.

"I'll never be able to preach like you do, Chaplain, but I can live a good life and I can pray," Major said with such heartfelt sincerity.

"Never say never, son. Never say never." I just smiled. "Well, get your wallet out, the bill is all yours. I'm going over to the station to pick up our young friend, Jason. You better be doing some heavy duty praying in all this."

"Sure will. See you in a while," he said, picking up the check the waiter had left with us.

I could tell he was feeling a "man moment" in paying the bill; he smiled all the way to the cashier. I looked back through the window as I walked to my car and saw him leave a nice tip, too. He's a great kid; just the kind of man our country needs in the military. I was so proud of him.

As I drove over to the station, I was recalling what I said about revival. Am I witnessing the beginning of one? There have been so many things going on lately and many lives changing pretty quickly. I smiled as I thought on this.

"Oh, Lord," I prayed, "please keep the fire going. I volunteer; use me as You will in this place."

Upon arriving downtown, I saw a bit of a crowd and quite a commotion over at the police station. The lieutenant was outside, talking to a reporter, and there was a camera crew there! Oh no, now what?

"As a matter of fact, here comes the Chaplain now. She may have something to add," the lieutenant said as he reached out for me as I walked toward him.

The reporter didn't wait for me to step any closer. He walked very quickly toward me.

"Chaplain Fontana, Roger Appleby from KWAT-TV, our local TV station. Is it true that you are going to take in the kid who destroyed your property and threatened to kill you?"

I responded, "I think you have your information incorrect but I'm sure the lieutenant can answer all of your questions over the next few days. Excuse me, I have a meeting inside."

Someone yelled out, "I heard the Jesus-hater had a 'come to Jesus' meeting with you yesterday. Is that true? What do you think about that? How did you brainwash him so fast?"

I hurried into the building.

"What the heck is going on, Lieutenant?" I asked incredulously.

I could feel the anger rising up within me and spoke quite loudly with that anger spilling out, "How did anyone in the media know what happened with that kid while I was with him in that interrogation room? Why did you ever in the world tell another soul?"

From the back of the large, open office area came a quiet voice, saying, "I'm the one to blame, Lieutenant." It was the guard who was watching us yesterday.

He sheepishly continued, "I went home and told my wife. She was so excited that she called her prayer group that had been meeting every week in our home. She said they were specifically praying for the young people in our area and she was ecstatic at the news. I guess someone in her group must have opened their big yap about it."

"As far as I'm concerned, it's nobody's business. Let this kid have a fighting chance with this opportunity and without the paparazzi up his. . .well, in his way," said the lieutenant.

We both agreed but the lieutenant said he would have to tell the reporters at least some general information.

"Is the reporter who wants to meet with me still out there?" I asked.

"Yup," he replied. "He's the one that had the mic shoved in your face."

"Could you ask someone to go out and tell him I'll talk to him, but in here and without the cameras rolling?" I asked.

"Sure," he said. "Hey, Ed, make yourself useful and tell the reporter we'll talk to him in here."

"Roger that."

"But no cameras in the station!"

"Got it," he yelled back as he ran outside.

As soon as he came inside, the reporter introduced himself and started the usual inquiry; my name, what I do, if I knew the kid, etc. And then the corker came.

"So you took advantage of a young kid to proselytize him for your church?"

"It wasn't exactly a chance meeting there, fella," I said.

That old anger and sarcasm rose up and practically choked me at the throat. I took a long, deep breath and continued.

"What would make you say that?" I said, with a begrudging smirk.

"Well," he said, "the word is around that you prayed with him and he changed in an instant. Said he wanted to learn how to forgive his parents. . .you know. . .stuff like that."

"Those are things involving that young man's personal journey, and if he did want to try to forgive his parents, wouldn't that be a good thing? I get the distinct feeling that you're looking for some story that really isn't here. And for your information, I am only here sporadically, so even if I did talk to him about going to a certain church, which I didn't, it would be to one locally, not my own. So I'd appreciate it if you didn't stretch the story into something that it isn't. In due time, you'll know if he's sincere or not anyway."

"And how will we know that?" the reporter asked.

"You'll know it if he gets in trouble again and shows up back here at the police station! In the meantime, let the kid just give it a try. Do you have son?" I asked.

"Yes, I do," said the reporter.

"Would you try to keep him protected from others, too?"

"Of course."

"Well, this kid has a dad who is struggling and struggling so much he told him not to come home and that he was on his own. So you want to do the community a favor. . .let this kid have another chance, but without bugging him, pre-judging him and following him around. Let him stabilize out and see what happens. He'll be under the tutelage of a good family. Try praying for him instead of 'prying.' If it all falls apart and he plays the game and goes right back to his mess, then I'll be the first one to call and you can use him in your investigative report. Right now, he's not a number, he's a kid in trouble, and we want to salvage what we can so he doesn't jump off the bridge of life into some pretty nasty stuff. Kapeesh?"

"Ka-what?" he said with a funny look on his face.

I rolled my eyes and said, "It's an Italian word, properly spelled c-a-p-i-c-h-e, meaning 'Do you understand?'"

"Oh never mind!" I continued. "Just give me a little leeway with this kid and see where it goes. You don't need to know where he's going or what those details are. But I tell you what. . .if he turns out a success story, can you cover it from that angle instead?"

"Yeah, right," he said with disdain. "These kids are a pestilence on our town. We need harsher sentences. Lock 'em up and throw away the key, as far as I'm concerned." He took his paperwork and went outside.

"Now that's one cheerful dude," I said.

"Ma'am, we deal with these guys all the time. They only want the gross and negative stuff; it sells newspapers and keeps a person 'liking' their Facebook page. He'll be back for some other reason, I'm sure. I'll hold him off as long as I can. He'll find out what the sentence is, because that will eventually be public record. But he'll have to dig a while. I may not get to file my paperwork any time soon." The lieutenant smiled broadly.

"Let's get our paperwork done at least," I said. "Did our boy get any breakfast yet?"

"Yes, he had some juice and sandwiches a bit ago. He'll be ready to leave with you once we get everything signed off."

"Let's roll then," I said, and walked back with him to his office. I was excited at what might lie ahead for our young man.

18

*Y*oung Jason sat quietly next to me in the front seat of my car. It was warm, so I had the windows down. He was sitting with both arms leaning on the window frame, his chin on his hands and the wind blowing through his hair as we sped along the winding country roads heading out of town. He looked like a kid on his way to camp; you'd never know he had just come from a brush with the police and that his family had disintegrated before his very eyes. Youth. . .it brings such resilience with it.

He was quiet a long time. Sliding back upright in the seat, he quietly said, "Thanks. I don't really know what to say after all this. I'm sorry I broke your window and wrote that stupid note. I was all caught up with a dumb group online that kept talking about hating religion and how it just brainwashes people to be robots. It talked about how there isn't really a God, so it's stupid to pray. After all that happened with my family, I kinda believed all that. I'm pretty dumb, huh?"

I waited a moment then said, "Jason, you're not dumb, you're just hurting after all the sad and bad things that have happened to you. Like I said before, 'hurting people hurt people,' and that is still true. I'm not giving any excuses to your mom and dad for their actions, or to you for yours. It's just that there is a bigger picture here that we usually all miss out on. But God doesn't. He *is* in charge, but you have to *let* Him be in charge of your life. He will not force Himself on anyone; but He does pour out a lot of help and mercy on us when we are in trouble. See, God knows your heart and when He sees that someone really has room for Him in there, He goes after them to help them come to Him. It's like a lifeguard at the beach. He watches everyone on shore, but they are not drowning. The lifeguard jumps into action to save someone when they are drowning. Just like us; we often are not interested in God as our Lifeguard. . .that is until we're goin' down!"

"Yeah," he said. "That's sort of what happened to me. I was so angry at God, but He sent you at the time I needed it most."

"Yes, but it's not me that is important, Jason. Look at all that went on in your life. Most people, just like you did, get angry at God because of all of the cruddy stuff going on, but God was just lining things up. What so many people think is just circumstance is really the awesome, exact plan of God for rescue and remedy. Unfortunately, some people just stay in their anger and hatred of God and of everybody else, and it just prolongs their agony. . .and their rescue! I am so glad to have had the privilege of being present when you gave your heart to Jesus. But God has been working on you a long time, honey. There have been people and situations that God has been using to bring you just to that right moment, when you would bend the knee of your heart to Him and actually invite Him in and let Him start you on the biggest and best changes in your life. It's quite a difficult ride at times, but oh, brother, you will love the changes and the miracles that start happening. People who don't know the Lord will think what you say and do is nuts; but remember, the word of God is foolishness to those who are perishing."

He just looked at me, and as seriously as I've ever seen a young person speak, he said, "I don't know what God did back there the other day, but like I told you then, something very dark and very heavy left my chest area. It scared me at first, but then it felt really good. After the junk left, it was almost like a warm blanket or something was placed on me."

"Not surprised that happened," I said. "You've had a lot of sad things happen, a lot of loss for a young kid. Your sister and mom are gone; your dad is confused and has rejected you; and you were sitting in jail facing imprisonment. . .that's a pretty heavy load for anyone! When we go to God, He very often removes the loads we were carrying."

Jason just looked sad, but then said, "I am going to be okay. I don't know how I know it, I just do. It's sort of, like when all that dark stuff left me, something else came in. You won't think I'm crazy if I tell you that I actually smelled like a 'fresh' smell, you know, like when someone has the dryer going with that nice smelling stuff they put on the clothes."

"No," I said, "I don't think you're crazy. Some unique things happen when we come out of our darkness and into what is called the 'marvelous light' of God. I don't want to be demon-oriented here, but there are evil, impure spirits roaming around, just like there are good, pure spirits. When we go against what God has said to do, it's sort of like inviting the 'opposite' to come in, and gladly they do. When we have our broken nature of anger, hatred, or lust. . .or whatever, that is the territory of Satan and he fits right in. In rebellion, we open ourselves to Satan, magnifying our already broken nature. So the hatred of someone, or the need to hurt someone, or to steal something. . .it's almost more than we can handle. We often don't control the urges and then we just give in to it and get off on the wrong track. . .way off."

"Oh no, I don't want that to happen again," he said, with quite a bit of concern. "How can I stop doing the wrong things and only do the good?"

I looked at Jason and smiled. "It's a long journey, dear. It takes time and effort on your part, to learn the better ways of God, and then to practice long enough that His ways then become your ways."

His eyes widened as he said, "But I'm not too good at this stuff! What if I do more stupid stuff? Do I have to chase God down again?"

I smiled. "Oh, so many questions, but that is really good. Now, you're searching deeply into your own heart, and will learn as each day goes by. One thing you always have to remember, though, is that God has promised that He will never leave you or forsake you; that nothing will ever separate you from Him, not even more actions that are foolish. But He does warn us that if we disobey, we often have to deal with the consequences that are the inevitable result. He will still love us when we're stupid, but the whole goal is to get wiser and wiser, in His wisdom, and avoid so much of the junk we tend to spill out all over the place. Kapeesh?"

"Ka-what?" he asked.

"Oh, never mind! Well, here we are," I said as we rolled into the Garretts' driveway. Aimee happened to be on the porch with a load of laundry she had just taken off the clothesline.

"Aimee," I shouted, "I thought you had a clothes dryer? You must be a glutton for punishment!"

She just laughed and shouted back, "No way, but on sunny days I like to hang out my bed sheets. Just something about the fresh air that makes them smell so clean. Don thinks I'm nuts, too!"

I looked over at Jason. I don't know what he thinks of working here at the farm or how all this will work out, but I have a sneaky suspicion it's going to work out just fine. And that suspicion was confirmed when his face lit up as he saw Major and Josh walking in from the barn. Don was with them. They were covered in hay and dirt and you could smell them coming. Jason would probably look and smell like that tomorrow, but he seemed ready for it. Time will tell. Time will tell.

We exited the car and headed toward the porch. Jason was carrying the small backpack he had been living out of before his arrest. It had been returned to him before I picked him up at the police station this morning. *Hm, I thought, I'm sure his clothes will need some of Aimee's laundering and fresh air system.*

"Welcome," bellowed Don. "I hear you're going to be working with me and the boys for a while."

"Ah, yes, quite a long while," Jason said nervously.

"Well, that don't bother me if it don't bother you," Don said quickly.

Don had pulled his sons together yesterday, and told them of my wild plan to have Jason work off his sentence by working the farm with them. They at first were hesitant, saying that he might "steal them blind" or "destroy some of their stuff." They remained at ease when Don shared the whole story of my interaction with Jason, his changes, etc. They prayed about it and as far as I understood it, these boys were in it for the long haul. Major and Josh will only be here for the rest of the summer. That leaves just Don and John on the farm when the boys head off in the fall, so the extra hands will be welcomed. All the boys were eager to give this kid a fresh start, and especially so when they realized the entire back-story on Jason's family situation.

These guys are such a blessing to this family. Heck, they're a blessing to me and the rest of this community, too. There is such a fire in my heart for all of the community. Oh God, I ask You to really stir up our young people to be full of Your Spirit and not all the garbage that inundates their world today. So many of our young people are like "dead men walking." Well, Lord, this is a beginning; at least we are witnessing one of the "dead men rising."

As we entered the house, the smell of homemade bread filled the air. Aimee is such an awesome cook. Jason is going to love it here; at least the meal times, anyways.

John's wife, Melody, was helping Aimee as we walked in.

"Well, just in time, everybody," she said with a broad grin. "You boys had better go get showered and changed. That dirt and stink isn't going to sit at this table"

I looked over at Jason. He was still smiling. This was going to be a good journey for him.

"And you, young man," Aimee said, looking at Jason, "you can set the table for me, if you would, please. The plates are over in that cupboard and the silverware is in the drawer under it."

I watched as Jason quickly did as he was told. It almost seemed as if he was eager to help, sort of like he was very comfortable here; almost a part of the family already. My, my. . .if it ain't a miracle I'm watching!

Jason and the boys chatted about "guy stuff." Don started talking about the workload for tomorrow and who would do what. I saw Jason wince a bit at the 4 am wake up, but there was a lot of hay to cut, bale, and store, as well as the myriad of other tasks required in the daily routine of the American farmer.

Aimee, Melody, and I started to clean up the table after that sumptuous meal. Aimee stopped a minute and said, "You men can feel free to go in the other room. The girls have the dishes covered this time. Don't expect us to spoil you too often, though. This is just a special occasion cuz of our newest member here with us."

She looked over at Jason and winked. He turned his head as if he didn't see her, but he had a big grin on his face as he went into the other room with the "men."

When they left the area, I began to speak.

"Aimee and Melody, I can't thank you and your husbands enough for this opportunity you're giving to young Jason. So much of this is all based on a hunch, so to speak. I just feel it in my bones that this is the right way for him right now. I just want you to know of my deepest appreciation."

"You pay it no mind now, Chaplain," Melody said. "There is enough work around here that young boy will be too tired to get into trouble. The boys and John will keep a close eye on him so he won't die of exhaustion while he's working."

Aimee laughed and chimed in, "That's for sure. We'll take it easy on him. But I gotta say, I have that same feeling too. It's like somehow he belongs here with us. I feel really good about helping out now, seeing as there was nothing we could do before when all that horrible tragedy was hitting his family. That poor kid. No wonder he got in trouble."

We could hear them howling in laughter in the other room.

Aimee said, "Don is probably telling them his favorite story."

"Which one is that?" I asked.

"It's about the time when he was a young boy, while he and his brothers were growing up here on the farm. They'd go to the nearby river and invent games to play once they tired of swimming. He said his older brother was famous for a game they called 'Bombs away.' His brother would wait until he had to have a bowel movement, then he would climb up on the rope swing, swing out over the river, let 'er rip, and drop the poop on certain river targets. They said he had deadly aim! For some strange reason, the boys loved Don telling that story. They would ask for it over and over again. I swear that's why Don Jr. ended up going into the military pilot program before he started flying civilian airlines!"

I exclaimed, "Oh, that's just gross."

Melody, with nose scrunched up, repeated the same comment, also adding, "I hated that story every time he told it. But John still laughs his head off when he hears it."

18

"Guy world, such a strange place," I quipped.

We all laughed heartily at that comment.

I asked the women if they would like to join me in a prayer before I left for my place. They warmly agreed. I prayed, "Life is good, Lord. You are so right when You said that all things work for good, to those that love God, and are called according to His purpose. I call upon Your many blessings to be showered on the Garrett family as they take this precious wounded bird under their care. May Your glory be seen in all that is done. In Jesus' name, I pray." We all said, "Amen."

19

*T*he next morning, I mused on all that had happened over the past few days. Things were moving pretty swiftly, but I had to trust the Lord in all He did. As I prepared the coffee for the morning meeting with Major, I looked out over the field.

"Well, well, what do my eyes see," I said out loud. "Here comes not only Major, but Jason and Joshua. That's good, Lord, that's good."

"Good morning, Chaplain," said Joshua. "I'm not here just for the goodies, just to let you know up front. Jason, Major, and I were up really late last night, just talking. Major was sharing with us some of the things you've been sharing with him, and I want in on it. So does Jason. I talked to my dad and John and we all worked out a schedule with them. We would work as late as needed to finish all the farm work, as long as we could all come over here first thing in the morning. The only problem is that my dad asked if we could meet earlier than 10 o'clock, so we could get out there before the heat gets too brutal. Would 8 o'clock in the morning be too early for you?"

I rolled my eyes and jokingly said, "Oh brother, what I don't do for you guys, sure. . .I'll have our coffee and goodies ready by then."

They all laughed and I was surprised when Jason said, "See, I told you she'd do it."

"And how did you know that, buddy?" I replied.

Major laughed and said, "Because you have to love us. . .a 'God rule' you know!"

It was a great discussion. Jason joined right in and was unashamed as he spoke of his challenges growing up. Major was just as bold in admitting his recent wrongdoing and the changes he was experiencing in dealing with his friends and the issues of mercy and compassion. Joshua opened up about the doubts and concerns in his heart about missing God in his life and how the changes in Major had really caused him to cry out that he wanted to have God as important in his own life as he saw that He was in his brother's life.

It got quiet as we finished up. Then, as unexpectedly as it was to have all the boys show up this morning, Major piped up. "Joshua, I'd like to pray with you to ask Jesus to come inside you. You know Him in your head, like I did. But you really gotta have Him in your heart if you want any real change. Bro, are you ready, or do you want to wait?"

Joshua stood up, straightened up his back, squared off his shoulders and said, "I want Him in my heart, not just my head. I need Him to help me figure out my life and what He wants me to do."

Right then and there and to my surprise, Major led Joshua in a prayer of repentance, with Joshua confessing that he was a sinner and needed Jesus to save him and be his Lord. Joshua breathed a sigh of relief as they finished, and with tears in his eyes, gave his brother a big bear hug. Jason just stood by on the sidelines. But once the two brothers had finished hugging each other and taunting each other about crying, Jason said, "I know how you feel, the same thing happened to me." He went on to relate his story about the dark thing that left his chest the day he gave his heart to the Lord. They continued with excitement, in their conversations about Jesus.

Have I lived to see the day? I thought. *This is just too awesome. The very thing I prayed for is happening before my eyes. Young people, the future of this great nation, are talking, without shame, about the power of Jesus Christ and what Jesus has done in their lives.*

"Gents, I hate to break it to you, but you better get back or your dad and brother are going to think that you're just milking it for extra time over here."

"Chaplain, they'll be fine," Major said. "We'll prove ourselves to them in the hard work we do each day to make this happen."

"Okay, guys. Then see you tomorrow," I said.

"Ah, Chaplain," said Joshua. "I've been talking to my friends about how you and Major have been meeting and how it's kinda neat what you talk about. Some of them asked if they could come by too."

"Whaaat! I mean, sure thing, as long as it's okay with their parents," I said almost dumbfounded.

Major noticed my puzzlement. "Hey," he said half-jokingly, "just cuz we're part of the youth of today doesn't mean were a bunch of criminals, you know."

He looked over at Jason and said, "Oh, sorry man."

Jason just laughed. "Word up, not offended, man, not offended."

Major continued, "We just never heard about living in God's wisdom. It was always just a bunch of rules that kinda sounded stupid. You make it so we understand it, and the other kids wanted to hear it, too."

"How many will be coming? Just need a head count for the coffee and goodies."

Joshua continued, "So far, four guys said they want to listen in. And one girl, but I said I didn't know if girls were allowed."

"Of course girls are allowed. . .I'm here," I joked.

They all laughed. "No, seriously, can girls come too?"

"Sure, fine with me, but this has certainly changed from its start," I exclaimed. "We better ask Major, because he's the one with the questions he wanted to send my way. If it's okay with him, it's okay with me."

They looked over at him and Major boldly said, "Chaplain, the main reason I wanted to come over was the pregnancy issue with my ex. It just took me a while to get around to that. That's sort of now resolved on my part. The stuff we talked about, our country and the changes and all, well, that really got to me. So I'm open if anyone else wants to come too and hear about what you're sayin'."

"True that," said Jason.

"You mean, 'that's true'?" I responded.

All three of the guys laughed heartily.

"No Chaplain, that's just what we say when we agree with something."

"Duh," I replied, while crossing my eyes.

They laughed again. Major said, "You're so funny, Chaplain, I mean for someone who is. . .I mean, for someone who's like older, I mean."

Joshua said, "Like Dad says, 'Better quit while you're ahead'.""

I took a turn at laughing. "No problem, guys. Getting older is going to happen to you, too. That's when you look in the mirror and the twenty-five-year-old that lives in your head looks and says, 'Who the heck is that old person?'"

They all hopped down the stairs and chased each other back across the field. It was ever so good to see Jason fitting in so well, so quickly.

Just then, I heard my phone ring. It was such a beautiful morning that I returned to the front porch to take the call. It was the lieutenant.

"Good morning, sir, how are you?"

"Just fine," he replied. "I'm calling to see how it's working with Jason. Any problems I need to know about?"

"As far as I can tell, Lieutenant, it's going just fine. The Garretts have hearts of gold and have surrounded that young fellow with love, guidance, support, and great food to boot!"

"I figured as much," he replied. "You sure called this one right, at least so far, Chaplain."

"I'll keep on praying for it to continue."

"Oh, and by the way," he said. "Thought you'd like to know that my deputy, Ed, you know the guard that was helping to monitor your interview with Jason here at the station; well, this morning he came into my office and asked some questions about God. He asked if he could borrow my Bible for his morning break. Said he ordered one, but it wouldn't come in for a few days. What do you think of that? There sure are a lot of strange things going on here in this town. I mean good things, don't get me wrong. That prayer stuff you talked about is sure working!"

"I think so, Lieutenant. God has waited a long time for a response, especially from His young ones. Looks like He's turning up the heat a bit, I guess. Let's see where it all goes."

"Yeah," he said a bit hesitantly. "Let's see where it all goes. Have a great day, and oh, yeah, God bless you."

"And God bless you too, sir."

I hung up and sat in amazement at all that had just transpired. My head was spinning.

20

❧

"*J*ason," Major yelled, "it'll work much better if you take the hay hook and kind of jab it into the top of the bale in the middle, like this." He demonstrated what he meant.

"Oh, I get it. Yeah, that's much better."

Joshua yelled over the roar of the old flatbed truck. "Hey, you two, we got nine hundred more bales to get loaded. Let's get going, will ya'?"

The field was wide and flat; the open sky and bright sun looked down on the workers, almost as if with a chuckle, knowing that the unabated sunshine and heat were going to add a challenge to the strong, young bare-chested minions below. With sweat pouring off all three of them, they continued their work.

Don was running the baler. It would swish on through the high grass, grabbing up bunches of it at a time, as the blades rotated up and down the rows. And then, as if almost like magic, it spit out the neatly wire-wrapped, seventy-pound bales at even increments. From a distance, it looked like a large science fiction movie monster, leaving its droppings throughout the field.

The three young men would follow the rows of bales. Joshua expertly pulled the flatbed truck up alongside each one; Jason would hook the bale and toss it up on the truck, then Major would stack it, alternating the placement of the bales for each new row. Then they drove off to unload it all in the barn. They repeated that process until they had filled the barn to the ceiling.

When it was all done, they looked at each other and grinned. There was a great satisfaction in a man's heart at having done a man's work, and these boys were no different. As they rode back to the house at the end of a very long day, Don started telling his stories again. The boys howled in laughter at some, winced in disgust at others, and all around enjoyed the company of a man who was skilled at his work and extremely happy in his life.

Jason, who had been holding his sides while laughing so hard he thought he'd puke, finally piped up and said, "Hey guys, this has been the best day of my life. Thanks."

Joshua jokingly said, "What a sad life, bro. Holy crap, your best day was when you almost killed yourself working?"

"YOLO," Jason responded. They all howled.

"True that," said Major, "True that."

"Is this when you say, 'Word up'?" interjected Don.

They howled again. Major said, "Dad, don't even try to keep up with our language!"

More laughter abounded. Joshua then said, "Be careful, Jason, when my dad gets real happy, he belts out a song or two."

Jason was reveling in the camaraderie. He was wistfully thinking, *If only my dad could be here.*

"Hey, Jason, did you hear what I said?"

"Yeah, sure did. I was just wishing my dad was as happy as your dad."

Everything got somewhat quiet in the crowded cab of the truck. Then, without warning, Don belted out, "Ninety-nine bottles of beer on the wall, ninety-nine bottles of beer. . ."

"Ahhhhhgggghhhhh," shouted Major and Joshua in unison. "Look what you did!"

Jason was beaming. He loved his new home and friends. He thought a moment and said to himself, "God, You are real. You are good. I want to know You more. Thank You for helping me and taking me out of my dark place. Please help my dad and do the same for him. Amen."

Off they went, chugging on home in the old, dilapidated truck; Don singing at the top of his lungs; the boys just rolling their eyes, hoping to get home sooner than later.

After supper, the three exhausted young men went up to their shared room. Two beds and a cot; they couldn't care less. They could've fallen asleep on a cold steel beam, they were so tired after such a long hot day in the field.

Jason was the first to speak while they each lay in their beds in the darkened room with only the moonlight coming in around the window shade, which was only half pulled down.

"I was thinking," he said. "Would you guys pray for my dad? He's still so sad about my mom and my sister. I just wish he could have just one good day like we had today."

"Sure," Major said. "I'll bring it up in my youth group at church, too."

Jason replied, "Speaking of youth group, do you think I could just go to church with you guys this Sunday? I don't got any fancy clothes or nothing, but I have some clean pants and a shirt I could wear."

"Don't worry about dressing up, bro," said Joshua. "We dress very casual at church and I like it that way."

"Oh, good," Jason continued. "That makes me so happy, I think I'll sing a song. Ninety-nine bottles of beer on the wall. . ."

He was pummeled with pillows and loved every minute of it!

Don stood at the bottom of the stairway. "Hey, you guys," he yelled. "Long day tomorrow, too. We get to clean out the barn while the cows are out, so you better get some shut eye! Oh, and nice tune there, Jason," he joked.

He went out to the kitchen to sit for a few minutes with Aimee.

She tenderly said, "Honey, I love how you work and play with the boys. We are blessed with five great kids, but you've really been such a great mentor to them and I thank you for it. They are as fine as they are because of you."

"Well," he jokingly whispered, "you kept 'em well fed and that made my job easy! And besides, we have that fine daughter, Rebecca, and you were the instrument used on that one."

"I love you, Don Garrett," she said.

He replied as he always did when she said that, "I love you more!"

"I guess we both 'done good,' partner" she replied." They kissed a long and tender kiss. Don followed her upstairs with a happy gleam in his eye. He started to sing the old song, "Tonight's the night."

She turned around on the stairway and with a beautiful, big smile said, "You just might be right." They both laughed. He chased her up the rest of the stairway, just like when they were first married. As they entered their bedroom, Don had a wry smile as he quietly closed the door behind them.

Later that night, the whole household was rudely awakened by loud yelling and banging on the front door.

"What the heck is that?" Don yelled out.

"Be careful," Aimee said.

Don grabbed the gun he kept by his bed and ran downstairs. The boys heard the noise too and rushed down the stairs after him.

Don looked out the window. The boys did the same. Jason's eyes got wide and he screamed, "Dad!

21

"Oh, what a beautiful morning," I sang as I looked out at the stunning panorama of reddish layered clouds, patch-worked over the azure blue sky. The mountains stood tall and majestic in the foreground. "Wow, it doesn't get any better than this," I sighed.

While the coffee was brewing, I whipped up a batch of pancakes and bacon for the "gang" who'd be showing up for our morning rendezvous. I loved to cook, and this was not a chore but an enjoyable gift for me, as well as the eager hearts who would soon be gulping it all down.

The sound of a number of people talking and laughing stirred me to peek out the front window.

"Oh, my Lord, what in the world is this?" Up the road from the Garretts, a whole troop of young folks was excitedly talking, play-fully pushing each other, laughing and. . .heading this way.

"Better make some more grub. Hmm, do they even drink coffee?" I said out loud. "Ah, just figure it out when they get here," I mumbled to myself.

I poured a cup of the hot brew and went out on the porch to greet my visitors. I could see Major out front. "Oh how I love that young man, but I have to keep it all inside a heavy heart," I sighed. The painful reminder of the burden of past sins flickered in my head and inner being. *Maybe someday I can tell him who I really am. God have mercy on me until that time,* I silently prayed.

As I looked at the approaching group, I also saw Joshua and Jason. There were six other young men and one young girl that I didn't recognize. . .and Don! Why was he heading over? "Hmm, must be pretty important if he's taking time out from the field. Surely hope everything is okay," I mused.

"Hey there, good morning, did word get out about my free breakfasts or something?" I shouted.

Don piped up, "Must look like that, Chaplain, but as good as they are, we are all here for different reasons."

Jason was so excited he could hardly contain himself. "You are never going to guess what happened last night!" he blurted out.

"Well, come on in and let's hear about it over some chow," I replied. We retreated inside, with each one helping themselves to heaping portions of steaming pancakes, crisp bacon, and what seemed a swimming pool's amount of coffee and juice.

Don started first and recounted the surprise visit from Jason's dad, Richie Westfield, with Jason excitedly chiming in to fill out the details.

"Yeah, we were all pretty surprised when Richie came banging on my door in the middle of the night," said Don. "He apologized for the lateness of the hour and asked if he could come in." At this point, all the young chowhounds were listening intently, and so was I!

Jason said, "I was afraid he was drunk again and was going to make a scene, then tell me to leave the Garretts' house! But that wasn't it at all!"

Don continued, "I was just as perplexed as Jason. Richie came in, sat down in our living room and started pouring out his heart. He told us he knew that the courts saw that Jason was not being helped by his own father and just considered Jason another troubled, bad seed. He told us he heard what had happened to his son this last time around and had felt so bad that Jason had caused all those problems. He then went on to say how shamed he was that another man was willing to step up to the plate, in his place, to do what he should have been doing all along. At that point, he started to sob. We were all shocked and just sat there listening to him for over an hour. Richie said he was finally jolted out of his own bad attitude by what had happened.

He related the horrific events of the past few years and how he had drowned his own sorrows in bitterness and booze."

Jason joined in and said, "And then, the best thing in the world. In the midst of all his sadness, he said he didn't want to live like that anymore and wanted to have the peace, wisdom and the understanding that Mr. Garrett has!"

Don took it from there and said, "I asked him if he was a praying man and if he had any spiritual preference. At which point he told me he was always a 'church floater' and didn't really have any bond with God. I asked him if he was ready for the change needed and told him that only Jesus inside of him could bring what he was asking for."

Jason jumped in again and excitedly said, "Yeah, my dad said he was tired of messing up our lives and wanted to be a good dad again. And right then and there, Mr. Garrett prayed with him to ask Jesus to forgive him, save him, and give him another chance. It was awesome. I cried too."

I had tears in my eyes as I listened to the account of last night's intrusion turned rescue mission.

Jason continued, "And that's not all. As my dad and Mr. Garrett went on talking, I could see something different in my dad. At first, I didn't know what it was, and then I realized that he wasn't so sad anymore. Couldn't put my finger on it, but I felt like my real dad that I used to have kind of came back into him."

"Well, he's probably going to be even better than that now, Jason," I said, wiping the tears that still lingered in my eyes.

"And on top of that," Jason went on, "Mr. Garrett found out that my dad is a certified mechanic." Breathlessly he continued, "But my dad doesn't have any steady work right now, um, well, because of the drinking thing, you know," he said with a bit of an embarrassed tone. "But Mr. Garrett said that his regular mechanic just moved to another state. The mechanic said it was to help a brother with getting through a tough fight with cancer and that he wouldn't be able to work for Mr. Garrett anymore and. . ."

"Whoa," I said, "slow down, Jason. You're running everything together. . .so you mean your dad can now work on the farm with Mr. Garrett while you are working there too?"

"Yeah," he screamed in jubilation. "He and I will be working together. Well, at least at the same place during the day. I'll get to see him again. And best of all, my dad said he wanted to see me again, too!"

The tears were welling up again in my eyes and I said, "Who could have ever thought this was even possible just a few weeks ago?"

Don entered the conversation again. "I can sure use a good mechanic with all the machines I have to tend, and especially with harvest time upon us. Richie will start work with us tomorrow. I've heard of his good work before all his world blew up, and I really want to be the one to support him. I think the Lord has arranged it for me to have this second chance to help out."

Jason excitedly spoke again, "And that's not all!"

I raised my eyebrows and said, "I don't think I can take any more surprises, what else could there be?"

"Mr. Garrett and me, and Joshua and Major are going to help fix up the trailer my dad is still living in. My dad started crying all over again when Mr. Garrett told him that!"

The eager group that had descended on my cabin continued chatting and sharing the meaning of the myriad of changes in people. . .both older and younger. It was an exciting moment in time for us all.

Don interjected, "Well, now that breakfast and the good news are finished, I think I'll head back to work. I want Richie to get off to a good start. Jason, you, Joshua and Major hustle on back over when you're done here. Thanks again, Chaplain, for the grub. God be with you as you share with this bunch of hoodlums."

They all laughed while he fist bumped each one as he headed off toward the door.

"Wow, that was some great news, guys, ah and gal!" I shouted with gusto in my voice. "Do you all still want to have a little gathering, seeing as the time has gone by so fast?"

One of the boys piped up and said, "I do have some questions. I been talkin' to Major and he said he really has been able to understand more about who he is as a man and what he is supposed to be doing in life. I kinda don't know and thought you might help me, too."

I replied, "Well, I don't know if I can help you, but I do know that God can. Let's start with intros on who you are and a little background on each of you and what you may want to get out of our meetings."

The young girl, Julie, replied, "Major told us to just talk to you and you like tell us what's in our hearts and all."

I smiled and said, "It's not like I'm some carnival attraction, or magician or something! It's just that when you look through God's wisdom in every portion of your lives, it makes no difference if you're younger or older. . .something good comes your way. It isn't a matter of 'feeling' holy; it's a matter of 'being' holy. That's what God wants."

"I never thought of it that way before. I think I'm going to like this," she replied.

We did a round of introductions. Some of the young men jumped right in and expressed some concern at the sexual urges they were feeling and the proliferation of pornography. They also had questions about homosexuality, and gay marriage.

I thought, *Whoa. . .they're going right into the difficult and contentious issues, right up front. They must have been thinking on this stuff long before they decided to come on over here.*

"Let's cover a few principles first," I said. "One is that we are born with a broken 'thinker,' 'wanter,' and 'feeler,' so to speak. So just trying to think through some of these challenges is not going to bring us the highest level of success. Nor are your feelings and emotions or desires going to sift through and figure out what you need to do, either."

I went over the information about Adam and the broken nature; the need to have the nature of God within to even try to achieve the things of God; and the football game with no rules example. Again, much to my surprise, there was agreement and understanding of what was being said. These young people were ready to hear some tough, unrestrained truth, not just religious gobbledygook!

I went on to say, "I am not surprised that you all have a lot of sexually oriented questions. Your generation is inundated with sex, sexual scenes, and sexual expressions. The humanist philosophies that have saturated all parts of your generation have lowered sex down to dog levels instead of the beautiful, holy experience God intended it to be."

One guy, with a confused look on his face said, "Sex...holy...what in the world do you mean?"

I replied, "Seeing as we are all adults here, so to speak, I can talk candidly. God is not some Providential Prude up there, making rules about sex and our bodies. God made it perfect in the beginning. There was no lust or perversions in the Garden of Eden; all of that junk started after Adam disobeyed God, and he and Eve were removed from that perfect place."

Someone quickly said, "I guess when God gets mad, He just throws you out!"

Jason just as quickly said, "No way. I am proof that you aren't just thrown out when you disobey God. God sees your heart and knows you want to change, but just may not know how to. He also sees your sorrows and the things that deceive you or drag you down. He is a loving God, I can surely attest to that!"

"Hey, let her finish," someone else piped up.

"No problem, guys, your comments and questions are good for each other," I said. "Anyways, God invented sex."

One of the boys whispered to another, "What? God invented it?"

"Yes, but His intent was totally different than the broken intent today," I went on to explain. "Men and women are significantly unique, and it's not just the plumbing that's different. We have different hormones, different temperaments, different leanings and nuances distinctive to maleness and femaleness. Even science can attest to that! That doesn't mean that one is above the other; it's just that men and women can often have different functions and roles in the scheme of life. It's sort of like right hand and left hand; together they work better. And it's not just the 'togetherness' that's important, it's the one-ness that God relishes.

"The man was supposed to be the head of the union, not the boss or the master, but the head, meaning that he was supposed to be the 'Christ' to his wife. To love her, nurture her, and be whatever help he could be to bring her to her fullest capacity emotionally, physically, and spiritually."

"Whoa," said Major, "that's a tall order for us guys!"

"I know," I said. "That's why it's so important to have God's Spirit inside you to lead you and guide you in all that you do."

Julie then asked, "Yeah, but what about the women?"

I replied, "The Bible often uses the word 'helper' or 'help' to describe a wife. But that really isn't as close to the original word used. . .the original meaning of being a helper is that the wife is the 'lifesaver' of the husband. Because she is so different in view-point, intuition, temperament, etc., she brings 'the rest of the story,' so to speak. She literally 'saves' him from himself and any of his one-sided actions. So any decision a wise husband makes should be based on an in-depth inclusion of input from his wife."

Our young female smugly looked around at her male counter-parts, half a smirk on her face. It was sweet to watch their interactions.

"What about single people then?" someone else asked.

"God doesn't call everyone to be single. But He calls some to be single so they can be unattached, so to speak, to be 'on call' for Him. If someone is single, then they don't have the other responsibilities of children or mate and can be used in a different way in God's plan. It doesn't mean they're better nor have it easier; it's just that God has a complete plan and knows how to cover all the bases."

I looked over and noticed that Jason and Major were feverishly writing down most of my comments. *Hmm, I see a couple of bright faces coming up to the plate for the Lord,* I mused.

"Ah, excuse me Chaplain. I have a question," said one of the young men. "What about sex and single people then?"

"Hey man, why are you going there?" quipped our lone female.

"That's okay," I quickly interjected. "Great question, really. You guys aren't holding back, and that's good. There are a lot of life's questions that you are going to have to find the answers to, and find it fast."

I continued, "Your generation is wading through what I call the 'sexual sewer' of our current culture. Without some positive intervention or clarification of the truths of life and its realities, you won't be able to step out of that sewer and be clean in any respect."

They were still glued to their seats. It wasn't the physical food they were hungering for, that was long gone; it was the spiritual food that had been so lacking in their lives. Much to my amazement, they were listening to and taking in what I had said. That amazement continued on my part because there was not one sigh, not one watch checker, nor an eye-roller in the group! I pondered how it was happening yet again. I had seen more and more youths who seriously wanted to hear that it was okay, even wiser, to make solid, moral choices; choices not based on some religious list of rules, but based on God's inherently better ways to live a better life.

Jason slowly said, "Uh — back to the sex and singles please."

I then asked them, "Well, what does God say about sex?"

One young fellow raised his hand and with a mischievous grin said, "My mom said if I had sex before I got married that my dick would turn black and fall off!"

A hearty laugh rose from the group. I couldn't help laughing, too; mainly at their innocence in some respects and yet sadness at how such coarse language had crept into their everyday life and even into their common responses.

"Well," I said, "I don't think that will actually happen. But seriously, you could get an STD and have something bad happen like get warts and oozing sores on it."

At that comment, quite a few of them said in unison, "Eww!"

By that point, all of them had wrinkled up their noses or were frowning in disgust.

I waited just a moment, then said, "Ah, I think you might then understand, as I said before, God is not some Providential Prude to come up with His guidelines on sexual behavior. He just knows that if you've never had sex with anyone and you marry someone who's never had sex with anyone, then the likelihood of you having an unwanted pregnancy or a sexually transmitted disease is nil, nada, zero, and zilch. So you see, God is not up there thinking that sex is nasty. He's just trying to warn us it is so unwise to have sex before you're married. You're inviting not only misery upon misery, but also those unwanted pregnancies and possibly life-threatening or at least life-altering diseases. And even if none of those things happened to you, you would still be 'practicing' fornication or adultery, which is the broken way to pursue relationships."

One of the kids piped up at this point and said, "You mean like friends with privileges?"

"Yes, we used to call it 'shacking up,' but call it whatever you want. . .it is outside the boundaries of what God has set. That is a bitter pill for many people to swallow nowadays. But I'm telling you, not all the condoms and birth control pills in the world will cover your immorality and the wrongness of your actions. Disobedience to what God has said is the problem. And He said that if you say you love Him and yet don't obey Him, you're a liar."

"Boy, that sounds like a boring life if you can't fool around a little first," said one young fellow.

"Pete, what are you talking about? Like you even have a girl-friend!" said Jason.

Major at that point stood up.

"Guys, the Chaplain is right. I know. I had sex with my girl-friend, now she's pregnant."

"Whaaaaat?" a few souls yelled out in utter surprise. The group seemed stunned.

"Yes," Major continued. "It turned out that it wasn't my kid, cuz she had sex with another guy about the same time. But it really screwed me up for quite a while. It's not just the sex part; it's what it does inside of you. I'm not talking about guilt or anything, even though that was there, too. It's that I didn't really love her and had no plan for her in my life. I just really liked her, that's all. After I found out she was pregnant, I felt confused and angry and I didn't want to think about having to stop school and have to raise a kid, either. How could I tell my parents? I could have been really screwed with all this. I know now that God knows what He's doing and I have promised myself that I will live the rest of my life finding out what He says to do and then doing it. God really saved my butt on this one, and I want to tell others that the stupid stuff you do can have some pretty stupid results."

The room got pretty quiet then. He continued.

"I want to help this girl and her boyfriend. I don't want to avoid them for sure, cuz I wouldn't want that to happen to me. They have decided to keep the baby, well, at least so far. I'm really glad they didn't decide on an abortion. I got to thinking about that. That poor little kid growing inside her. Why should it get a death sentence for what its parents did? Things get really messed up sometimes."

You could hear a pin drop at this point.

He continued, "And ya' know a lot of it we bring on ourselves cuz we're cowards. We just take the moment of pleasure and think nothing of it. We lie about everything or use excuses or steal some-one's stuff and think nothing of it. What are we doing, guys? Why are we groveling at the bottom of the heap like dead men? We should be rising up. . .yeah, dead men rising. . .standing at the front of this mess, leading with a better way. . .even if we're laughed at or lose a friend or two. I don't mean putting out our ideas, but God's ideas. Not preaching, but living it in every thought, word and deed. We can do this. We're the next set of leaders. If we're sick of the cheating in school, let's not cheat, and tell others the same. If we're sick of having our families all screwed up, then we need to be sure we don't screw up ourselves, and teach others the same. We can take back this town, our families, our school, our lives, heck, even our country!"

"Wow," yelled Jason. "I want that too. Count me in."

"Me too."

"Me too."

"Me too."

Right down the line, everyone said, "Count me in."

I hesitated to step in at this point with any comments, but said, "You all have made quite a commitment to a cause today. I hope you tie down a few more details on what you have just said to each other and carry it through. Don't let that fire die out. Go for it. For now though, we had best wrap up and meet again in a few days. If there are going to be this many coming, maybe we could change the format a bit, ya' know, not daily, but a couple of days a week? And we're going to need some more space, too."

"Chaplain," said Joshua, "that big old barn out back of your cabin is just sitting there, uh, do you think we could use that?"

21

I replied, "Well, sure you could. It just holds some junk I've been storing for a while. I'll clean it out; maybe even have a garage sale over at the church or something.

"Hey, I have an even better idea. Come on back this Saturday and we'll all work on it together. We can even paint inside and put in some benches or chairs too. Sort of a special meeting place, if you'd like. Decorate it and set it up however you want to."

"Hey," Major said, "sort of like our own clubhouse!"

"That's so juvenile," said Julie.

"Well, we'll just call it our 'office' then," he said, as he smiled at the idea.

"Whatever!" said another young man. "And I'm going to tell my brother too. I think he'd like to come by and start up with us."

Major said, "We need to come up with a plan and I've got a bazillion ideas going through my head right now. I'll get with Jason and Joshua later on and we'll talk to the rest of you at our next meeting."

"Aw," said one guy, "I wanted to hear about God inventing sex and all."

At that point, I said, "There's more you need to know about some of these important issues. Remember, even though some of you know the Lord and He is in your heart, your head is full of the ideas of the world. We had better have a fact check on that stuff!"

"Sure thing," said Major. "We're outta here for now."

The whole group left chatting and laughing; such eager, bright, and wonderful young people. Just what our country needs. Not brainwashed as some think. Rather, heart-washed!

Part II

Count Me In

22

That evening, as I sat in my living room, reading and writing out some thoughts in my journal, the phone rang. It was Major, and he was so excited.

"Chaplain," he said, "You would not believe how excited my friends are about fixing up the barn and having some meetings out there. They even have a name for the group too!"

"Well," I said, "I'm excited for you, too. You young ones are our future and we depend on you to do things better than we did. What's the name going to be?"

"Remember when I said something the other day that we were like dead men, but after Jesus comes into your life, it's like you're dead men rising? Well, Pete really liked that name and said we ought to call our group, 'Dead Men Rising.'. Definitely cool, right?

"Oh, definitely cool," I responded with a chuckle. "I like it, it's catchy."

"And even better," he said, "Julie's aunt works in a shop where they make those colored plastic wrist bands. We are going to have some made up for each of us with DMR on it. We thought it would be a good reminder of how we want to live now. . .and also, it might open up some questions from our other friends when they see us wearing them. It felt really good talking about all this new life and everything with each other; and it was really cool when we came up with the name and the wristband thing. I'm even more excited and motivated now! This isn't some kids club, we are young men and women on a solid mission to be holy, not just feel holy. We want to tell others that we can bring back the good standards that will fix broken families, as well as make our whole country strong and good again."

I listened with a smile on my face, and I'm sure there was one on my heart.

"That's really good news," I said. "It sounds like you guys are on a mission. Go for it. See you on Saturday, and then after that on the next few Wednesdays and Fridays. Looking forward to it. Hey, pretty soon, you won't need me to hang around; you'll get your own leaders coming up and can really take off in spreading God's good news!"

Major laughed and said, "Don't drop us too soon, Chaplain. We're just starting out and need some more of your 'listen up lectures' before we fly off into the wild blue yonder!"

At that point, we both laughed heartily.

"Okay," I said. See you day after next. God bless."

"God bless you too, Chaplain. Have a nice day tomorrow. . .hey, like a day off, cuz we won't be there!"

I could hear the smile in his voice.

Then he abruptly said, "Oh, I almost forgot to tell you. Tomorrow, Dad, Joshua, Jason, and I are going over to Mr. Westfield's trailer and start working on fixing it up for him. I feel really good about doing that. And Jason is jumping all over the place today just thinking about working with his dad. I'm happy for him, too. Funny thing, it just feels so good helping people, it just makes you want to do more of it."

"I know honey-pie, I know. And I'm really happy for you, too. You make me so proud of you."

"Thanks, Chaplain," he said.

Then he broke my heart and filled it at the same time when he said, "I'm so glad you're in my life. You're just like a mom to me and I love you very much."

"Well, I love you too, buddy. . .your whole family is very special to me."

I hung up the phone and cried my all too familiar bittersweet tears. Love, life, longing. . .they get so mixed up sometimes, but we must go on, always for the better, we must go on.

23

*S*aturday came pretty quickly, but I was prepared, as I had gathered together all the cleaning and renovation materials I had. As I spoke to Don about what we were doing, he offered to send over some boards and building tools for shelves or a makeshift desk. I was looking forward to the tidal wave of youth that would be showing up soon to fix up their "office."

As I stood outside, enjoying the cool of the morning, I could hear the "gang" coming up the road. They sounded like a happy mob heading toward me; yelping, laughing, pushing, shoving, joking; some were even singing some of the songs from the youth group at their church.

"Good morning," I shouted. "Welcome to the Saturday morning work party. How y'all doing?"

"We're good; ready to start working."

"Did you make breakfast, Chaplain?" someone piped up.

"Hey stupid, we're not here to eat, we're here to work!"

"As a matter of fact," I said, "I did throw together some muffins, juice, and coffee and. . ."

"Wait a minute, Chaplain. We didn't come here to eat, really. We all met earlier at the coffee shop and got a bite," said one of the boys.

"Speak for yourself, butt head. I'll take a muffin before we get started," said another.

I laughed and said, "I've set it all up on the porch. Just help yourselves whenever you want."

Someone yelled out, "You're the best, Chaplain."

"No," I said, "YOU'RE the best!"

They all laughed and got to work. I just stood by and let them figure out what they wanted to do. I got the feeling they would soon be meeting here without me anyways. It was a good feeling, though. I think something had started in their hearts; a real fire for the Lord and that needed time to grow, for it would surely spread quickly.

It was such a joy to be on a common task, the comradeship growing and the job being done. As we all worked together, some of the questions they had the other day came up again. I was glad they did because this was a relaxed circumstance in which to approach some of the questions that often were unanswered in this age group.

"Well, what about pornography, then? Single people can do that, can't they? Isn't that like you're just lookin' and not touchin'?" said young Pete.

I smiled, not at the question, but at the eagerness of these young people to hear what God had to say about the pressing issues that faced them all the time.

I kept working alongside them and said, "Because sex is pleasurable and our nature is broken, God had to put it within some boundaries. You see, when Adam and Eve were in the Garden of Eden, they had God's kind of love for each other. Once removed and sin had entered into them, what they originally had would now be reduced to 'lust'; primitive, emotion-based lust. And unbridled 'lust' carries with it such destructive tendencies. After Adam's fall, God developed a system whereby that 'lust,' within the boundaries of course, would then allow them to enjoy each other, grow in love and commitment to each other, and, as God directed, would also procreate more humans. It was a safe and holy way to allow more humans to enter the plan. That way, so many more than just Adam and Eve would have an opportunity to be born, even if with a broken nature, and thus eventually be able to be rescued and redeemed in Jesus. Sort of 'the more the merrier' aspect!

They laughed. We continued working.

"But, back to the pornography," I went on. "The perverted, erotically extreme format of pornography tends to demean sex; brings it down to that 'dog' level experience. It gives guys the wrong idea about women and gives women a degraded idea about themselves.

Remember, the 'sex is supposed to be holy' thing? You see, the sexual act was not just for our pleasure, recreation, or procreation. It does all of that, but it means a lot more to God. In His eyes, it was designed to be a word picture of His relationship with us."

"What? God, sex, us? How does that fit together?" asked Julie, as she picked up some broken pieces of wood from the back of the shed.

I replied, "When a man and woman have sex, the act itself is supposed to be like worship to God. I don't mean a perverted thing, like in the old pagan temples with prostitutes and all. Just think of it, a man, who has the seed of life, actually enters into a woman, who is the one in which the seed can grow and nurture. . .it is a mirror image of God and us. God takes the seed of life, spiritually enters us and plants that seed, which grows into a 'new you.' That very special meaning is lost with any other combination of sex partners. That's why God has required a 'one man-one woman' marital and sexual relationship. Anything else is a mockery of God. People don't mean it to be; but it is.

By this time, everyone was either leaning on a broom or shovel, or stopped loading the wheelbarrow and was intently listening.

"In addition to that aspect, pornography, in actuality, isolates you. It is a fantasy world and we were made for the real world. Porn is just you and sexual pleasure, and God did not invent sex just for the pleasure end of it. He wants sex to be combined with building and binding affection with someone. We all long for affection and that, duh, requires someone else besides you!"

"Never thought of it that way," said Jason.

"Neither have I," chimed in some others.

"And neither had I until God showed those things to me," I said.

"God talks to you?"

Major answered, "Yes, and He talks to me, too. Not like out loud like we're talking now, but deep in my heart. Chaplain told me it was simple; just quiet yourself down in the presence of Jesus, fix your eyes on Him and use the 'eyes of your heart' to hear Him, then let the spur-of-the-moment flow of His thoughts come to you, and then write them down. You ought to try it, it really works!"

"Sounds like work to me!" answered another.

Jason piped up, "It is work, sort of, and it takes a lot of effort on our part. It's not like you sit in church and get sugar sprinkled on you or something to make you good. You have to crucify your flesh and let God's nature rule. I just read in the Bible the other day that God says we can't serve two masters. You're either a slave to one or to the other. Well, I decided that I was not going to be a slave to my stupid thoughts and feelings anymore. And it is working. Some of the things I used to think and feel are just gone. And if they try to come back, I just act like I am a soldier in a war and I run it off, shooting at it with things that God has said that are the opposite of what I was thinking."

"Yeah," said someone else. "I want that too. This is exciting, tell me more!"

Major said, "It is exciting, cuz you never know what God is going to do next. But because I know He is good and just and kind, all at the same time, even if I get in trouble or someone else tries to cause trouble, it will all work out for good."

They were talking to each other with such eagerness and excitement. I just watched with joy. God was really training up His soldiers for the spiritual battles they would encounter. My heart was full.

Jason said, "It's sort of like we said before, we are dead men coming to life. We were dead in foolishness and darkness and far from God but now we are alive."

Major then said, "Yup, we are. . .Dead Men Rising."

"Hey, what about me?" said Julie.

Major said, "It includes girls, too, don't worry. What 'men' means is not 'male' but humans. . .like a general term for mankind."

In unison they chanted, "Dead Men Rising. . .Dead Men Rising. . .Dead Men Rising."

I then said, "I hate to interrupt your meeting folks. . ."

They laughed again.

"But," I continued, "I think we need to finish up building your meeting hall and then get on with the rest of the day. Let's meet Wednesday as planned and we'll talk some more along the same lines as today. Bring friends and questions too, if you'd like."

23

Major said, "Don't forget, seeing as our group is growing, we'll just skip the good Chaplain's breakfasts here, everyone just eat at home or someplace, and we can get going as soon as we arrive. But of course, any time the good Chaplain may want to throw in some of her homemade biscuits or muffins, I'm sure we could make a bit more room in our stomachs."

Still smiling at his comment, Major then said, "Don't forget to bring your Bibles along with those questions. Now, all in favor say yes."

These bright young faces were glowing; I was watching a miracle unfold before my very eyes.

They all shouted, "Yes." Then, without any direction, they all together shouted, "We're Dead Men Rising!"

24

Wednesday came quickly and an even larger group of young people attended the meeting. "Can this even be happening?" I still asked myself.

"Hey guys, I have something I think you'll like."

"More muffins?" chimed one of them.

"You idiot, quit thinking about food," said Jason.

"Back off, dork."

Major interrupted and said, "Nice going guys; great way to start practicing a better way of living!"

"Oh, yeah. I forgot, I'm sorry," said the muffin man.

I smiled at them and said, "I was trying to come up with something simple that you could remember and share with other young people; sort of a common standard to remember to base all your decisions on. And this is what I came up with."

I handed out postcard-sized pieces of paper, on which I had printed five principles; they were:

1. Integrity first
2. Sexual purity
3. Sobriety
4. Service to others
5. Excellence in everything you do

They took a few minutes to read it over. One by one, smiles started plastering their faces. They looked at each other with great excitement.

"Chaplain, this is awesome, just great," said Major.

Pete, Julie, Jason and all the rest were excited, too.

One fellow said, "This is really simple. I can do this. It's hard, but I can do it. My little brother could even understand this stuff."

Major stopped and had that deer in the headlights look on his face.

Jason said, "What's up, bro?"

Major replied, "I just got this great idea. For our wristbands, let's put 'DMR-5'. . .that would add a reminder of these five principles too!"

"Yeah, I like that," said another.

"Sweet," said Julie. I recognized that look on her face. She just might have an eye toward Major, her new hero.

Two more boys piped up with suggestions.

Ryan, a tall and lanky young fellow with red-blushed cheeks spoke up and said, "Yeah, and the wristband should be black."

"Yuk, black, that's dumb," someone said with a smirk.

"No, it isn't," said Ryan. "The black stands for the old dead life we rose up from."

"Yeah," said Joseph, a much shorter, pale-faced young man. "And the DMR-5 should be in white to stand for the new, clean life we're trying to live."

More smiles and laughter erupted in the group. They were all talking and agreeing with the ideas floating around. The noise and commotion was quickly quelled when Major stood up and told everyone take a seat. He called the meeting to order and indicated they should start their meetings with a prayer.

One young man piped up and said, "Just what I thought; this is just another church youth group. How boring."

Major was quick to answer. "This is not a youth group; this is the beginning of some big changes in our lives and in our town. I can't put my finger on it; I just feel this pressure or something in my chest."

"Holy crap," said another guy. "You having a heart attack or something?"

I stood in the back of the "office" and just smiled at all the comments.

"No, not like that," Major impatiently replied. "More like an anticipation, or feeling like something big is going to happen. It just keeps coming back to me. I have even been having some dreams like I'm in front of a really big group of kids our age and they really understand what I'm talking about."

Jason said, "Remember, this has nothing to do with religion; it has to do with relationship. . .with God through Jesus."

As the sense of surprise kept mounting in my heart, I watched in amazement at the sincerity of these young men and women. The message of freedom, integrity, and purity had been pushed away from the center of our culture for so long that it sounded like something brand new to them. I was just going to roll with this and enjoy their coming into maturity.

When Major stepped up to speak, he looked over the scene. The area had been swept clean of hay and debris. The long, rough-hewn bench seats they made last Saturday filled the center portion of the barn. They decided to use them instead of trying to round up some chairs. The walls were freshly splattered by these young amateur painters and it looked pretty good for a makeshift meeting place. An old table was placed up in front of the benches and held some papers, notes, and a Bible. Major stood nodding his head at all that had been accomplished.

He banged on the table edge with his open hand to get their attention and said, "Let's take a minute to ask God to help us understand what it is He wants us to know and do."

Jason raised his hand somewhat self-consciously and said, "Would it be okay if I said the prayer?"

"That's just what I'm looking for; someone to step up to the plate and be bold for Christ."

The group remained in respectful silence while Jason prayed.

"Dear God, I thank You for giving me another chance to do things right. I thank You for giving me back my dad, and even though really bad things have happened to my family, I am glad that

You have shown me a better way to live and how we both can go on. I ask You now to please bless our meeting today. Fill our minds with your wisdom, our hearts with your compassion and give our hands the strength to do Your will. Amen."

"Thank you. That was pretty good, Jason. And now, Chaplain has a few more things to tell us. Listen up."

"Thanks, Major, for all your hard work in pulling this together," I said. "I love all the fresh and new ideas coming up from you all. This is really exciting."

From the back of the group, a young man raised his hand, stood up and began to speak.

"Before you say anything, Chaplain, I wanted to tell you guys just how different I feel, too. I heard what happened to Jason and his dad. I knew Jason was turning into a jerk when he was hanging out with those losers he used to hang with."

The young man turned to Jason and said, "I'm sorry man, I mean. . ."

Jason stood up too and said, "Don't be sorry. You're right. I really was turning into a jerk. I was sad, lonely, and felt abandoned by everyone I knew. My family was gone and I was heading to a bad place. I never knew the truth about a clean life, a new life in Christ. All I ever knew was the religious junk. But I found out that God wasn't upset that I didn't love Him. He never held it against me; He just waited me out, set up the right circumstances and captured my attention for sure."

"Yeah," the young man continued. "That's the way I feel. I talked to Joshua the other day. We just prayed and this special 'thing' just happened to me. I just didn't feel like doing some of the dumb things I used to like to do before. Don't know what happened but those ideas and feelings just kinda left me. It was weird, but good. Am I making sense?"

Chaplain answered the young fellow, "Yeah, you're making plenty of sense. Keep sharing that with others and I bet it will make sense to them too. You all have those cards with the five principles of life decisions on them. I have a good way to remember them, too. When you look at the black DMR-5 band on your wrist, look at the fingers on your hand. Hold your hands up and go along with me on this."

The room was soon filled with hands shot up in the air.

"Your index finger, go ahead and stick it up there as if you were pointing upwards. That stands for integrity. . .totally upright, number one so to speak."

Pete took his index finger and stuck it up his nose. "You mean like this, Chaplain?"

"You are such a sorry piece of. . .ah, horse dung, if I ever saw one," said Ryan.

"That's okay," said Chaplain. "He's pretty funny. I like the humor!"

Major laughed and said, "Okay, settle down. Let's get back to business."

"Now this could get dangerous," Chaplain continued. "Stick up that middle finger. You all know what that means and that is to remind you of sexual purity. Uh, and try not to use that outside of explaining your five principles, okay?"

The room echoed with hilarity at that one.

"I am really glad that no one is looking in on this meeting. Here we have a room full of you young dudes all giving the finger at one time. That surely would look strange to the uninformed."

They all continued to chuckle when I made that observation.

"Now, hold down your other fingers with your thumb and try to hold up only your ring finger. It is usually a little weaker and doesn't come up as straight without help. That is to remind you of sobriety."

The group giggled and teased each other as they attempted to move their fingers as directed. They were poking and joking; it was good to see them relaxing and understanding all that was said.

Jason stood up this time. "Okay, guys. Let's get back to work here, listen up."

Major looked over at Jason and gave a nod of approval at his leadership.

I continued, "Your little finger can be made into a hook. And that's to remind you of the fourth principle, which is service to others, to prompt you to help people, and rescue them in their time of need.

24

"And lastly, put your thumb up, like the 'okay' sign. That is to remind you to have excellence in everything you do.

"Now go ahead and practice that a bit on your own. And while you're doing that, let me remind you of something else. It's not laws that God is interested in; it's your love for Him that is important. Because when you get to know Jesus and all Who He is and all He has done for you, then it won't be 'laws' that you are bound to; it will be such a love for Him that you actually will want to please Him, by doing His will. It sounds really weird sometimes to say it that way, but it's true. It might start out like that, hearing about all His rules, I mean. But sooner or later, all that falls to the side and nothing is just a rule to you anymore, but what you want to do for Him."

One young girl stood up and said, "It does sound really different from what I usually hear at youth group or at church service, but I like it. I'm going to try harder to make all my decisions with those principles. I think knowing them will make it easier for me to get started."

Major then wrapped up the meeting with a profound statement.

"I think God has given us a mission. This is real, this is serious, and you need to back out now if you don't want to continue with us."

Not a word came from the group.

"Good," said Major. "Then we're all in. And I have an idea. At first I thought it was dumb, but the more I thought on it, the better it seemed."

Joshua stood and looked over at Major. With his finger tapping over his right eyebrow he said, "Now, my brother can have some wacky ideas." They both smiled. "But this one I like. Go ahead, bro."

"You know how they took prayer out of school a long time ago?" asked Major. "Well, you're going to bring it back! I'll be off at boot camp but this is how you can do it. You just gather every school morning before school starts, right there at the flagpole, and say a short prayer. No one can stop you, because you have the right to freedom of speech. It's voluntary, and run by the students. So you're fine in doing it. Besides, other kids will probably want to join you once they know what you are doing."

I was grinning from ear to ear with all that was going on here.

They all smiled too. "That's brilliant, man, brilliant. Yes, *every* morning," said Pete. "I can't wait to get it started. There'll be a ton of kids who'll join us!"

"And," Major continued, "I have another bright idea for our meetings. At the end of each meeting, just before we all leave, I will ask, 'Who are we?' And we will all answer at the same time, in one loud voice, "Dead Men Rising.""

"Oh yeah, I like that too," said one.

"Me, too," said another.

Major saw the barn was filled with chatter and laughter, some were trying to remember the finger notations; others were talking with each other about all that had just happened and the school prayer idea.

"Okay, okay, let's finish up here." Major took a deep breath, and shouted to the crowd, "Who are we?"

In unison, they thundered back, "Dead Men Rising."

What a great ending cheer for their meetings. This was going better than I ever thought.

I chimed in then and said, "Good start to your DMR-5! You guys clean up; I've done all I think I can today. Just close the door and hook the latch when you leave the barn. Now that we have your stuff in here, we need to keep the stray animals out. God bless you all. See you next go round."

They chattered with delight, and then, one by one they started leaving the barn and heading on home. Some to finish their chores, others to enjoy the relaxed treasure of school vacation time, but overall, none would ever be the same again.

"Thanks, Chaplain," yelled some in the group, as I walked off back to my cabin.

Now, I better get going. I have a meeting with some of the local church pastors to present my latest idea on working with the youth in this area. It's called "The Crucible," and I'm excited at what can be achieved if it is implemented.

25

*P*astor Jeffries stood and shook my hand when I entered the conference room. It was a large area on the west side of the church, just off the parking lot. Windows lined one entire side, allowing a beautiful view of the distant fields and an abundant flow of sunshine to flood the whole place.

There was a large table around which sat twelve pastors from surrounding churches. I must say, the good pastor did an amazing job to get this many leaders from so many different churches to gather in one place. It must have been like chasing cats, but he did it.

"Good morning, ladies and gentlemen. I'd like to introduce Dr. Jeanne Fontana to you, more commonly known as 'Chaplain.' She's been one of our favorite visitors over the years. Although she lives in Atlanta, she seems to spend more time over here in our neighborhood. And we're glad she does.

"Dr. Fontana has come here today with an idea that I think you'll like and can build on in your home churches. She has a heart for our youth and this is another avenue to reach them and to teach them. So, we'll just go round the table and you can introduce yourself and tell Chaplain a little about you and your church, and we'll hear what she has to say after that."

Each one of the pastors shared as requested. They seemed warm and genuine; true warriors for Christ. We finished chatting, shared some stories, dove into the coffee and pastries provided, and then I started my presentation.

"It's great to be here today and meet so many of God's finest workers in His vineyard. I have a few slides to share with you as I go through the presentation, but don't worry, it won't be 'death by PowerPoint'!

The participants laughed at that comment.

"What I propose today is a program that you can offer in your communities that will both challenge and change the youth who join in. I call it "The Crucible." The name came to me when I was teaching a series on suffering. The example in the Scriptures of the refiner and the gold reminded me that our lives in Christ are just like that.

"God is the refiner and has us in His 'crucible'. He turns up the heat, not to destroy us but to purify us. As you know, gold is a heavy metal and sinks to the bottom of the crucible, while the dross rises to the top. When it does, it is skimmed off. But the process is not complete yet. The refiner turns the heat up over and over again, until all the dross is gone and what is left is pure gold.

"The program I propose is just like that, it turns up the heat, so to speak, on the young people who participate."

"Is this a youth group at church, or a Bible study?" asked one gentleman.

"No, it is not a Bible study as such. It is a program, lasting a number of weeks, which you can offer at your church, or any place, really. It is designed as an afterschool program for high school students in your area."

"Hmm, you have me curious now," said another.

"It's designed for about thirty kids for each class. The target audience is at-risk kids, but any high school-aged student can join. It is a twelve-week program spread out over the fall semester and then repeats for a new group in the spring semester. There is ample room to accommodate school requirements and holidays."

One man asked, "Is this for both boys and girls?"

I replied, "Yes, but with a few rules. The boys and girls are separate in class time but are together for the 'challenges' portion of the program. The challenges will include four areas: hiking, obstacle courses with over water zip lines, team-building dynamics, and public speaking presentations. It is intended that, in addition to the classes, one challenge is to be completed each month."

"And just what is the daily time frame you suggest?" asked another.

"Three days a week, after school from 3-6 pm. I highly recommend working on getting transportation opportunities set up for those whose parents cannot drop off or pick up. Some will be walkers, but probably not that many.

"This is set up to be very flexible. Make it your program. If you stick by the basic format, it should work very well for all involved. I've done this in four small communities outside of Atlanta and it works great. There are superior results if the program is followed and you have committed adults involved. But hey, isn't that always a winning proposition?"

Another participant then asked, "What does the basic format look like?"

"While I am getting my computer set up to the projector, you can take a look at the handouts that Pastor Jeffries gave you when you arrived. Follow it along with the slides explaining the format."

Each of them studied the papers in front of them. Some were smiling, some looked a little puzzled and, thankfully, there was only one eye-roller in the group.

I reflected, as they looked over the materials, that change can be difficult, especially change or new ideas that involve a lot of work up front. But work is a huge part of the Christian existence, that and sacrifice, patience, love, overcoming. . .all the uncomfortable parts of our lives are an integral and recurring part of serving the Lord and serving each other. But the results, if led by the Lord, are really golden.

My thoughts were interrupted when Pastor Jeffries indicated that they were all ready to begin.

"I'm all set up too. Let's get started. As you can see, there are six types of classes."

The group intently looked at the slides on the screen.

This is the basic outline. It is purposely vague so it can be molded to fit the needs of the unique groups that will be involved in the varied communities that adopt this program."

"The Crucible" Program—Basic Class Format:

Character Development: Integrity, sexual purity, sobriety, serving others, excellence in all you do.

Finding your gifts: Academic, carpentry, electrical, welding, masonry, medical, dental, veterinarian, plumbing, engineering, chemical, law, other areas of interest

Health and Nutrition: Healthy eating and exercise, meal planning

Security: Martial arts, personal discipline, strong physical education program

Family life: Dating, marriage, parenting

Financial: Use of check books/online banking, investments/savings, and computer games to practice financial skills

"The Crucible" Program—The Challenges:

- Hiking (a weekend long challenge)
- Obstacle course (including ropes courses, zip lines and over water traversing)
- Team building dynamics
- Public speaking

"It is a full scope of life skills to be reviewed and renewed. And, at the very least, the sections on Character Development, Family Life, and Financial are presented through the lens of a Christian perspective. It is a tough program both physically and mentally and few get through it; that's why it's called 'The Crucible.'"

Someone then said, "It sounds like a military outfit."

I smiled. "Yes, it has uniformity, discipline, high standards, and you must complete it all to finish the program. So in that way it is similar to the military. There are also standard uniforms the participants must wear. They look similar to the Coast Guard or Navy work uniforms. It consists of a navy blue shirt and pants. Over the left breast pocket is an embroidered nametape in white lettering that reads, 'Crucible,' and over the right breast pocket is a similar tape but with the individual's last name. Black running shoes and a navy blue ball cap with 'Crucible' in those same white letters on the cap front, complete their attire."

Someone asked, "That's a little expensive for the uniforms, don't you think? Especially if this will be offered to some at risk kids in the poorer sections of town."

"It is expensive and that's why it is imperative to get local businesses and groups on board to help finance the scholarships that will be needed for some."

"Do they wear those uniforms to their schools before they come to the Crucible program?" asked another.

"It is optional. But I have found that the kids really like the uniforms. Sort of gives them that unique identity among their peers so they tend to wear them to school on their Crucible class days. That is, unless the school's policy does not allow it."

"Sounds like a walking advertisement for the program if they do wear them all day," said another pastor.

"It has worked that way many times. This program is catching on in other areas. Its popularity is a sign of the times, because what this program does used to be an integral part of every school's curriculum, sans the uniforms, at one point or another as a kid progressed through high school. It is a sad commentary that these teachings are not still in schools today."

"You can say that again," quipped one woman. "And I have another question, if I may. Who in the world can teach all of that information and handle all of those activities?"

"That's where your leadership skills and creative thinking come in," I said. "There are many generous people inside and outside of your church and community that you could call on to come in for their portion of the training. CPAs and financial management people can help with the finance section; nurses and doctors can help with the health section; parents as well as pastors can help with the character development and family life portions; law enforcement or military members can help with the security section, and guidance counselors or shop teachers, skilled community employers can help with the finding your gifts section. It's really wide open for many churches to share resources, plan together for the future of our community, state and nation by touching that future through a solid life skills program for our youth."

"So what's the difference between this and any other youth-oriented organization?" asked another.

I paused a moment, then said, "Well, the biggest difference is that the students have to continually earn their spot, with rule compliance and Challenge completion, to stay in the program. If they don't, they are dropped. That's not a popular idea in schools these days, where everyone passes whether they make the cut or not."

"It seems a lot of kids would just say to heck with it, it's too hard and just not make the cut on purpose so they could be dropped," quipped another female pastor.

"That's what I thought at first, too. But what we found is that even though there are a few who may do that, the majority of the kids really like the challenge to push themselves further than they would have on their own. They seem to relish the competition and camaraderie they find in the program, especially in the Challenges. The high moral standards, the discipline, even the uniforms are so unique in this anything goes, mediocre morality world we live in, that it seems to draw many more than it repels. It's quite amazing to see and that's why I wanted to share this with you today.

"If anyone has any more questions or specific details on this program, just call my office in Atlanta. We don't have a massive staff there, but we do have some dedicated workers committed to the mission I am on to reach our youth in unique and unusual ways other than the typical church youth group. No offense pastors, but I think you catch my drift here."

There was a quiet hum of activity as the pastors talked to each other. Some were really excited about the prospects of starting something of this magnitude; others were passive in their response.

"Well," I said, "I am not here selling this program. It's yours for the taking should you choose. I have found it to be very effective in drastically changing lives at its best, and steering the young ones in a more favorable life direction at its least. Anyone who has set up a strong program has had extremely successful results. The word gets around; parents see the changes and want to get involved. Once it starts, it's almost self-promoting and self-perpetuating. Surprisingly, many dads have wanted to be involved."

Pastor Jeffries stood up and asked if there were any more questions. None being asked, he thanked me for coming and added that he would be starting the program in his community. He continued telling them he intended to offer "The Crucible" to the two foster homes near his church, and any homeschoolers, as well as the high school near him during the next school year. He also would be contacting any interested pastors to come to a planning meeting where they could brainstorm and share resource contact information to get the program off the ground.

He's a good man, I thought.

We ended the meeting with a prayer. Many of the pastors took my contact information, too. Let's just hope it wasn't a courtesy move but a good faith start to a real revival for helping develop a vibrant and morally sound "next generation."

26

While driving home, I couldn't help but feel the excitement that rose up within me at the prospect of the "The Crucible" program gathering steam and spreading all over the county, heck, the country even. I kept thinking how all across our wonderful nation, many of our young people have been short-changed on the moral legacy of our forefathers, and it is time to stand up and make a massive transformation. As forcefully as opposing agents have worked to stymie that legacy, we need good people to rise up and make a stand for moral excellence, not a lower set of moral mediocrities.

Confirming the value of the family with mother and father present and aggressively engaged in guiding their children in decent, morally excellent principles was a start. We needed more conversations in that area in our homes, schools, and community forums. We needed more parents involved in the running of their schools. We needed conservative-minded people to be active in the political arena; and we certainly needed more teachers and leaders inundated with godly principles directing their every move, thus influencing the next generation of Americans. Without these things firmly and unwaveringly in place, I fear our nation is doomed to the failures and weaknesses we so abhor.

The ringing phone interrupted my line of thought; the screen indicated Aimee Garrett was calling. *Hope all is okay*, I thought as I answered it.

"Hey Aimee, what's up?"

"Thankfully, no problems!" she said. "Just thought I'd ask if you'd like to come over for dinner tonight, relax a bit with us and talk about some of the great things that have been happening lately. I just don't remember seeing the boys so excited about something."

"Perfect timing, my friend," I replied. "I've just finished up a lengthy meeting with some pastors, and that on the heels of all the fun this morning at the DMR-5 meeting. I'm famished and ready for a break."

"And that DMR-5 thing sounds fantastic!" she exclaimed.

"Yeah, the young ones really floored me with that one," I said.

"Well, can you make it tonight?"

"Oh sure, wouldn't miss one of your meals for anything!" I laughed.

"See you at 6 o'clock?" she said.

"6 o'clock is perfect. I have time to shower and change into my sweats. Informal, right?"

Aimee laughed. "You have to be kidding. My family is 'casual' personified."

I laughed with her. "Great, I'll see you then," I said.

As I arrived home, the mountain air somehow seemed cleaner and fresher. Or was it just me, being jubilant over the past few weeks? I continued to muse on the many hearts that have come to a greater understanding that a person can have a vibrant and lively relationship with Jesus, instead of the stodgy, old religious one people are so used to hearing about. I leaped up the stairs and into the cabin singing, "Oh happy day, oh happy day. . ."

The crisp early evening air invited me to walk over to the Garretts'. I saw the cattle in the field, the machines and trucks tucked in and near the barn, and the dog lying down on the porch. I thought, *This must be what Norman Rockwell saw, no wonder he captured so much of it on canvass. What our country was back then, it can again be today. Well, at least with some updated electronics!* I laughed.

My knock on the door was greeted with a group reply, "Come in."

As I entered, the wafting smell of baked beans, potatoes and gravy, hot biscuits, pot roast and some sort of cake filled the air. It brought back such pleasant memories of my own childhood that my face was beaming as I entered.

Don introduced Jason's dad, Richie, as I walked toward the dining room table.

Don said, "Well, you're one happy lady!"

I answered, "You guys are just so much like family to me. You not only fill my stomach every chance you get. . .you also fill my heart and soul!"

"Oh, jeez, that's pretty serious," Major quipped.

Then he flashed that handsome smile of his, jokingly pretended to toss his hair back from his forehead with his calloused, farm worker's hand and said, "Here, sit by me tonight. I saved a place for you."

My heart always melted at these opportunities. Funny it seems sometimes, how even the sad and bad things in life somehow get resolved. Maybe not how we'd like them, but God is so very, very good at filling the desires of our hearts. . .just framed up a little differently than we would have liked.

"Thanks, any charge for that?" I joked.

"Nope, you get the pleasure of my company, Ma'am," he responded.

We all laughed and proceeded to enjoy another of Aimee's delightful and delectable meals together.

As we finished eating and Aimee and Joshua served us some cake with whipped cream, I said, "Someone, and I just don't know who, once said that 'children are the living messages we send to a time we will not see.' I really liked the way it was stated."

Don furrowed his brow as he looked at me and said, "Whoa, that's deep. What made you think of that?"

I answered, "You and your family."

Aimee blushed, Don smiled broadly, and I could see Richie pondering that statement.

I continued, "I really admire how you have loved your kids and yet have not spoiled them."

Joshua piped up, "Yeah, we sure have not been spoiled, I can vouch for that!"

The boys all laughed, including Jason's dad. It was good to see him relax after all I've heard he'd been through. He looked healthier and more vibrant than what my imagination had supposed. This whole mess had turned around for sure. And I mused again on how God has such a unique way of working things out for those who follow Him.

As we were laughing and enjoying the meal and the company, I summoned up my courage and asked Jason, "So, how has it been going with you and your dad?"

Both Jason and Richie looked at each other and smiled. No other comments were needed!

Richie answered instead of Jason. "Well, I can't speak for my son, but I can tell you that I have gotten to know him again and I am so proud of what I see."

Out of the corner of my eye, I saw Jason sit up a bit taller, just beaming.

He continued, "I know he's changed for the better and that makes me happy. The only thing is that I really regret how I let everything get so erratic and out of control. I hurt Jason so much; I've had a hard time forgiving myself."

Jason put a hand on top of his dad's big calloused hand as they sat next to each other and said, "Dad, I really screwed up, too. But I learned that hurting people hurt people. But God is fixing both of us right now. He's given both of us a second chance, so you gotta give yourself that second chance too. I forgive you for everything, and I hope you can forgive me too, especially 'cuz I hated you so much."

Richie said, "I think I hated me too, but I never hated you, son. I just was lost for quite a while, you know, sort of like in a fog and I couldn't see where I was going. But that's all changed now."

Richie looked over to Don and Aimee, and with tears in his eyes and a halting voice said, "And I want to thank you so much for helping with that change. I've seen what you've done with your family and how your dependence on God was not weakness all these years, but was a lifeline to some pretty powerful strength. I want that too. And I want you to know just how much I appreciate all you've done for me and my boy."

Don looked serious now, and looking down at the table said, "Glad I finally stepped up to the plate myself. I should've done it when your whole world started falling apart, but didn't."

He looked up at Richie and said, "But I'm glad God has given me a second chance too, and I'm not going to let it fly by again. You're a good man, and I'm glad to call you a friend."

The two men got up and hugged each other in that manly, bang your back until it hurts kind of hug. Then they went off into the living room, with the boys following behind them.

"Don't worry about the dishes, I'll call the maid," Aimee yelled after them facetiously.

Don came back in the kitchen.

He said apologetically, "Oh, honey. I'm so sorry. You worked so hard at getting dinner and all." He held up his thumb and index finger with about a half-inch space obvious between the two digits and said, "I should have offered at least a little help."

Aimee lovingly pushed her shoulder against his, as if trying to move him out from her kitchen. She had expressed to me earlier that she was always so grateful that her husband remained aware of her hard work. He honored her many times, not only with words, but often by helping with the laundry or dishes after dinner; and that was after his own long day of toiling in the fields. He was such a great example to the boys and she knew that example was part of the legacy he diligently wanted to pass on to them.

"Scoot," she said jokingly. "You'll only mess up my system."

I piped up, "Hey, I have a degree in cleaning up too and I'll help Aimee. You go on now and get in the other room with the rest of the guys."

Don laughed and said, "Two to one, I lose!"

From the other room we heard Major say, "Yeah, right Dad, you know you won!"

It was uplifting being in a house of love and merriment. Like all families, the Garretts have had their bad hair days, but overall, they are and have what many people dream of, but sorely lack. As I thought on that, I was reminded again of the old saying that, "If you want what someone has, then you have to do what they've done to get it!" So true, so very true.

26

And, as is so very true of people who are experiencing moments of sheer enjoyment, Aimee and I were able to sing and laugh during the common chore of cleaning up after such a large group.

We enjoyed our "girl talk," while the men were in the other room enjoying their "guy talk."

Life is good.

Aimee interrupted our little chitchat with a question. "So, what have you been up to lately? I know you've been busy, because you're just that kind of person; boots on the ground, as they say."

I answered, "Yes, 'boots on the ground.' Well, I have been doing a lot of praying for God to pour forth His power on peoples' hearts, and that He would convince and convict them like no church service or sermon could ever do. And boy, has He!"

Aimee smiled and nodded in agreement. "You can say that again, Chaplain. Say, didn't you have a meeting today with a bunch of the local pastors? And how did that go?

I replied, "It went very well," and I proceeded to share about the "Crucible" program.

"Wow," she exclaimed. "I love that idea. And Pastor Jeffries wants to start it up at church? Count me in, for sure."

I laughed a little and said, "And you say I'm busy."

We both grinned and continued our work in the kitchen.

27

As it turned out, I couldn't make the next DMR-5 meeting because of a last-minute schedule change of a speaking engagement at the local Christian Businessman's Association; that just held the lead for priorities and I had to go. After coordinating the change with the Association, I called and explained the situation to Major. He agreed to go ahead with the meeting anyways. I was glad to see that he was taking the reins on that and I told him so.

"Chaplain," Major said, "I've been feeling lately that God is calling me to do an even bigger job for Him. I get to practice some of that right now, and I don't mind running the meeting. I want to do it, really.

"I'd like to hear all about what that call might be. I'll let you know when I get home and maybe you can clue me in then," I said.

"Sure thing, Ma'am," he briskly said.

"You're a nutcase, kid, but I still love you."

He just laughed. "See you later then."

"I'll be praying for your meeting today," I replied.

"And I'll be praying for yours too," he said.

As I was driving to the speaking commitment, I was wondering how the DMR-5 meeting was going. It should go just fine. God is in charge and will deal with those young pups better than I ever could. A smile came across my face as I started thinking on what those jokers would do while I was not there. As I kept on thinking, the smile turned to a plea for God's safety and wisdom to reign. I felt

God's return smile on both me and the DMR-5. "Thank You, Lord," I whispered and continued on my journey.

Back at the barn, the meeting of DMR-5 was bristling with excited young people. Major explained that Chaplain would not be able to make the meeting and that he would take her place this time.

The joking started immediately.

"You gonna get a sex change?" said one.

The howling crowd kept it up.

Laughter bellowed through the barn as another young man stood and imitated the Chaplain in a feigned female voice, "Now, now, just let me explain what Major said. . .Kapeesh?"

Major took the joking in stride. He held up both hands to signal for everyone to quiet down. Surprisingly, they did.

"Very funny, but I think you know what I mean. Let's get on with our meeting."

Just then, the new guy, Thomas said, "I'd like to say the prayer today. Could I?"

"Sweet, go right ahead," said Major.

Thomas began in earnest. "Father God, I'm glad this group let me come and join them. I feel good being around them and want to learn more about living a better life. We ask You to guide us today and show us what to do at our meetings." He then struggled a bit with what else to say, finally blurting out, "And help us to discipline our lives better. Amen."

"Hey," said Ryan, "he didn't say, 'In Jesus' name.' Isn't that the rule?"

"Remember, said Major, "we don't want to go all legal on each other. We're talking to God, and we know that the only mediator between God and us is Jesus. For now, let's leave it at that. Amen is good."

"Okay, bro. That's good with me then," Ryan answered.

Major asked if anyone had any information about the direction they might want to take their newly formed "DMR-5" group.

Julie spoke first. "Well, this isn't about direction but my aunt has ordered the plastic bracelets." With obvious jubilation, she then declared that her dad was so excited about all of this that he said he'd pay for them.

The room lit up with a spontaneous cheer.

Major knocked on the table for the noisy group's attention.

He then said, "I have something to share with you all. As many of you know, at the end of the summer I was going to go into the Marine Corps."

One young fellow shouted out, "What do you mean, 'was'? You turning chicken or something?"

A slight murmur went through the meeting room.

"No, nothing like that," Major continued. "After a lot of prayer and talking to my parents, I've made a slight change. I'm still going to go into the Marines, except not as I thought. I talked to my recruiter and told him I wanted to go in as a Chaplain."

"A Chaplain!" Julie yelped. "But that will take so long, won't it? Does that mean you'll be gone for years?" she said with an obvious distress in her voice and thinking, *I need to tell Major how much my heart yearns for him and I better do it soon if he's going away. I have such deep feelings for him and really admire who he has become. I couldn't bear it if he went away that long.*

"Not really. The seminary is only twenty-five miles away, well, the one I want to go to anyways. It means I'll be staying here for four years to finish it before I head off anywhere."

One of the boys said to Julie, "You're sweet on Major, aren't you?" He continued in a singsong manner with, "Major and Julie up in a tree, k-i-s-s-i-n-g!"

Julie's countenance changed and with a scowl, she turned to the young man and snarled, "How juvenile!"

Major smiled at her reaction. He had had an eye for Julie for quite some time now, and was glad to see that she seemed a little miffed at the thought that he might have to be gone for a long time. And he was further delighted to see her relieved expression when he said that he'd be staying fairly local for a longer time frame.

Major said, "Funny, funny, bro." He wasn't angry with the teasing but was more amused, if anything. "As I was saying, the recruiter's helping me now to apply to seminary. The military will pay for that and then I'll owe them a bunch of time to serve with the Marines once I graduate. The good thing, though, is that I'll go in as an officer. It's sort of like God knows my heart and what I really want and is shaping it up in a way unique to me and heck, even better than what I planned in the first place."

Thomas, a tall, skinny teen, still bearing a face full of acne, said, "There are an awful lot of situations that are working out pretty well around here lately. Even my dad started going back to church. What's going on? Is it the end of the world or something?"

Joshua said, "No, stupid, it's not the end of the world."

Thomas' face showed that he was hurt by Joshua's comment. He was pretty sensitive because he got a lot of teasing about the acne that still plagued him.

Joshua softened up a bit and said, "Hey dude, I'm sorry. You're not stupid; I am, for saying that. We okay?"

Thomas looked up, quite surprised. No one had ever apologized for teasing him. A slow, broad grin spread across his face as he said, "Sure, we're good."

Major then had them divide up into groups of four. He distributed paper and pens and told them to brainstorm ideas for further meetings, how to get the word out to other young people, and in what community projects they wanted to participate or develop. With some serious gusto, they broke off into their assigned groups and delved into their work.

28

As I was being introduced to the Businessman's Association, my mind wandered off into vain imagination land for just a moment. My worrywart personality started seeing visions of someone back at the DMR-5 meeting breaking a leg or something even worse. Could it be they were horsing around at the meeting without me being there? I struggled with the onslaught of bloody horror scenes, but had to give it all over to the Lord. He was in charge and had more power over those kids' meetings than anyone present or absent. After that momentary mental discourse, I settled down to the task at hand. Before I started to speak, though, I made another mental note to stop calling them "kids"; they were young men and women on the cusp of adulthood and needed to have that affirmed more frequently.

I was abruptly brought back to full attention as I heard the audience's applause after the moderator's introduction. "And now, Dr. Fontana," he said, slightly turning his head as he moved his right hand and arm, pointing in my direction.

"Thank you, Ed," I began. "I am so glad to be able to speak to our community leaders today. How you think and what you do sets the tone for the positive growth of our community and its families. As Christians, we know the difficulty in this ultra-busy world to stay tuned to and in touch with Lord. So now, I'd like to address a subject that we all struggle with at one time or another. The title of my speech today cuts to the chase: 'Balancing Worship and Works.' And, as I proceed, please feel free to ask questions as we go along.

This isn't a lecture; it's a meeting of the minds. . .and by the looks of this audience, the best minds around!" I joked.

I could see a few people settle down more comfortably in their chairs. A gentleman loosened his tie; one woman flipped off her shoes. As they relaxed, so did I; and this being a Christian group, I felt free to share whatever the Lord would have to pour forth from my heart.

"Ever suffer from the Martha and Mary syndrome?" I asked.

An unspoken affirmative answer to that question was given when soft laughter floated through the room.

"You want to be in intimate fellowship with Jesus Christ; flowing in His Spirit; full of power and wisdom, oh hear the angels sing!" I quipped.

Smiles and more laughter erupted with that remark.

"But you end up working late many days each week; all of that in addition to cleaning the church, teaching the Sunday School, visiting the sick, delivering Meals on Wheels, volunteering at the Senior Citizens Center, and painting the homes for the local 'Restore the Neighborhood' project. You lie down each night exhausted, saying, 'Oh, no, I didn't get in devotions again. I didn't get in any scripture time. I didn't even say good morning to You, Lord.'"

Many nodded in agreement; some with dramatic, exaggerated looks on their faces.

"We all struggle to keep balance in our lives—duties vs devotions, worship vs works, what shall we do? For starters, follow Jesus. He was the most balanced person ever to come into the world. He served His Father AND served His fellow man. He taught, He rested, and He prayed, He traveled, He worked. He did all that we do, but He did it with a peace and deep satisfaction, knowing that His obedience was pleasing to God. When once asked what someone had to do to inherit eternal life, Jesus' answer was to have a balanced life when He said, 'Love the Lord your God with all your heart and with all your soul and with all your strength, and with all your mind; and your neighbor as yourself,' as we read in Luke 10:27.

"See—worship and works, devotion and duties. It is not one or the other. . .it is both. It is a flow, one to and from the other. If you really, really love God, you will really, really love your neighbor, meaning 'the one near you.' That way, you will worship freely and do His works freely. You will have devotions with Him and gladly serve Him by serving others. As Tim Hansel writes in his book, *"Holy Sweat,"* God provides the "holy" and we provide the "sweat"!

"God intended for us to worship Him; we were made to do that and have fellowship with Him. But His love example is so great, He also intended for us to share that love with our fellow man. Yes sir, that is our joyful life, serving God AND man, devotion AND duty.

"I think it was Tony Blair, former Prime Minister of England, who said that in leadership, it was easy to say 'no' to something; the harder thing was to say 'yes' and then do it. Be quick to say yes to God, but you don't have to say yes to everyone. When we fill our schedules with good works, it is so very easy to drift away from the well of the water of life. We have the voices of the needy screaming at us to help them and that can sometimes drown out that 'still small voice' of the Lord. God is talking about service, not slavery, folks. Find out what God wants you to do and do it with all your might! That way you are worshiping God AND serving His people. By hearing from God, you end up doing what is in His plan, not just every good work that crosses your path. What's that old saying that someone's bad decision doesn't make it your emergency?"

"Can we make that a banner we post at work?" someone joked.

I smiled and said, "Now that needs to be on a billboard in the middle of town!"

This audience certainly understood the value of hard work and sacrifice. *Hmm, which gives me an idea,* I thought. I prayed that God would bring it back to mind before I left there today.

I continued. "The same God who leads you to the service you gave your 'yes' to, will also bring along someone to cover the service you said your 'no' to—voila, it's all good and it's all covered. So we can put down our superhero capes and just listen to God. Stay in that worship and devotion to Him and you will then know what portion of 'duty' or 'works' He has in His plan for you. He is much better at the God stuff, anyways!

"Now how can we succeed in what was just discussed?" I asked them.

"Hire another exec!" proclaimed another attendee in jest.

"Hey, I like that idea," I jested back.

"Seriously, think about it. Does that mean one hour of service for one hour of devotion; tit-for- tat? No, the Adam nature tends to think of 'balance' in that way, sort of like a balance scale; especially you type 'A' personalities here today. . . . One pound on that side means one pound on the other side to keep things 'balanced.' Not exactly, folks.

"Balance in God's realm really means more of a flow. The Greek word for "spirit" is *rheo*, meaning "flow." We get our English word rheostat from it. So, the balance we so eagerly desire is really a "flow." And the flow we are talking about is from God. So it is not so much a stiff devotion vs duty thing as it is finding a right rhythm. . .sort of like dancing. God wants us 'flowing' through the day. . .duty, devotion, duty, duty, devotion, devotion. In listening to the Lord, He will set the rhythm of your dance for that day. Boy, is that freedom or what? Don't worry about how to serve Him, just seek Him and obey Him; the 'service' will come as a wonderful flow through you. The key is just to be open to the Lord for both. Be ready for devotions OR duty, worship OR works at any point in time, according to His plan and timing. That way you won't feel guilty if some of the works don't get finished while you bask in the devotion, or some of the devotion doesn't get included while you toil in the works. Yup, just like dancing — sometimes you are stomping and sometimes you are floating across the floor, and it's all good. Work, worship, duty, devotion, it all flows together. In this total submission to God, He'll show you how to tend to both priorities."

Someone in the audience raised a hand and asked, "Yes, but how can we get back into balance once we're all skewed in one direction?"

"Glad you asked," I said. "That just happens to be the next subject area to cover. Now let's say that you've been leaning a bit too far in one direction — not only is there no balance, there is no flow.

"In Joanna Weaver's book, *Having a Mary Heart in a Martha World*, she makes some great suggestions. Here are a few signs that she notes, that may give you a hint or two what to do."

One woman asked, "Do you mind if I take a few notes on this?"

"Oh please," I responded. "I hope you will. Feel free to share this with anyone. God holds the copyright anyways."

They laughed at that comment.

"Ms. Weaver notes in her book [34], you may need to do a bit more 'service' and 'works' if:

♦ You are tending to be a bit unhappy and depressed
♦ If you are resenting people being in your life
♦ You feel a bit lost and don't have a sense of direction and purpose
♦ You are becoming too self-indulgent with foods, clothing, hobbies, etc.
♦ You find yourself not caring; you just don't give a hoot!
♦ No or low energy levels

"So, get out there, bubba, and volunteer someplace—church, school, local hospital, or the like."

They smiled one to another at that statement.

I continued, "But a little caveat here. The things I just mentioned could also be signs of something more serious, physically or emotionally, so don't let faith throw away common sense. . .be wise in what they may be indicating in your life.

"Now, on the other side of the coin, you may need to spend a bit more time in worship and prayer[35] if:

♦ You are wrapped a bit too tight, so to speak, lashing out at people for the smallest things; REALLY frustrated at everything
♦ You have to have noise around you all the time because you are uncomfortable being quiet and still
♦ That "abundant joy" the Lord talks about is far from you
♦ You feel like you are on a desert island, all alone, "nobody likes me, everybody hates me, I'm going to eat some worms!"
♦ You keep doing more and more "works." You suffer from an increased drive for more duty and service time
♦ You feel dry and empty; no kidding, you keep giving out and don't stop to refill!

28

"If these things are happening with any frequency, best get out the devotionals, keep a prayer journal, or go on a weekend retreat. And you had better do it fast if you want to have the fullness and joy of the Lord to be yours and in abundance.

"Remember—a balanced life is really a dance before the Lord. Devotion and duty; worship and work; they go hand in hand, a flowing together.

"Say, that's not a bad idea. Just dance every day with Jesus. Wow, why didn't I think of that?" I said, smiling as I ended my comments.

With that last remark, laughter erupted. I took a drink of water from the condensation-covered glass set beside the podium for me. Some dripped on the front of my blouse as I drank it. I was glad for the humbling moment and said, "Well, I hope some of what I said will water you as quickly as I have just watered myself."

I held the glass up as in a toast, and said, "Continue with excellence in our business community. We need you to be the best and the brightest out there to pierce the moral darkness surrounding us all. God bless you richly."

Warm applause and smiles greeted my final remarks. The audience was politely quiet as the moderator returned to the podium and said, "Thank you so much, Dr. Fontana, for spending some time with us today. We appreciate your wisdom and humor in sharing the good and godly truths that can benefit us all. Please feel free to mingle as we finish up today."

"Oh," I said, "you mean go ahead and schmooze?"

He grinned again and said, "Yes, that too!"

As I mingled and schmoozed, I saw that the members of the group were pleasant, educated, and of various backgrounds and specialties. I have always enjoyed speaking in the community and meeting so many different people who love the Lord. Some of my speaking venues were not as open to or aware of God and His principles as these people were, but God always managed to do a marvelous work wherever I went. And just to make sure I remained humble, He had me spill water all over the front of my clothes this time!

Just then, that previous idea I had popped back into my head. I proceeded back up to the podium and said, "Ed, I have just one more thing to share. May I?"

"Oh, please," he said. "Feel free to continue."

I cleared my throat and began. Before I even knew it, my heart was pouring out about the young people and the DMR-5 group. . .their ideas, and the new "mission" they were formulating to change their lives for the better and to share that with others. This group of professionals gave their utmost attention to what I was saying. I further explained "The Crucible" program too. Their looks portrayed a deep understanding and their eyes conveyed a willingness to be involved somehow. Was I dreaming? In my own fire and passion for our young people to have access to God through Christ, and thusly a better life, was I reading something into these business aficionados' responses that wasn't really there? Those questions were soon answered.

A man in casual attire stood and said, "May I call you Jeanne?"

"Please do," I said.

"Well," he continued, "My name is John Madison and my son was killed in a diving accident four years ago. I was very active in all his sports and youth groups and I have been looking for something to continue that mentoring and giving process. I have access to many people in the community and God has blessed my business with enough to 'overflow' to others. This, to me, is an answer to prayer. I would love to be involved with these young people, Jeanne. Count me in."

A few tears welled up in my eyes. "Thank You, Lord," I whispered.

He continued. "I was thinking that I could best help by rounding up some resources for those kids for any of the projects they come up with. I'll give you my contact information after we wrap up today. But I really think I could best serve by organizing those teachers and mentors for the "The Crucible" thing. Logistics is my gift and specialty area, and I would be glad to work with Pastor Jeffries on getting that program off the ground. I'd also be more than willing to develop a framework of instructions so that the program could be easily shared with others. The more I talk about this, the more excited I get."

He wore a broad grin, but his smile could never beat the one that grew on my own countenance!

He continued, but a somber look slowly came to his face and he said, "On his deathbed, my son made me promise that I would be a dad to those who needed one. And this will most certainly honor him if I have this on my 'work and worship' list!"

When he finished his comments, wonderfully so, a number of these fine leaders gathered around him to exchange contact information so they might also participate helping DMR-5 and "The Crucible" program.

We all exchanged small talk for a few more moments, then the group dispersed, each to their work and life.

Wow! What a God we serve, I thought as I made my way to the exit.

"Good meeting today, good meeting," I mumbled as I left to return home.

29

When I arrived at my cabin, I was surprised to see Major and Jason waiting for me on the porch.

I teasingly said to them, "Let me see, it's too late for breakfast but too early for dinner; so what could possibly be the reason for your presence at mi casa?"

They laughed, looked at each other, smiled, and Major began speaking.

"Well, Chaplain, I've made a decision I want to run by you." He slowly and deliberately shared his seminary plans and desire to serve as a military chaplain, just as I had done.

I was silent for a long time. Tears, my all-too-frequent companions, began to fall, only this time in a deluge.

Major, with a concerned look on his face, put his hands out in front of him, palms up, shrugged his shoulders and looked over to Jason, who seemed just as puzzled.

Jason then said, "Uh, is this a bad time to talk to you?"

My eyes were closed as if I could hide the tears.

I began, "No, it's just that when a woman's heart is happy and full, it sometimes spills out in tears."

Major said, "You're not unhappy then with my decision?"

I stood up and danced around, yelling with excitement and delight. "Yahoo, thank You, Lord. This is just so awesome!"

Their eyes bugged out at me as I danced. They exchanged looks of sheer confusion.

Jason said to Major, "She cried but she's happy?"

Major just said, "Girl world. . .who knows? And she says 'guy world' is puzzling!"

I sat down, looked tenderly at Major, and said, "You have made me happier than you could ever know. I have watched you grow up to be a fine man, and now I get to see that you will be a fine man of God too. My prayers have been answered. I can die a happy woman!"

I cried so much that my nose was running.

"Sorry boys, excuse me a minute. I need to go inside and get a Kleenex."

As I went inside I heard Jason whisper, "She's going to die?"

Major whispered back, "No, you butthead, it's just a saying."

Their comments made me laugh while I was crying.

When I returned, those two young men were smiling and joking.

"There," I said. "That's better now. It's hard to look serious with snot running down your face!"

They both laughed.

Major said, "I'm glad you're on board with my decision. I've always valued what you have to say to me. I haven't told you all the time," he hesitated a bit, "but I really love you. You've been my second mom. Some guys might think that would be a pain in the butt, but it just made me more spoiled than most."

I smiled with that comment and humorously said, "Don't you blame me for how you turned out!"

He stood and walked over to me and gave me one of his big bear hugs. I cried again.

His eyes grew large once more as he saw my response.

Jason said, "You squeezed the juice out of her, idiot!"

"No, no," I quickly responded. "I'm crying cuz I'm happy again, very, very happy."

They both took a deep breath and looked at me with that puzzled look again.

Major said, "Okay, if you say so. See you later."

Jason smiled and said, "Ditto."

As they jumped down the porch steps, Major turned, smiled that gorgeous smile of his and saluted as he often did when leaving.

"You coming over for supper tonight?" he shouted.

"Wouldn't miss it for the world; lots to tell your parents."

"Hey," he said, "no squealing on me!"

"It's all good," I retorted.

30

*O*ften, in researching materials for my speeches and books, I have preferred the older published works, especially from our country's beginning years. These past few days were not any different, as I worked on some ethics teaching outlines to give to the DMR-5 from a book titled, *Ethics, An Early American Handbook*. Published in 1999 by David Barton of the Wallbuilders Publishing group, it was based on a book by Benjamin Comegys titled, A *Primer of Ethics*.

The *Primer* was originally written in 1890 and was based on a book written even earlier than that, by Jacob Abbott titled, *The Rollo Code of Morals*. Mr. Abbott was a popular author of his day, fiercely interested in cultivating moral truth, and morally based character traits in the young men and women of his era. With that, I totally concurred.

I appreciated many of the older writings because they were saturated with ethical teachings and methods. Sadly, this is not the case today. But I am surrounded by the young ones of my era who are hungry for the solid things in life that will help diminish the widespread shakiness of the world on which they tread. I can do no less than those who have gone before me and remain deeply compelled to leave a legacy of moral rightness and solid directions for this generation's success.

I chose fifteen of the lessons from the *Handbook* text that I thought would nicely dovetail with what I had recently discussed in the DMR-5. And as I reflected on the unbelievable occurrences over this past summer, I remained amazed and ever grateful to the Lord for the outpouring of His power and His conviction laid on so many hearts.

Tomorrow the "gang" will be meeting here and I wanted to get these lessons wrapped up before then.

I prayed, "Lord, I am so grateful for Your presence, Your mercy, Your wisdom and Your justice to reign upon all of us who deserve none of it. I ask for Your hand to be upon me that I could finish up the last of this information to be readied for that meeting. Amen."

I gathered my materials and sat out on the porch. That has been the all-too-familiar vantage point from which I watched Major and his family as they worked in and around the fields and the barns. For years and with a heavy heart, I have observed him at a distance. "So close and yet so far," I said to myself.

I have been so blessed, though, to watch him grow into such a fine young man over these many years. Someday he will know the truth, and I hope he can find forgiveness for me in that great and loving heart of his.

"Well, get going, Chaplain," I said to myself. "Tomorrow's meeting will be here sooner than later."

Smiling and laughing, looking like a fool for speaking to the wind, I dove into my work, knowing that I had to finish up before I left to visit with Pastor Jeffries. I was excited at the prospect of meeting with him to work out some details on the coordination to start the "Crucible" program in his area.

Silently I said, "God, I love my life. I really screwed it all up, but you rescued me and gave me the desires of my heart anyways. They were packaged a bit differently than I had planned, but Your love overcame my foolishness and You blessed me in spite of me. I love You, Jesus."

31

The waiting room at the hospital was filled with the DMR-5 gang. A somber atmosphere pervaded the place. Some were crying, some were praying, some were just staring off into space, wrapped in the solitude of their thoughts.

The Garretts were there, all lined up in one row against the far wall. Major was sitting beside Aimee with his head resting on her shoulder. His eyes were closed. Don Sr. was beside him, his arm draped on the back of the chair and his hand resting on Major's other shoulder.

Don Jr. and his wife, JoAnne both were there, as well as John and his wife, Melody. Joshua and his sister, Rebecca, who had flown in all the way from New Mexico, were quietly chatting in the far corner.

The lieutenant was standing by the waiting room door, almost as if guarding it; he looked over at the family with grief etched all over his face. Standing beside him, almost as backup guards, were Jason and his dad, Richie. They too were pale-faced and weary-looking.

Pastor Jeffries stood up and began to speak.

"This is a sad and difficult time for us all. As frail human beings, we can barely understand the ways of God and why He allows things to happen the way they do sometimes. Our dear and precious friend, our Chaplain, our mentor, was seriously injured yesterday in a car accident and now is in the Intensive Care Unit, fighting for her life. I can't take away our pain, but I can urge us to look to the Lord to take away our fears."

As the pastor prayed, Major was hearing him as if he was in a barrel. It seemed a hollow echo, barely audible to him. Major's sorrow was more than he could bear, but he was trying to hide it in front of his young compadres as best he could. This fine young man was determined to maintain a firm course with the Lord and not abdicate his leadership role to his emotions.

After Pastor Jeffries concluded the prayer, Major called the DMR-5 group to the other end of the fairly large waiting room.

"We can't stop the work that Chaplain started. I am going to continue with our meetings. Anyone with me?" he asked.

"Count me in," "Me too," and down the line they went. They all agreed to continue the work that was so dear to the Chaplain and as she put it, "so important for our country."

Then, quietly, and in unison, they put their hands together, and they whispered, "Dead Men Rising."

At that moment, a man clad in green scrubs, the cotton unisex garb of the operating room, came over to the Garretts. His head was wrapped in an O.R. cap banded in sweat. A facemask hung dangling on the front of his chest like a miniature sail in full wind, but it could not mask the grave look that hung heavily in his eyes.

"Mr. Garrett, I am so sorry to tell you, but the surgery was not successful. Her injuries were just too extensive. She is on life support right now; we have not stopped the machines, as it was thought some of you might want to be in the room when we do. Her brother is in there with her now and wants you to be there with him when that happens."

Don slowly stood and responded with obvious sadness, "Sure, thanks, doc. I'm sure you did everything you could."

Aimee was sitting, sobbing, bent over onto her knees with her head resting on her hands. Major was leaning onto her back, trying to console the inconsolable. People could hear a pin drop in the room. Except for the sobbing, it was as quiet as the impending death down the hall.

All of the Garretts followed the doctor out of the waiting room. As they passed Jason, Major said, "C'mon, you need to be with us too, that is, if you want to."

Tears still in his eyes Jason said, "It's sort of like when my mom died. I'm really sad all over again, but I want to do this. Thanks."

The room was peaceful in a weird way. The sun streamed through the windows; the sheets covering the Chaplain were clean and crisp, almost like they were starched. She would have liked that. Her completely bandaged head was propped up on a pillow; copious amounts of wine-colored blood covered its left side. There was a tube protruding from her throat, held in place with cloth strips attached to a strap that wrapped around the back of her neck. That tube was hooked up to a breathing machine, in which was visible an accordion-like piece of equipment rising and falling to the hissing sound of forced breaths going into her lifeless body. Another tube extended from her nose, leading to a drainage bottle. Her face was bruised and swollen. Both legs and one arm were encased in splints with gauze wrapping covered with ace bandages.

Oh, the quirks of life! How often had the Chaplain seen this scene repeated in Vietnam and now she was the central character herself!

For all the sadness, serenity bathed the landscape in this most difficult place. The "Chaplain, Doctor, Colonel" was about to end her tour of duty here and PCS to her eternal home.

All present were comforted that they could reach out for a final loving touch to their once vibrant, joking, jogging, hiking, preaching-her-heart-out friend and mentor. They stayed at that bedside with her for a long time, just as she would have, had it been any one of them.

Some might have thought it strange at these somber moments that the occupants of this room were smiling, reminiscing, and even laughing at times. But to those holding the dear memories of a dear woman, it was a fitting complement to a life well lived. They were assured the Chaplain would have been in hearty approval.

Quietly the door to the room opened. The surgeon, who had so compassionately relayed the horrendous news to them earlier, was standing in the doorway. As all eyes looked toward him, Aimee gasped. When she looked up from the dimmed room, the light shining in from the hallway made a shadow of the doctor. That, in turn, made the brightness behind him seem to increase. To her and even a few others, it made him look like an angelic figure, as if sent to escort their beloved Chaplain.

Softly, delicately, the doctor interrupted their final moments and said to Steve, Chaplain's brother, "It's time. Are you ready?"

"Yes. We are."

The doctor left the room and returned with some nurses. They too were in green scrubs, and were quiet, respectful, and professional as they turned off all the machines and removed the tubes. Some of the Garretts turned away, as they could not bear to watch. Major stood stoically beside his Chaplain and watched every moment. There was a warmth and love in his heart for this woman that he could never readily explain. He always thought it was because she was just really special to him and had always been in his life since he could remember.

Once all the paraphernalia was removed, Chaplain looked so serene. They all stood there, some just rubbing her arms and legs saying, "It's okay. Go home to God. We love you so very much." She never moved, never took another breath. It was over then and there.

32

Major and Jason, the elder Garretts, Richie and even the lieutenant spoke at the funeral.

Chaplain's relatives were there, en masse. She certainly had not exaggerated when she said she came from a big family. Her youngest brother, Steve, gave a moving and humorous eulogy that touched everyone in a deep and unique manner.

Major was overcome with grief but remained calm during all the comments and ceremonies. Before people filed by to say their last goodbyes, Major went up to the casket, laid a rose across the Chaplain's folded hands, leaned in and kissed her forehead. He was unaware of it, but as he lifted his head back, one of his tears gently fell onto her lips. He then stood at attention at the foot of the casket, with his hand respectfully placed on the dark oak box; a true Chaplain's Assistant to the end.

He was strangely proud of this woman he called his second mom. She crawled into his heart at an early age and was always there for him through all his developmental years, the good times and yes, the bad times. He smiled through his tears as he looked at her laid out in her dress uniform. The chaplain's cross, placed above her many medals, caught his eye. He thought that she didn't just wear her cross; she bore it, she lived it, and she died under it.

As the room emptied and the visitors went to their cars, Chaplain's immediate family members, Major, all of the Garretts, Jason and his dad remained as they closed the casket.

Major whispered softly, "Chaplain, count me in. . .forever."

The graveside service also was attended by almost the entire local community. Chaplain had touched the lives of so many; and yet she was often unaware of the great work God had accomplished through her. Oh, but so much more was yet to unfold in this part of His vineyard.

33

About a week after the funeral, Major received a phone call. "Hey, Major, phone's for you. It's Chaplain's brother, Steve," shouted Don up to the boys' room.

Major took the call in the kitchen.

"Hello," said Major.

"Hey there," said Steve somberly. "I have something to give you before my flight leaves this afternoon. It's pretty important. Will you be home then?

Major replied with a puzzled look on his face, "Ah, sure. I'll be here all day.

"I'll swing by in about thirty minutes."

Okay, see you then."

When he hung up the phone, Aimee asked, "Everything okay?"

Major said, "I don't know. Steve said he had something for me. He'll be here in about a half hour."

Steve's taxi pulled up to the farmhouse. He knocked on the door and Don answered saying, "Come on in, can you stay for dinner?"

Steve said, "Not really, I'm running a bit late." He laughed at his own comment and said, "It runs in the family!"

"Can you come in for a moment?" continued Don.

"No, I just wanted to give something to Major," he said.

Just then, Major came into the kitchen and said, "You have something. . .for me?"

"Yes. My sister gave me this letter a few years ago and said that I was to give it to you when she died," he said as he handed an envelope to the perplexed version of the otherwise pulled-together young man standing in the kitchen.

"Oh," Major said awkwardly. "Thanks."

"Well, thanks again for all the love and care you gave to my sister over all these years. She certainly loved you and your kin-folks. She often said God gave her a second chance and a second family, seeing as her own family was so far away. And oh yeah, I took everything out of the cabin that our family would want for mementos, so the rest is yours to do with as you see fit. And one last thing; in her will, she left the cabin and all her savings to Major. I'll have my lawyers get with you to go through all the legal stuff to finalize the paperwork."

Don, Aimee, and Major just stood there and looked at each other as Steve left. The taxi took off and left a trail of dust as a new chapter of Major's life was about to begin.

Aimee looked tenderly over at Major and tearfully said, "I think I know what's in that letter. I think I've known for a long time."

She walked over to Major, cupped his face in her hands, and gently kissed his cheek. She then went over, took Don's hand and said, "I think Major needs to be alone for a few minutes while he reads that letter."

They both quietly left the room as Major pulled out a chair to sit down at the table. He slowly sat down and placed the envelope in front of him, putting his hands, palms down, on either end of it. Neatly printed, in large letters, was his name. He just sat there for a while, looking at the writing. He felt a lump thicken in his throat and that strange sadness returned. A longing to see Chaplain's face and hear her voice rose up in his heart as he looked at her handwriting. He slowly opened the letter, wondering what in the world was so important that she had to write a letter about it instead of telling him directly. His curiosity was really piqued.

Aimee stood at a distance in the other room, but in a position so that she could see Major and watch his reaction as he read what she suspected would be a life-changing missive.

Dearest Major,

If you are reading this, it means that God has called me home and I am dancing in heaven on the streets of gold! I hope you spoke well of me at my funeral. I know Steve did a good job and probably made everyone laugh, too.

I write this with a heavy heart because I know you may be mad at me for not telling you sooner. I am counting on you having a huge well of forgiveness from which to draw and apply towards me.

I have always loved you with a special love and I know that over the years, you have felt that from me. You have unknowingly covered my errors and filled my heart when you so often called me your "second mom."

I am so sorry, honey, that I never told you, but I am your birth mother.

Major slowly lowered the letter down on the table and looked out through the kitchen window, up to the cabin where he spent so much time with "her." His head was spinning; hot tears ran down his face and onto the letter. His head just couldn't wrap around the fact that he had grown up next door to his real mom.

He thought, *No wonder I had a special bond with her. I can't believe she didn't tell me. But I loved her so much, I can't hate her now.* He put his head down on his hands for a long time before he started reading again.

Aimee watched her son's agony and shared it in her own heart. Even though she wanted to run into the kitchen and rescue Major from his pain, she remained in the other room, sharing his shock and grief vicariously.

He continued reading, "*It's just that I was young, and traveling so much in the military as a Flight Nurse and to be honest, just knew I couldn't do it alone. Your father left me once he found out I was pregnant. He then moved to California and was killed in an accident shortly thereafter. I just couldn't bear to have you grow up in a home without a dad and practically without a mom because of my incessant travel, so I took the coward's way out and put you up for adoption.*

Your father's name was Adam. Great name, huh. He was really a very good man, but ran from responsibilities once they got heavier. I hated him for that for a long time. We weren't married, and that made it worse for me. I didn't know the Lord back then and didn't live a holy life, to say the least. After I gave you up for adoption, the pain was unbearable. I lamented at my lifestyle and the loss of you, my precious son. But in all that misery, God reached down and had mercy on me. The reality of such a lost life finally made me cry out to Him and He answered me with forgiveness and healing of my broken heart. I gave my life to Him that very day and everything from then on changed. It even changed what I did in the military and eventually I went into the chaplaincy.

And, in my personal mess, God still had a marvelous plan. A friend of mine worked at the adoption agency and I was able to find out who the adoptive parents were. It wasn't legal, but I was desperate. In the crazy world of miracles, I got the biggest one ever, when I found out that the house your father left me was right next door to the Garretts, who had just adopted you. I always considered that as an outright miracle; sort of God's way of telling me that I was forgiven and that He would work out what I could not. I never told the Garretts I was your mother, so don't blame them, but I think Aimee always suspected it. We women just have a sense about these things.

When I saw how much they loved you, I couldn't bear to tell them the truth. They let me hold you and feed you and change your diapers. I watched you as you grew up, and was blessed beyond measure that Don and Aimee allowed me to be such a cherished and long-standing part of the family, and your life.

My heart ached every time I held you, but I could not ever bring myself to tell you or them who I really was. Eventually you knew about the adoption and eventually I feared you would somehow want to find me. But now God has worked it out in this special way and I have to trust Him to make it right in your heart.

Just know I <u>always regretted</u> giving you away. You are a treasure beyond measure and I lost the grand opportunity to live with you as your mom. But God in His great grace and mercy gave you Aimee. If I could have looked all over the earth to find someone to replace *me, I would have chosen her. She is a loving, hardworking, self-sacrificing woman who has loved you and raised you with all the care you deserve. Her love for you is matched only by Don's and you are as much a son to him as if he were your real father.*

I again ask you to forgive me for not being truthful with you. I know now I should have told you all a long time ago. I have paid for my sins by living with the pain of your loss all of these years.

I prayed for you every day, and I am the most proud of you for how you have grown into a godly man in Christ. Carry on your legacy; it is a mantle God has given you.

My son, even though I have been in the background of your life, I have loved you every minute of every day and have cherished every moment with you.

I am so sorry. Please forgive me.

Major finished reading, put his head down again and wept bitter tears. After a few moments in that hellhole of regret, he felt the steady, warm grip of Aimee's hand on his shoulder. He got up, turned around, and hugged her tightly.

"Mom," he said. "She was my mom!"

"I know honey, I know," Aimee whispered.

"How did you know?" he sobbed.

"I could tell by how she held you and looked at you. I never said anything because I was afraid if I was right, she might try to take you back. But over time, I grew to love her too. I saw her hidden sorrow and knew how strong she must have been and how very much she must have loved you to give you up so you could have a better life."

"But why didn't you ask her, Mom?" he pleaded.

"Honey, sometimes it's best to leave things alone. We both loved you dearly, your dad would have died a thousand deaths had he known, and you may have become angry or confused, and God knows what you would have done," she said with utmost understanding and tenderness.

"Mom, I love you. And I loved Chaplain. I guess it will all work out in my head and my heart someday," he lamented.

At that point, Don entered the kitchen.

Major looked over at him and said, "Dad, we have to talk."

They went into the living room and Major let Don read the letter. When he finished reading, Don looked up at Major with such love and compassion. He said not one word but just held Major in his arms for a very long time.

Major pulled back and said, "Dad, I need to go up to the cabin and sit for a while. I'll be back for dinner. There's a lot on my mind right now. Can Jason help you for the rest of the day? I don't have it in me right now."

"Sure, son, you take all the time you need. These things hit us like a jackhammer and we need to step back for a bit. You want Joshua to go with you?"

Major replied, "No, Dad, I need some time alone up there."

As Major walked through the kitchen, he handed the letter to his mom and said, "I want you to read this too. We're all in this together."

Aimee and Don stood holding each other as they watched Major make the climb up through the field and onto the road that led up to the cabin.

"He's a man now, Aimee. This is his crucible and I trust God to find all the gold in him."

Aimee looked up at Don and sweetly whispered, "I love you, Don Garrett."

Don held her closer and whispered back, "I love you more!"

34

*Up at the cabin, Major sat on the porch. He looked over the same view that helped brighten each day the Chaplain was there. He went inside and looked around. This was his place now, but he could hardly process all that had happened.

He walked through the rooms, reminiscing in each one. The games of hide and seek when he was little; the sleepovers with his friends and the patience Chaplain always displayed with their noise, antics, and all around mess they made.

He looked over at the window that Jason had smashed and remembered pulling guard duty. He thought about how good he felt that he was able to protect her, and now know that it was his real mom he was protecting.

He looked through her closets, bureaus, and file cabinets. He touched her clothes and looked at her jewelry. It was strange to be here, and yet familiar. This woman was his own mother and it hit him like a ton of bricks. He fell down on her bed and wept himself to sleep.

It was dark when he awoke; he saw the bright moonlight through the window. Pushing himself off the bed, he turned the lights on throughout the house. As he was looking through some paperwork on Chaplain's desk, he saw a pile of papers entitled *Ethics, The Lost Heart of America.*

He smiled as he read it. *Just like her to get this ready for the DMR-5,* he thought. There were notes, books, and research items all over the desk. Some in neat piles, others scattered about, but each set was labeled with a large sticky note with a description of what the papers entailed.

Boy, she poured her heart into gathering information on the moral issues of the day, he thought. *I think I understand what she meant when she wrote in the letter that I must carry on that legacy and wear the mantle God has given me.*

Major went out on the back porch and looked up to the stars. The events of the past few days crowded his head and his heart. He felt that lump in his throat again. He stood tall, wiped those ever-returning tears from his eyes, and shouted, "Chaplain, ah, I mean Mom, I will make you so proud."

He went back in, gathered a bunch of papers on various subjects, and headed on home. He was determined to continue the teachings Chaplain had started. Comforted with that thought, he went straight to his room and slept like a baby.

The next day, he was having breakfast when there was a knock on the door.

"I'll get it," he shouted.

It was Julie. She had a casserole in her hands; a cardboard box was at her feet. It was stuffed full of more goodies.

"I hate to bother you," she said sheepishly. "But my mom and I made some dinner for you guys. We thought there might be a lot going on here with Chaplain dying and all and that your mom might appreciate not having to think about cooking, for at least one night."

Major softened his glance as he looked at her. She seemed prettier than he'd ever seen her before.

"Oh, where are my manners?" He chuckled. "Come in, come in. Let me help you with that."

He went to help her lift the box. As they both bent down, his cheek brushed against hers. He blushed as their eyes met. He'd never felt anything as soft as her cheek. He wished he could touch it again.

Julie smiled but was a bit embarrassed. "Sorry, didn't mean to almost knock your head off."

"I'm the clumsy one. Just put the casserole on the table and I'll get this box," he said happily.

Just then, Aimee came over to see who was at the door.

"Well, hi, honey. What do we have here?" Aimee said with delight. "Oh, thank you so much," she continued. "This is a real help for me tonight. You and your mom are angels!"

Major just kind of rolled his eyes around and didn't quite know what to say. Julie just asked if the DMR-5 meeting was still on as scheduled.

Waiting for his answer she thought, *I love being with Major. I wonder how long I can stretch this out before he gets suspicious about me hanging around.*

"Oh yes," he said. "We'll get together tomorrow as usual. I think we should just keep going. Chaplain would have liked it that way."

Julie replied, "She sure would. Oh, excuse me a minute while I help your mom put these things away."

She helped Aimee put the foodstuffs away for later then Aimee went outside to the barn to help Don. Julie and Major, alone in the kitchen, just looked at each other.

Before Major could say anything else, Julie looked at him with such a love and warmth in her eyes and said, "My heart breaks that Chaplain is gone, and I feel so badly for you."

She gently touched his arm, stood on her tiptoes, and kissed him softly on his cheek. As she turned to leave, he took her arm, looked her in the eyes and said, "I really appreciate you."

They smiled at each other and then she left.

Major stood at the door and watched her drive her dad's old truck back up the road. He watched until the truck disappeared over the horizon. He felt good inside. He liked her a lot.

35

At the DMR-5 meeting, a somber mood prevailed. The young men and women present had been deeply touched by the death of the Chaplain and were now even more determined to carry on the work they felt was their destiny.

Major came to the front, asked for prayer, and told the group of the change in decisions for his life path. He excitedly shared that he was accepted at the seminary and would start in the spring semester.

Julie could hardly contain herself with the joy that bubbled up within her heart when she was near Major, or for that matter when she even thought about him. She had listened intently to Chaplain and was in total agreement that relationships should be based on a life in Christ and not just how well someone danced or how handsome they were. She was willing to wait for Major and be prayerful in that waiting and seeking the will of God. She already had been chided by some friends for her hesitancy to pursue those feelings for Major overtly. But the most hurtful rebukes had come because of her stance on sexual purity. She had resolved to maintain that stand, even if it meant losing a friend or two in doing it. This commitment was real and deep; a conviction that came to her from God and not just some religious rule she was told to obey.

She mused a moment while Major was speaking and thought about the many things they had discussed on the "porch meetings" and the many more at DMR-5. She was excited to be a part of such a growing movement of young people who were determined to take back control of their moral lives in such an immoral climate.

The sound of Major's voice became loud and clear, as she ended her daydreaming hiatus.

"And that wraps up the update of what I'll be doing and some of the places I'll be bringing our DMR-5 message. I appreciate your support with all that has happened lately, but I have one more thing to share with you."

There wasn't a dry eye in the place as Major related the revelation of who Chaplain really was. There were no comments, no murmurs in the group. Most of the young ones just stared straight ahead at Major, swimming in surprise and disbelief. It took quite a while for it to sink in.

Julie just sat there, slowly moving her head from side to side as if saying "No, no." Her mind was swirling with thoughts. Her heart was overflowing with love and deep compassion for Major and concern for what he must be dealing with at this time in his life.

When Major finished sharing, without signal or sound, the group went up and each one hugged and patted Major on the back or the arms. They were not afraid to show such love. To an outside observer, one might have thought, "My, how they love one another."

As the days went by, Major spoke at any and every youth setting they could find. He spoke at the Boys and Girls Club, the local DeMolay, the Young Civitans, Boys and Girls Scouts, and the YMCA. And in all of this, he was ably assisted by the casually dressed businessman who promised Chaplain that he would commit his time and resources to DMR-5 and "The Crucible" program.

Within a short time, there were so many young people at the DMR-5 meetings that Pastor Jeffries opened the church's fellowship hall. The young exuberance of youth permeated the meetings. Yet, they never turned into some fight fest or carnal music concert, rather the meetings were filled with young hearts ever so open to the messages of hope that Major would bring.

There was something spreading in this community and many of the older residents recognized just what it was. . .the spiritual revival they had been praying for, for years! Many of them often wept with joy as they drove by the schools and saw hundreds of kids gathered outside for the voluntary prayer time as a start to their day.

Pastor Jeffries was just as excited because "The Crucible" program was a huge success. The quarterly meeting of the local pastors that he started years ago was full of a new excitement regarding this program, an excitement at the prospects of such an effective community service and the spreading of the good news of a life in Christ.

Some in the area were skeptical that such a young man as Major was at the helm of the DMR-5 group, but after they saw the deep-rooted changes in the attitude, behavior and all around lifestyle of their teenagers, all disbelief was alleviated.

36

After dinner one night, Don said, "We need to talk."
He was addressing the boys, including Jason.

John said, "I've got some work to do in the barn, so if you don't need me at the meeting, I'm going to head on out."

"That's fine. I'll meet you out there later to help finish up", Don said.

Don, Major, Joshua, and Jason went into the living room.

Don Jr. had gone back to work a few days ago, but JoAnne was still visiting after Chaplain's funeral. JoAnne, standing at the sink, looked over at Aimee and said, "I love our family."

Aimee answered, "Me too, honey, me too. We are so blessed."

The boys were all seated and looked over at Don.

Major asked, "What's up, Dad?"

"Well," he started, "I've been thinking about all the changes that have taken place over such a short time. When the stuff hits the fan so to speak, things can get very confusing, and I want to make sure we continue to pray about every decision we make; now and in the future. So this is a good time to tell you my thoughts."

He turned to Jason and said, "I've been talking with your dad. We discussed the possibility of him moving his trailer over to this property and you can live there with him. You'll still be carrying out your community service with us, but you'll be able to be with your dad at the same time. With Major and Joshua not here, I'm going to really need the both of you to keep things going."

Jason's eyes widened and he said, "Oh yeah, man cave coming up!"

They all laughed.

He turned to Joshua and said, "You'll be leaving to go back to law school next week and I just want you to know how much I appreciated all the help you gave me this summer. I know it was a lot to ask you to give up your school break; but what may look like random circumstances to some, really turned out to be planned of God because you were here when John was down with his injury. He's back in the saddle now, but I don't know what I would've done without you. Major worked his butt off, but we couldn't have done it alone."

Joshua stood tall, looked at his dad, and man-to-man said, "Dad, I love you and Mom so much. And besides, it builds character, remember?"

They all laughed again at that comment. There surely was a grand amount of character in this family.

Don then turned his gaze to Major and said, "And you Major, have made us all so proud. It seems you just picked up where Chaplain left off. I have seen you grow, not only as a man, but as a man after the heart of God. We need that kind of leadership among our young people."

Joshua teased Major when he said, "Oh, yeah, now we know who Dad's favorite is!"

Major leaned over and hit Joshua on the shoulder, laughing and pretending like he was going to fight with him and said, "Yeah, if you weren't such a jerk, maybe you'd be his favorite."

Don piped up and said, "Quiet down or I'll start singing."

They all immediately shut up, looked around with mischievous grins, then started howling. Jason laughed so hard his sides hurt. He loved this family, and being a part of it had started him on the right road to manhood.

Don continued, "Now that I have your undivided attention, I have more to tell Major. Son, and you are still my son, no matter what, but I think it's time for you to move on."

They all became seriously quiet.

Major looked a little puzzled, but Don continued, "What I mean is, since you'll be going to seminary and it's only a short distance away, it might be a good idea if you moved up to the cabin. Seeing as it's yours now, you can get your stuff up there and have a quiet place to study and start figuring out the direction God has for you."

Joshua and Jason both smiled, and Joshua said, "Parrr-tay time!"

Don pretended to scowl and said, "Yeah, right!"

Major said, "That's cool Dad. I was going to ask you if it would be all right to go up there anyways. So I guess that's going down sooner than later and I'm good with that."

Don stood up and said, "All right, boys. Let's finish up the chores."

They all stood in the middle of the room, fist bumping and hugging those manly hugs, then off they went to finish the long farm day.

Major then turned to his dad and said, "I'll meet you in a minute. I'm going to call Julie, okay?"

Don smiled. He recognized the stirrings of a young man's heart and was excited for the plans God just might have in store for them.

"Sure," he said. "But don't think for a minute she's going to visit you up there at your new hacienda. All visits are restricted to my house, not yours," he said with a hearty laugh and concurrent broad smile.

"No problem, Dad. I ain't gonna mess up all this good stuff God is doing. . .no way."

Julie answered the phone. Her stomach filled with butterflies when she heard Major's voice.

Major said, "I hope this isn't a bad time to call you."

Julie smiled and said, "Oh no, it's fine. I've finished all my work and was just catching up on some email."

Major loved the sweetness he always heard in her voice. She was so different from the guys he always hung with, and he liked that difference.

He started telling her all that had transpired with the cabin being his and also with Mr. Madison's help with "The Crucible" work. He also told her more of his plans to start seminary. The conversation went on for well over an hour. When they finished, Julie had agreed to help him if they actually did have that upcoming conference being planned by Mr. Madison. He was glad she was so eager, and he was realizing they had some serious feelings for each other.

Out in the barn, Joshua said to his dad, "Do you want me to see what's taking Major so long?"

His dad answered with a wry smile, "No, son, he's got some business to be tendin' to, some pretty important business. We'll just finish up without him tonight."

Back at the house, "Oh," Major said, "before we hang up, can I pray with you?"

Julie's heart soared with affection for his willingness to remain humble and open to God.

"Of course, anytime. I like it when you pray. It brings me closer to God." Under her breath she said to herself, "And closer to you, Major Garrett."

37

A few days later, Mr. John Madison was on the phone talking to Major.

"Yes, sir," said Major. "Nice to hear from you again. I can't tell you how much I appreciate your help and advice. You're the oil for this machine, if you don't mind me saying so."

Mr. Madison said, "No, I think you're that oil, I'm just the oil can."

They both laughed.

Major asked, "What's up?"

"I think it's time to pump up the message. You've done a great job getting out there, but I'd like to provide those DMR-5 bracelets for you from now on, and I'd like to start sending out some T-shirts with you when you go to speak."

"Wow," said Major, "That's a great idea. Wearing the bracelets has opened up so many ways to get the attention of the young people around here. I see the bracelets all over and it would be awesome to see the shirts, too."

Mr. Madison continued, "I'd also like to finalize the plans for a huge city-wide conference for the young people. You know, you talk to them in that unique way you do, and I'll set up the rest. I was thinking of an all-day thing. You know. . .the obstacle course, zip line, and some of the other challenge games from "The Crucible" program so we could get that word out, too. I'll even provide the food and security."

Major was shocked. "Mr. Madison, I don't know what to say. This is beyond anything I thought about and it will continue to spread the word of DMR-5 as well."

"Don't mention it. I'm getting a kick out of all this. I think I've found my calling. You've given me a reason to live again after the death of my son. I haven't felt so good in years. I have energy; ideas are flying through my head. I have the money and the motivation and you have the 'moves,' so to speak."

They both laughed again.

Major replied, "I don't know about that. I just know there's a fire in my gut to tell my story of how the morality is the problem and how my generation can be instrumental in making huge changes along that line. . .changes for the better, that is."

"Good," said Mr. Madison. "It's a deal; we're partners. This is quite a ministry you've started, and heck, you're not even in seminary yet!"

"Well, let's see where God takes all this. My motives have been a bit changed too. I really want to do well by Chaplain and all the groundwork she provided. She's left a legacy that I am determined to live out in a way that brings honor to her and glory to God."

Mr. Madison finished the conversation saying, "Sounds like a match made in heaven. I'll get with you on the date and place of the DMR-5 conference. God bless you, talk to you soon. Goodbye."

Major hung up the phone. He stomped his feet, threw his hands up in the air and let out a shout of joy. "Yes. Thank You, Jesus!"

He ran out to the barn and told his dad; then he ran to the far field and told John, Jason, Richie, and Joshua. He ran back to the house to find his mom, Melody and JoAnne and excitedly related to them the conversation with Mr. Madison.

That was one happy farm family that day.

38

A few months later, after many meetings and hours of preparation, Major and Mr. Madison stood off on the side of the stage area at the front of the auditorium.

"Well, the big day is here," Major said. He was wired for sound and ready to go.

Mr. Madison answered, "You'll be fine. Just go out there and follow your heart. You speak their language on the need to pursue moral excellence. You've been gifted so that what you say doesn't sound like some lofty and boring sermon. You hit them right in the heart. We both know that's God's Spirit working through you. And, of course, you have a ton of prayer cover from the Christian Businessmen's Association and the many people who care for you. Go ahead now, do your thing."

Julie was in the front row. Major gathered his strength as he looked at her, looking at him. He wished that Joshua could be there too, but he was back at school now. They spoke on the phone earlier, at which time Joshua delivered a well-timed "pre-game" encouragement speech to his brother.

Don and Aimee were busy in the back of the auditorium, giving out T-shirts and bracelets, basking in the joy of the success of all of their children. They considered it a privilege to help at the conference.

The lights dimmed; the energy in the place was palpable. A myriad of cell phones lit up to express the unity of the moment. It looked like candles lit at a music concert.

Major took a deep breath, looked up heavenward and said, "Chaplain, this one's for you."

He walked out to center stage before thousands of late teens and twenty-somethings. They cheered and chanted, "DMR, DMR, DMR." He raised his hands in a call for silence. A hush came over the audience.

He began, "We are here because we want change. We are here because we are the agents of that change. . .a change for the better."

The crowd roared in agreement. Major held up his right hand, brandishing his black wristband with DMR-5 written in gleaming, white letters. In the darkened auditorium, filled with eager faces looking up to their new emerging leader, Major bellowed to the crowd, "Who are we?"

In unison, they thundered. . .**"DEAD MEN RISING!"**

Work Cited

Part I

1. "Too Sexy, Too Young," http://abcnews.go.com/2020/video/young-sexy-15031065
2. "Too much TV," www.familyresource.com
3. James Warner, *Manning Family History Compendium*, (Ozark, MO: Dogwood Printing, 1997), p. 92.
4. Michael Lowman, *United States History, Heritage of Freedom* (Pensacola, FL: A Beka Book Publication, 1996), p. 31.
5. David Barton, *Original Intent: The Courts, the Constitution and Religion*, (Aledo, TX: Wallbuilders Press, 2000), p. 12.
6. Ibid.
7. Ibid.
8. *A Secular Humanist Declaration*, drafted by Paul Kurtz, reprinted from *Free Inquiry* magazine, Vol 1 #1, Winter, 1980, p. 11.
9. Ibid, p. 12.
10. Ibid, pp. 14-15.
11. Ibid, pp. 17-19.
12. Ibid, pp. 19-20.
13. William J. Federer, *America's God and Country*, (St. Louis, MO: AMERISEARCH, INC, 2000), pp. 4-5

14. L.H. Butterfield, ed., *Diary and Autobiography of John Adams* (Cambridge, MA, Belknap Press of Harvard Press, 1961), Vol III, p. 9.

15. William J. Federer, *America's God and Country*, (St. Louis, MO: AMERISEARCH, INC, 2000), p. 98

16. Tyron Edwards, D.D., *The New Dictionary of Thoughts- A Cyclopedia of Quotations* (Garden City, NY: Hanover House, 1852; revised and enlarged by C.H. Catrevas; The Standard Book Company, 1955, 1963), p. 90

17. William J. Federer, *America's God and Country*, (St. Louis, MO: AMERISEARCH, INC, 2000), pp. 239-240.

18. Carl Van Dorn, *Benjamin Franklin* (NY: Viking Press, 1938), p. 188.

19. *Abington v. Schempp*, 374 U.S. 211 (1963).

20. CAPP 265-1, *Values for Living* (Moral Leadership Guide, 1999), p.11.

21. U.S. National Center for Educational Statistics, 2008.

22. Mark A. Beliles and Stephen K. McDowell, *America's Providential History* (Charlottesville, VA: Providence Foundation, 1996), p. 246.

23. Ibid, p. 248.

24. Compiled from, David Barton, *Original Intent: The Courts, the Constitution and Religion*, (Aledo, TX: Wallbuilders Press, 2000), *Harris v. Joint School District*, 41F. 3d 447 (9th Cir. 1994).

25. Ibid; *Engel v. Vitale, 370 U.S. 421 (1962).*

26. Ibid; *Bishop v. Arnov*, 926 F. 2nd 1066 (11th Cir. 1991) and *Duran v. Nitsche*, 780 F. Supp. 1048 (E.D. Pa. 1991).

27. Ibid; *Stone v. Graham*, 449 U.S. 39 (1980) and *Ring v. Grand Forks Public School District*, 483 F. Supp. 272 (D.C. ND 1980).

28. Ibid; *Reed v. van Hoven*, 237 F. Supp. 48 (W. D. Mich. 1965).

29. Ibid; *Warsaw v. Tehachapi*, CV F – 90 – 404 EDP (U. S. D. C., E. D. Ca. 1990).

30. Ibid; *Roberts v. Madigan,* 702 F. Supp. 1505 (D.C., Colo. 1989), 921 F. 2d 1047 (10 Cir. 1990), *cert. denied,* 112 S. Ct 3025; 120Ll Ed. 2d 896).

31. Ibid; *Florey v. Sioux Falls School District,* 464 F. Supp. 911 (U.S. D.C., SD 1979), *cert. denied,* 449 U.S. 987 (1980).

32. Ibid; *Brittney Kay Settle v. Dickson County School Board,* 53 F. 3d 152 (6th Cir. 1995), *cert. denied,* 64 L.W. 3478 (1995); see also Dallas Morning News, "Court Rejects case of girl who wrote Jesus paper," Nov 28, 1995, 4-A; picked up on wire service from *Los Angeles Times.*

33. Ibid; *Olean Times Herald,* Monday, April 6, 1992, PA-1; see also *State of Florida v. George T. Broxson,* Case no. 90-02930 CF (1st Jud. Cir. Ct., Walton County Fl., 1992).

Part II

34. Joanna Weaver, *Having a Mary Heart in a Martha World,* (Colorado Springs, CO: Waterbrook Press, 2002) p.182.

35. Ibid; p. 183.

Dr. Linda J. Pugsley

Follow her blog on www.myghcf.com

Her first book, *The Climb* is still available at Amazon.com or by contacting Great Hope Christian Fellowship Church on the web site noted above

CPSIA information can be obtained at www.ICGtesting.com
Printed in the USA
LVOW101352040613

336920LV00002B/2/P